* * * *

Lord Terrance may have forbid her from coming to his manor house, but she was determined to clear his country home of its resident ghost.

"That is a desolate looking house, is it not?" Winfield said. "I would have it torn down and rebuilt in a more flattering style, but Terrance seems fond of this monstrosity. So what brings you so far north, my lady?"

She faced the gentleman. "I have come for a visit with Lady Terrance. She is my grandfather's friend."

"I had heard the countess still wore dark colors."

Before she could respond, a loud crack sounded. She sensed danger stab from above. With a shouted warning, she pulled Mr. Winfield out of harm's way just as an icicle crashed and shattered where they had stood. She protected her face as splinters flew in all directions.

Mendal screamed. The owl fluttered its one good wing and screeched. The dog barked ferociously.

Mr. MacBride spoke first, his voice quivering and eyes wide with terror. "It is an omen, ah tell ye."

"He is right," Mendal said, sounding unusually timorous as she crossed herself. "We should leave. Bad luck comes from going where we are not wanted."

The front doors opened then, and a footman descended. Immediately, the dog raced up the stairs and inside.

"Dog!" Belle called out in alarm. The animal might wreck the place. This was *not* how she had hoped to introduce herself to the countess.

An older woman, dressed in black, moved to the open doorway. Belle recognized her from a drawing her grandfather had shown her. This was Lady Terrance. She gave off waves of fear as she looked toward the roofline.

Belle's worries drowned beneath the lady's emotional assault, leaving her head pounding with a headache. Through that onslaught, Belle's purpose became crystal clear. This is why she had come here. Lady Terrance needed her.

Dedication

Thanks to my critique group for their exceptional insight and
unflinching assistance over the years.

Other Books by Shereen Vedam

Coming Soon
A Devilish Slumber

A Beastly Scandal

***

Shereen Vedam

Jace & Dari
To two beauties
in real life. Enjoy
Shere V.

Forever Regency
an imprint of ImaJinn Books, Inc.

A Beastly Scandal
Published by Forever Regency,
an ImaJinn Books, Inc. Imprint

Copyright ©2013 by Shereen Vedam
All rights reserved. No part of this book may be reproduced in any form or by any means (electronic, mechanical, photocopying, recording, or otherwise) without prior written permission of both the copyright holder and the above publisher of this book, except by a reviewer, who may quote brief passages in a review. For information, address: ImaJinn Books, Inc., P.O. Box 74274, Phoenix, AZ 85087, or call toll free 1-877-625-3592.

ISBN: 978-1-61026-124-1

10 9 8 7 6 5 4 3 2 1

PUBLISHER'S NOTE:
This book is a work of fiction. Names, characters, places and incidents are products of the author's imagination or are used fictitiously. Any resemblance to actual events or locales or persons, living or dead, is entirely coincidental.

Books are available at quantity discounts when used to promote products or services. For information please write to: Marketing Division, ImaJinn Books, Inc., P.O. Box 74274, Phoenix, AZ 85087, or call toll free 1-877-625-3592.

Cover design by Josephine Piraneo
Cover Credits:
Photo of Regency woman: RazzleDazzleStock
Background glitter: JaguarWoman

ImaJinn Books, Inc.
P.O. Box 74274, Phoenix, AZ 85087
Toll Free: 1-877-625-3592
http://www.imajinnbooks.com

Chapter One

Dear Lord, let us not have killed him.

In a panic, Belle clambered down from the carriage and ran to the fallen horseman lying on the snow-covered ground. She gently laid his head on her lap. Under the carriage light, her gloved hand came away bloody, and her heart skipped a beat.

She peeled off the hand portion of her right glove to check his breath. Was that a faint draft against her fingers? His body and long limbs looked properly aligned, but he was icy cold and lay utterly still. Other than for that one lump on his head, there were no obvious bruises to him or his horse. Could her carriage have merely frightened his horse, so that it reared and he had fallen? She just wished he would wake up.

Beside her, hoofs stomped, leads jangled and carriage wheels shifted. Feet crunched through calf-deep snow as the coachman and the stranded family she had offered to take to the nearest inn joined her on the darkened roadside.

"Is he dead, my lady?" The coachman held a lantern over the body so he could properly inspect their victim. "Oh, it be the hangman's noose for me for sure!"

"Hush," Belle said. "This was an accident. The puppy's barks merely startled the horses. This was *not* your fault."

It was mine. Belle's heart squeezed with guilt, for the young wolfhound had barked and jumped to get at the injured baby owl Belle had rescued from a stable at her last stop to change horses. She had refused to countenance them killing the tiny creature and took it along with her when they left. She had been keeping it warm and safe under her jacket. Until she stopped to pick up a family beside a broken down carriage. They had found a lost puppy in the snowstorm, and the children had brought it into Belle's carriage. Then the dog sniffed out the bird and . . .

The mother approached, her breath huffing out. "Imagine, riding along a main thoroughfare in the dead of night during a snowstorm. Anyone's coach could have run him over."

Belle shook her head in confusion. How could so many of her good deeds have caused such a catastrophe?

"What is done is done." The woman's husband hugged his wife close. "What are we to do with the corpse?"

"Bury him?" his six-year-old son asked.

"He is not dead yet!" Belle said. "At least, I hope not. Besides, we do not even know who he is."

"Right you are, my lady," the husband said. "No use putting out a grave marker without a proper name."

"My lady." Mendal, her maid, wrapped a blanket around Belle's shoulders. "Should you sit so close to a dead man?" At Belle's glare, she amended that to, "Near as dead, then."

Thick snowflakes settled and stuck to Mendal's black bonnet. None of them, children included, should remain outside much longer. But the coach was already full. There was no more room for a badly injured gentleman, especially one this long.

The large, fawn-colored Irish wolfhound pup that had been the crash's instigator padded over and sniffed the still figure. Then he stood on the man's chest and licked his face.

"Get off him, you big lug." Belle pushed the dog away. "If he is not already dead, he will be if you stand your giant weight on his chest."

"My lady," the father said, "I believe the gentl'mun blinked."

His wife gave a relieved laugh. "Oh, thank the good Lord."

Belle's heart, too, leaped in hope, for the talk of burials had made her doubt he was alive. She gently brushed his cheek with her bare hand. "Sir, are you well?"

His eyes opened, exposing exquisite deep blue eyes.

"Sir, do you hurt anywhere besides your head?"

"First, kiss me to prove I am alive, and you are not an angel," he said in a deep, husky voice.

At his audacious suggestion, Belle's gaze flew to his lips. The lower was full, the upper strong, firm and sensuous. His mouth curved up, as if smiling were his natural tendency. For a moment, from sheer happiness that he was alive, she had the scandalous urge to do as he bid.

"Go on, m'dear," the mother said. "Kiss the gentl'mun. 'Twill be the best entertainment we have had all night."

The little boy and two girls giggled.

The dog barked, as if he approved.

"I believe they insist." The stranger's entreating gaze did not waver.

"But we have not been introduced." Her mouth twitched with humor. Suddenly, despite the snowstorm, cramped traveling conditions, her fear for the abandoned owl, the stranded family, and this fallen horseman, joy stoked a fire in her belly. It was the first good sensation she had experienced since she had entered Cheshire. Of its own volition, her head descended.

His lips parted, and he raised himself to meet her halfway.

"My lady!" Mendal said. "What are you thinking?"

Pulled out of her dreamy state, Belle jerked back.

His head dropped onto her lap, and his heavy sigh puffed out in a white cloud of disappointment.

"Right, Mendal. This unusual storm must have addled my senses." Had she really meant to kiss him? *Yes.* And she felt utterly deprived at the foiled touch of his lips.

Belle had never kissed a man in her life, except for her grandfather's forehead, and that should not count. Her betrothed, Jeffrey, had only lightly kissed her cheek, his lips barely grazing it. And considering the sad state of her social status after Jeffrey begged her to break off their engagement, she might never kiss a man again. With a disheartened sigh, she made her introductions.

"Sir, I am Lady Annabelle Marchant. This charming family—"

"Marchant?" he interrupted. "Annabelle Lilith Marchant?"

She tenderly brushed his silky blond hair off his forehead. "My grandfather assures me that is my name."

She was unable to contain a bubble of laughter. His frown looked adorable. Had he heard of her? Then her smile faltered. Had he heard of her in London? That could not be good.

The gentleman scrambled to his feet and then staggered.

The husband and wife steadied him, but he pushed them away. He put a hand to his temple and blinked, as if in confusion. His skewed clothing pulled against his movements, and he straightened his greatcoat with impatient tugs.

He took a deep breath, and his eyes wandered over her face. Was that a tender look in his eyes? She pictured them kissing. Did he too? Or was it her shattered wish resurfacing to torment her? Just her, she realized with regret, for his face looked hard again. With a glum sigh, she rose onto her knees.

He extended a hand, and she used his strength to pull herself upright.

Once she was on her feet, he snatched away his hand and hid his arm behind his back, as if unsettled by her touch.

She lowered her gaze to hide her surprise and hurt.

He bowed. "Allow me to introduce myself. I am Rufus Marlesbury, Earl of Terrance."

A collective gasp drowned out her shocked, soft, "Oh no!"

Of all the people to run into, must it be *him*?

"May I inquire where you are headed?" he asked in a cold voice. "Other than seeking innocent riders to trample?"

She ignored the insult. "My lord, it is fortunate that we met, for I have come to stay at your home."

A bark of laughter escaped him, which did not foster her hope for a hearty welcome. Then he leaned in to whisper, "I am astounded you would dare follow me, Lady Belle. Please understand, even were I inclined to take you under my protection, I keep my mistresses far from my country estates."

She went icy cold with fury, and then flushed hot with consternation, for he had grounds for his wrong assumption. Grounds she inadvertently provided not six months ago on his father's front doorstep in London.

Her maid's arm wrapped protectively around Belle. She must have overheard his lordship's last remark. "How dare you, sir! My lady is a *lady*. You would do well to mind your tongue. You, my lord, are not in a tavern where you may say what you wish. If her grandfather were present, he would call you out!"

The earl's gaze never left Belle, and she laid a hand on Mendal's arm to calm her. "I believe you are mistaken, my lord." She defiantly tilted her head. She was in the right here. "I have come at your mother's invitation."

"Unlikely." He brushed snow from his sleeve. "My mother still mourns my father's passing so would not host a house party. Even if she did, she would hardly invite someone who delights in showing such a sad lack of decorum."

Lips pressed tight, Belle shook off Mendal's support and approached him. "The countess did invite me, my lord."

She had more to say, but not in public. She indicated the others. "May we speak privately?"

He led her away without argument. But before she could speak, he intervened, his tone deceptively soft and gentle.

"It does not become you to so boldly inflict your company on me, *twice* now. Let me make myself perfectly clear so we kill whatever false hope resides within your calculating heart. In friendship, I prefer women who are honest and well-behaved. In lovemaking, though London may consider you a belle of the ball, my personal preference is for women who sport a fairer shade of hair and more generous curves than you possess."

"You beast!" Her hand sprang up.

He caught it mid-swing. Behind them, the wolfhound growled, but his lordship ignored the dog and bestowed a kiss on the back of her naked hand.

A tingle shot up Belle's arm, and his eyes narrowed as if he, too, absorbed that shock.

She pulled free and attempted to slip her fingers back inside her glove, but the wretched tips went askew.

The dog barked.

"Silence." The earl pointed to the dog. "I will deal with you later."

The puppy scuttled back, head drooping, tail tucked beneath him. With a pitiful whine, he hid behind the mother's skirts.

Belle's anger built, not only at his abuse of her but of his bullying of the poor defenseless dog. "Sir, you dishonor me. Your mother would not approve of your disrespectful treatment."

"As my mother will never meet you, I have no worries there."

His superiority warranted a slap, but since recent experience had shown her that the swing would never connect, she ignored the impulse. Belle had left the comfort of her safe home to come to this God-forsaken part of England during this hellish weather for an important purpose.

"You do not understand, my lord," she said through clenched teeth. "The countess particularly requested my help. She is frightened of a ghost that haunts the manor."

"A ghost haunts the manor?" one of the little girls said, her voice high-pitched with excitement. The child must have wandered close enough to overhear their conversation.

"Ooh," her brother said. "There be ghosts at the manor!"

Belle could have groaned out loud. This was exactly the outcome she had hoped to avoid.

This time, the earl looked at her as if she had escaped from Bedlam. His voice rose, as if he no longer cared who heard him. "How dare you stir such preposterous ideas in my mother's head when she is still grieving over the loss of her husband. I will not have you whip up idle gossip and trouble within my family for no other purpose than your personal, twisted enjoyment. Time and again you have displayed a deplorable lack of judgment, which makes me believe you are not fit company for my sister or my mother. I forbid you to come anywhere near my home or my family!"

Tight-lipped, he stared at her and then at their audience. As if suddenly as appalled as the family and coachman by the violence of his outburst, contrition colored his gaze.

Belle had stiffened at each hateful word, shock piling over her like a snowbank forming, and then surprise gave way to an unbearable hurt that filled her eyes with moisture.

The earl backed away. He shook his head, apparently made speechless by her tears. Turning, he whistled to his horse, and the black gelding trotted over.

Lord Terrance picked his riding hat off the ground, put it on, and swung himself onto the saddle.

Oh! Belle bit her lip. He meant to ride away, as if he had not whipped her raw with his hurtful words. She swung around in search of a suitable weapon. Finding nothing but wet packed snow, she knelt and made a hard ball of the stuff.

He turned his mount toward her, his mouth opening to . . . to what? Apologize? *Too little, too late!*

She stood and whipped her missile at him. The ball of snow smashed across his face with such satisfying force, it almost knocked him off his horse. In quick succession, she sent more projectiles to shatter against his throat and shoulders.

Instead of shouting that she behaved like a hoyden, he took the bombardment in stoic silence, until her rage expired. With a sigh, she dropped the last of her snowy rounds and pushed past her flabbergasted audience to climb aboard her coach.

The rest of her companions, dog included, quickly joined her. The door shut. The coachman and the father scampered up to the outside seat, and the conveyance rolled on.

Belle sat with the owl secure inside a blanket on her lap. Her hands trembled until Mendal covered them with hers.

Instead of riding away, the earl edged his mount forward past the carriage window, toward the front of the coach.

"See they reach the inn safely." Coins clinked.

As the carriage rolled on, the young boy stuck his head out the window. "He is watching us leave," he said to his mother. Finally, he withdrew. "Too dark to see anymore."

"Shush, child," his mother said.

The hound lying by their feet sniffed at Belle's lap. The mother put her foot on the dog. "Enough of that!"

The puppy sighed and leaned against Belle's chilled feet, imbuing them with welcome warmth. This was the second time Lord Terrance had foiled her attempt to reach his home to help a member of his family. First in London, and now in Cheshire.

The last time she had lost her reputation and, sadly, he his father. If his mother's fear of a ghost haunting Clearview was true, the repercussions of her failure this time might fall on Lady Terrance's head.

Fists clenched, Belle forced back tears. Not again. She would not, *must not,* let him stop her again. But how to gain entry to a home that was barred to her?

* * * *

Rufus rode away with his temper as frozen as the surroundings. By the time he entered his home, some of his ire had thawed. Yes, he had behaved badly, but surely he had been provoked? The woman had abused his mother's good graces in order to reach him. He had to forbid her to come here.

Clearview's cavernous entryway was as deserted as the landscape of blowing snow outside. The cold delved deep into his bones, and his wet clothes added to his misery. "Felton!"

His butler's footsteps echoed as Rufus slapped his riding hat across his knee. White slush sprinkled on the marble floor.

"My lord." Felton's voice was smooth and calm as he approached. "Did you have a pleasant ride?"

"No. It will be a miracle if I do not catch my death of cold. If I am not warm, well fed, and undisturbed for the rest of the night, there will be hell to pay."

His butler's gaze searched the vast entry hall and the wide stairs curving upward. "Er, my lord, did you not find the puppy?"

Rufus ignored the question. The last thing he wanted to talk about was that ungrateful dog. He had spent hours in the storm searching for the hound, got knocked down for his efforts, and then the pesky hound had taken the lady's side and deserted him. How had his five-month-old wolfhound, Earnest, ended up in Lady Belle's company in the first place?

He shrugged out of his father's greatcoat, tempted to wish the intractable hound good riddance. He had put on this unwieldy coat because the confounded dog had soiled Rufus's garment. All in all, he had been thoroughly ill used this wretched night.

His scowl, in combination with the wet stain of snow on the greatcoat's rear, should give Felton all the explanation he needed. Rufus headed for the stairs and ordered his valet to be rousted from whatever corner of the wine cellar the man had secreted himself. "And he had better not be jug-bitten."

"Rufus."

The voice belonged to the last person he wished to speak with tonight. At the top of the first flight of stairs, he stopped and stood out of the entryway chandelier's candle glow.

"I can see you perfectly well, so there is no need to hide," his mother said.

He leaned over the banister. The open drawing room doors flanked Constance Isabel Frances Marlesbury, Countess of Terrance. His mother's full cheeks and curly blond hair made her appear younger than her two and fifty years.

Her face was as familiar to him as his, yet he understood her less than he did the hound. He could not remember a time when she had been less than good-natured. Even when he came home with the news that his father had unexpectedly died, his mother had merely worn a tired smile and murmured, "How like him."

"I am fatigued beyond measure," he said. "I have had a most disagreeable experience and simply wish to rid myself of the memory. No," he added before she could ask, "I do not wish to discuss it."

"I see," Lady Terrance said. "Well, once you clean up, would you be kind enough to lend me your ear? I have news."

"If it is about that Marchant woman, I have nothing to say on that quarter either. In fact, I have advised her she is not to call on us and is unwelcome in this house."

He gave a curt bow and continued on his way. The shock on his mother's face told him she had indeed invited Lady Belle. The knowledge burned his gut. So, his mother had written to her old friend, the Marquess of Alford, Lady Belle Marchant's grandfather. True, he was a family friend, as had been Lady Belle's late father, an earl in his own right. But his mother had written to ask for help about a *ghost*?

Even if she did have such irrational fears, why not come to him? His father had held a low opinion of him, but did that conviction also grip his mother?

His shoulders dropped as he entered his room. He stripped off his neck cloth with a vicious jerk, ignoring the burn.

"Gently, my lord." Ellison stepped away from the candles he lit by the bedside. "We have hope of reusing the material."

"What do I care about the deuced cloth? And let the devil take my mother for ruining our name yet again."

How could she be convinced of something as scatterbrained as their home being haunted? Worse, she must have discussed the idea with strangers. Or had that Marchant woman planted the worry in his mother's heart? How long had they been writing?

His valet slid away Rufus's fitted jacket, wool waistcoat, linen shirt and breeches, soggy from his fall. Rufus eased himself into a warmed robe and tightened the sash. The hearth's heat and smoky scent drew his gaze to the flames.

He accepted the glass of port Ellison offered and dismissed him. Restless, he strode to the window and stared at the bleak, white landscape. The storm swirled around the wide rolling grounds. He could barely make out his mother's rose garden or the elm trees that lined the pathway to the house.

Surprisingly, he had to fight an urge to go to the inn tonight to ensure Lady Belle had arrived safely. Remembering her tears, he worried that his harsh words might have unduly upset her. He had just taken a sip of the port, trying to let its familiar bite ease the discomfort of his guilty conscience, when a discreet tap told him his bath awaited next door. He entered the sitting room and discharged his valet with strict instructions he was not to be disturbed.

The door closed with a soft click. Rufus shrugged off his robe and stepped into the steaming bath water. He sank into the tub and folded his long legs to submerge as much of his body as he could. Slowly, the water's heat soaked into him and drove away unpleasant memories, but his head continued to pound.

He winced as his fingers brushed the sticky spot on his head. He soaked a thick cotton washcloth and dabbed gingerly at the tender area. Gritting his teeth against the pain, he rinsed the cloth and repeated the action until no more blood flowed.

A rap of the shutters startled him, and he dropped the cloth. Outside, the wind howled mournfully. The shutters rattled and then held. Cinders sparked as coals shifted, and the fire bathed the room in an orange glow.

He sighed and relaxed into the water, releasing the night's troubles, most prominent of which was his encounter with Lady Belle.

At a knock, he frowned. He had said no disturbances. A hushed argument preceded what must have been a struggle for the handle before the door was flung open, bringing in a gust of cold air.

"Rufus," his mother said, entering the room. "I must speak with you."

"I am sorry, my lord," Ellison said. "I tried to dissuade her ladyship but—"

The door slammed, cutting off Ellison's excuses.

"Madam!" Rufus said, indignant at her storming in while he was in the bath. He hurriedly spread a towel across the hip bath. "Can this not wait?"

The countess strode toward the tub, looking to be in high dudgeon. "No, it cannot. What did you mean when you said Lady Belle is unwelcome here?"

"I meant what I said."

"But why? How? Did you meet her on the road?"

"More like she met me," he murmured, remembering hearing Earnest's frenzied barks. Then a carriage careened out of the night. Goodwin reared. Rufus frantically drove his mount to the edge of the road. Goodwin stumbled, and Rufus flew toward the ground. He hit it hard, pain slicing through his head and blocking out the world in a blazing white light. His last thoughts had been of the barking pup and wondering if he had been trampled by frightened horses.

He came back to the present as his mother said, "You do not make sense. I have been expecting Lady Belle all afternoon and was worried the storm delayed her. If you have seen her, is she well? If she is not coming tonight, when will she arrive?"

"Pray, calm yourself," Rufus said in a soothing tone. "I have dealt with the matter."

His mother wrung her hands, looking worried now. "Rufus, what have you done?"

"It would be more accurate to ask what did she do? Did she run me down with her carriage? *Yes.* Did she steal our dog? *Yes.* Did she talk rubbish about ghosts and haunted houses? *Yes.* Did she . . ." He had almost said, *Did she steal my heart with one enchanting smile? Yes!*

Covered from neck to toe in white, she had looked like a lily in a winter garden. And like a lovesick pup, he had wanted to stay with his head on her lap, gazing up at her. He could hardly admit that to his mother. The thoughts bedeviled him enough. His head began to ache again.

"Then she had the temerity to fling snowballs at me." Even as he said it, an urge to laugh bubbled in his chest. Seeing his mother's eyes light up with interest effectively doused that humorous germ.

"How extraordinary," Lady Terrance said, and he could tell she was struggling to keep her lips still.

"I wonder where she came by her ideas about a ghost at Clearview?" He gave his mother a piercing glance.

That satisfyingly killed his mother's merriment. She backed away as she said, "How should I know? From what Alford has told me, his granddaughter is a well-behaved, kind child. One whose manner is tender and sweet and respectable. Certainly not someone to have flights of fancy. Or fights in the snow. Are you sure the young woman you ran into was my Belle?"

"*Your* Belle?" He could not recall ever being *her Rufus.*

"Well, Rufus, I feel I do know her. She sounds a charming girl. There must be a mistake."

"No mistake. Lady Belle Marchant is drawn to scandal, and I will not have her here."

"Oh, dear."

His mother departed before he could question her more on this havey-cavey business about alleged spirits.

The water had cooled while they spoke, his head still throbbed, and the topic of conversation had done nothing to ease the pain. He lost all interest in relaxing and stood.

Cold air brushed against his bare skin, and he shivered as he stepped out of the tub and dried himself before shrugging on his robe. Sighing, he leaned against the fireplace mantle and caught sight of his father's gold watch. A new purchase, by the polished look of it. He lifted the timepiece. The watch lay heavy on his palm and heavier on his heart.

On its backside was a tiny inscription. As he squinted at the words, the candles flickered out. A gust of wind descended into the fireplace and left scattered embers in its wake. The room went pitch-black, the temperature dropped, if possible, and a vaguely familiar odor invaded the room.

Rufus dropped the watch on the mantle and searched for a brimstone match. All the while, he bellowed for Ellison.

Running footsteps were followed by the handle jiggling. That was followed by a knock before his valet said, "My lord, you have locked the door."

"How could I lock it when I do not have the key?" he said with impatience. "The damned candles have gone out, as has the fire. You probably used inadequate coal. Wait, while I find my way to you." He took a couple of steps, and his foot struck the metal bath, causing pain to shoot up his leg. He swore, shaking his foot to ease the pins and needles, then hobbled over to the door and reached for the handle. Ice stung his palm, and he jerked his hand back.

His valet shouted in a high-pitched voice, "My lord, the handle be icy cold. It is bewitched. I . . . I shall go for help."

"Ellison," Rufus said in a deadly calm voice, "stay where you are, and do not spout such idiocy." Using the sleeve of his robe, he grabbed the handle again, turned and pulled. The door remained stubbornly in place and then suddenly gave way. He stumbled back.

Rufus pointed at the handle. "See, nothing but a sticky door. See that you oil the hinges so we avoid a repetition."

Ellison delicately reached out to touch the handle. "It seems fine now, my lord."

"Of course, it is fine. I have warmed it with my touch."

The valet stared at the handle with a doubtful expression.

"You are not to say another word about a haunting to me or anyone else," Rufus said, then added in a threatening tone, "If I find you have spread tales, especially to my mother, I will throw you out without a farthing to buy yourself ale. Do we understand each other?"

"Yes, my lord."

"Good. Then get on with your duties."

Unsettled, Rufus returned to his bedroom. He should have come home directly after his father died. Then he could have accomplished his two main goals—searched for his father's killer and cared for his family and servants. They apparently needed taking care of. Ellison was scared of shadows. His mother apparently imagined ghosts roamed the corridors. As for his sister, he had been home for days, and she had yet to greet him.

He paced around the bed. He should not blame his mother for turning to someone else for help. After all, he had not been here to comfort her after her husband died. But he was home now. He could make her trust in his goodness again, love him again, as she had when he was a child.

Beast. Rufus cringed at Lady Belle's unfair charge. Yes, he had erupted until he had sounded like a beast, but she had provoked him. Still, her allegation stung because it echoed his family's, his friends', even his Regent's, recent view of him. He paced to the window, flung open the curtains, and glared at the wintry landscape. It glittered back, cold and barren, like prison walls.

I am not a monster. A fine way to prove that to the world would be to clear all lingering suspicion that he had murdered his father.

Chapter Two

An oppressive mantle settled across Belle's shoulders as her coach clattered past the iron gateway guarding Lord Terrance's manor house. If only her carriage had not crossed his path last night. If only she had met his mother first.

She stopped herself. If onlys were as useless as snowballs thrown at a rock wall—or a man like Lord Terrance. The fact was, her vehicle *had* run across him, and he *had* forbidden her to come to his home. However, since his mother needed her, she must find a way to buck his frosty rebuff.

The carriage rounded a bend, and Clearview Manor came into view. Bare vines draped the medieval sandstone and brick building. High above, snow-capped gargoyles crouched over corner turrets, and rows of icicles stabbed downward from the eaves, like armed weapons awaiting the order to fire.

The conveyance drew to a halt, and the coachman jumped down to open the door. Normally, Belle would be the first to rush out, but a vision of Lord Terrance's furious demeanor kept her soles planted to the floor. She reasoned that she should wait for her companions to venture out first. But her maid Mendal wore a disapproving frown that rivaled one of those gargoyle's expressions and stayed in her seat, as if she never meant to leave the carriage.

At Belle's feet, the pup showed no sign that he wanted to go near the imposing manor. Despite his cowardly stance, Belle was pleased with his calm disposition. His behavior had changed dramatically since he instigated the carriage accident, and that suggested he had potential. On Belle's arm, which was encased in a long leather glove she had procured from the innkeeper, the owl sat and solemnly watched the dog, as if unsure about his changed character.

If the dog and her maid refused to get out, that left one last possibility. She turned to the man beside her who smelled of fresh baked bread. The moment the village innkeeper informed her that Mr. MacBride and Lady Terrance were close acquaintances, Belle had worked hard to persuade the baker to act as her escort.

She gave him a gentle elbow nudge. "Sir, would you please announce our arrival?"

The baker, shaking in his seat, refused to budge.

"There is nothing to fear, sir. Lady Terrance is your friend. She will be thrilled you have come to visit."

"But ah havena brought anything." He rolled his "r" in a strong Scottish brogue. "We should go get a few loaves."

"We are not leaving after coming all this way, Mr. MacBride."

The man did not respond, and with a defeated sigh, Belle accepted the coachman's help and stepped out herself.

The puppy followed, sniffing at the snow. He got a nose full of white powder and sneezed.

With grave misgiving, Belle contemplated the wide stairs that led to the imposing double doors. No one had come to greet them. She was unsure if she should be glad or worried.

The last time she had approached Lord Terrance's home was still fresh and mortifying. Then, it had been a clear spring night, at the tail end of her second Season, with a full moon in brilliant display. Belle's escort had tripped while he exited the carriage and landed on top of her, tearing her gown. From that point onward, the situation had gone from bad to worse.

Behind Belle, Mendal alighted onto Clearview Manor's sunny, snow-covered courtyard. Ignoring her maid's appalled protest, Belle handed her the spare glove and then the owl.

Finally, Mr. MacBride, too, stepped outdoors and offered Belle his arm. They were preparing to ascend the stairs when a clatter of hoofs sounded. MacBride jumped, and Belle's heart thudded.

"Ach, it be Lord Terror!" The baker whispered Terrance Village's nickname for their lord of the manor. "Ah am dun for. Why ever did ah listen to me wife when she said ta take ye here? She has not said a thing worth listening to since we married."

Afraid he would run away, Belle took a firm grip on his hand, prepared to drag him up the steps, if necessary. The horseman drew to a halt, and Mr. MacBride let out an audible sigh.

This was not Lord Terror. *Lord Terrance,* Belle mentally chided as her tension abandoned her shoulders.

The young buck, about the same age as Lord Terrance, shot an amused glance at Belle's and Mr. MacBride's clasped hands. The baker immediately pulled free.

Belle recognized the gentleman from her last disastrous Season. An ill sense about him had kept her from improving on their acquaintance. "Mr. Winfield, you reside in Cheshire?"

"Lady Belle Marchant, is it not? Good day." He tipped his hat. "My country estate is on the other side of the mere." Dismounting, he gave the coachman his reins and came over to give a handsome bow. "Dare I hope that you intend to grace our small village with your presence this winter?"

Suddenly, Belle's neck hairs quivered, but not because of the oily Mr. Winfield. Clearview Manor loomed over her shoulders like a shadow of doom. She gave the eaves a nervous glance. So Lady Terrance's grief had not conjured an imaginary ghost. There *was* an ominous presence here.

"That is a desolate looking house, is it not?" Winfield said. "I would have it torn down and rebuilt in a more flattering style, but Terrance seems fond of this monstrosity. So what brings you so far north, my lady?"

She faced the gentleman. "I have come for a visit with Lady Terrance. She is my grandfather's friend."

"I had heard the countess still wore dark colors."

Before she could respond, a loud crack sounded. She sensed danger stab from above. With a shouted warning, she pulled Mr. Winfield out of harm's way just as an icicle crashed and shattered where they had stood. She protected her face as splinters flew in all directions.

Mendal screamed. The owl fluttered its one good wing and screeched. The dog barked ferociously.

Mr. MacBride spoke first, his voice quivering and eyes wide with terror. "It is an omen, ah tell ye."

"He is right," Mendal said, sounding unusually timorous as she crossed herself. "We should leave. Bad luck comes from going where we are not wanted."

The front doors opened then, and a footman descended. Immediately, the dog raced up the stairs and inside.

"Dog!" Belle called out in alarm. The animal might wreck the place. This was *not* how she had hoped to introduce herself to the countess.

An older woman, dressed in black, moved to the open doorway. Belle recognized her from a drawing her grandfather had shown her. This was Lady Terrance. She gave off waves of fear as she looked toward the roofline.

Belle's worries drowned beneath the lady's emotional assault, leaving her head pounding with a headache. Through that onslaught, Belle's purpose became crystal clear. This is why she had come here. Lady Terrance needed her.

She strode past the servants and, ignoring Winfield's warning shout, crunched over the icicle remnants.

"Lady Terrance." Belle stood as straight as her backbone would allow. "Please allow me to introduce myself. I am Lady Annabelle Marchant. Lord Alford is my grandfather. I have come to help you, and I refuse to allow my servant, your son, or this house to stop me."

The countess stared at her wide-eyed. Then she let out a laugh.

Belle's concern spiked. Had this haunted house pushed the woman past the edge of reason?

"My dearest Belle, how glad I am to see you." Lady Terrance held out her arms.

Belle hesitated. After her son's rude reception, both in London and then on her way here last night, she had not expected such a warm welcome. In fact, since Belle's parents' death, no one had offered her a hug. Moisture filled her eyes, and losing all caution, she picked up her skirts and ran to greet the woman.

Lady Terrance's arms wrapped tight around Belle, as if they were old friends rather than strangers. She smelled enticingly of peppermint candy.

So this is how it feels to hug a mother. It had been so long, Belle had forgotten the wonderful sensation.

A horse neighing interrupted their heartfelt greeting. Belle blinked away tears and looked over her shoulder to see a man riding toward them. It was Lord Terrance, and his face was a mask of fury as he reined in.

Belle's shoulders dropped. She was too late. He would throw her off his property again. She tried to step away, but the countess's hold tightened. The lady pulled her into the house and shut the door. To Belle's shock, she then locked it.

Lady Terrance half led, half dragged Belle past a startled servant and into a room, then made to shut that door, too. The dog's body squeezing through blocked the action.

"You confounded dog," the countess said and gestured him in. As soon as he cleared the doorway, she closed and locked that door and pocketed the key. "Well, that should keep my son busy for a while."

"Aunt, will you introduce us to your guest?"

Belle swiveled and discovered several people present. A young lady in a simple black gown stood by the fireplace, her fine blond hair pulled into a severe bun. Beside her, a smartly dressed young man raised a quizzing glass to study Belle. On the settee, a matron, with a face full of wrinkles to testify to a well-lived life, eyed the wolfhound with obvious horror.

For a lady in mourning and not open to visitors, Lady Terrance did not want for company.

"Oh dear," Lady Terrance said. "How could I have forgotten you were all in here?"

"It is beyond us, Constance," the elderly woman on the settee said in a dour tone, "since you invited us here."

"Yes, aunt, what is this"—the gentleman waved his monocle in Belle's and the dog's direction—"all about?"

"Where are my manners?" Lady Terrance said. "Belle, allow me to introduce my family." She gestured toward the older woman. "Mrs. Henrietta Jones is my late husband's sister, and her son, my nephew, Mr. Phillip Crispin Jones. They arrived early this morning. The young lady is my daughter, Lady Susie Marlesbury. This, my darlings, is Lord Alford's granddaughter, Lady Belle Marchant."

Mr. Jones gave an elaborate bow. "So good to meet you."

"However did you find Earnest?" Susie asked.

Belle raised an eyebrow, confused by the unfamiliar name.

The young woman pointed to the dog sniffing the treats laid out on the side table beside the door.

"The dog belongs to you?" If she had known, she could have used returning the wolfhound as her excuse for coming.

"He belongs to Mama," Susie said, "though since my brother returned home, he has formed a strong attachment to the pup."

That was bad news. Not only had she invaded his lordship's home and been party to locking him out, now it looked as if she had also stolen his dog. She glanced at Earnest in dismay.

The hound, oblivious to being the center of attention, stood his forelegs on the table and gobbled numerous tiny cakes.

Belle pressed at her forehead. For someone not prone to fainting, she suddenly felt the need for a lie down. "I found him in the storm."

"How sweet of you to rescue him." Lady Terrance gave the dog an absent pet.

"My brother was heartbroken when he ran off," Susie said. "He went to search for him, despite the storm. I am surprised you did not encounter each other."

"They did!" The countess gave a delighted smile. "Or so Rufus advised me last night. I wish I could have witnessed it."

Belle, remembering the snowball pummeling, was heartily glad his mother had not been there.

"How did you meet Mr. MacBride?" Lady Terrance asked, thankfully switching topics. "He is a lovely man."

"Yes, he is," Belle said. "Should we invite him in?"

She had forgotten the baker and Mr. Winfield were standing on the doorstep. Not to mention Mendal. Then again, once Lord Terrance gained entry, she would be joining all three on the front steps expeditiously enough.

"I am sure they would have left by now." The countess gave a careless wave. "Rufus would have dealt with them. So, Mr. MacBride brought you, my dear? Good. After Rufus said he forbade you to come, I feared you might have left the village. I sent word this morning to the Briar Inn asking you to come."

"I must have left before your message arrived." If only she had waited.

"All that matters is that you are here now," Susie said.

"Highly inappropriate to drop by without permission." Mrs. Jones said, her frowning expression one of patent disapproval. "But then I had heard rumors in Town that your behavior is unorthodox."

A flush warmed Belle's neck and cheeks. Mrs. Jones sounded like the society patronesses who had banded together to withdraw her Almack's voucher. She raised her head to fiercely defend herself when she noted that although Mrs. Jones addressed her, the woman's gaze was fixed on her niece.

Mrs. Jones was not castigating Belle so much as instructing her niece on proper etiquette. Now that Belle focused on the older woman, she sensed unrest buffeting her like white-capped waves. Why so much concern over Lady Susie? Thus far, the young girl seemed perfectly well-behaved.

"Aunt, you must be mistaken," Susie said, drawing Belle's curious gaze. "There is nothing unacceptable about Lady Belle's behavior. She merely came to pay us a visit at Mama's request."

"She disobeyed my nephew's orders."

"It is my brother who showed rudeness in denying her the right to visit," Susie said with a stubborn tilt of her chin. "As long as Mama resides here, she may see whomever she pleases. Although visits can be tiring, on this occasion I am glad you grace us with your company, Lady Belle."

"Constance," Mrs. Jones said, "I do not approve of how you run your household. Most irregular. How can you allow your daughter to gainsay your son? If her respect toward her betters does not improve, no eligible man will have the chit."

So that is your worry. Belle's resentment faded.

"You are mistaken, Henrietta," Lady Terrance said in a placid tone. "Susie merely anticipates Rufus's actions. Once he meets Belle in these cordial circumstances, he can be nothing but charmed by the lovely figure she presents and invite her to stay." She took Belle's hand in hers and gave it an encouraging squeeze. "In any case, she is not here to merely visit. She is here to cleanse Clearview of our ghost."

"Balderdash!" a male said from behind Belle.

Startled, she spun around as Lord Terrance stepped into the drawing room and shut the door. He looked taller than she remembered. But then, last night he had spent most of their time together on the ground, with his head lying on her lap. Unfortunate that she had succeeded in finally waking him. He had been much more cordial while unconscious.

It appeared that a good night's rest had not improved his demeanor. His harsh frown suggested that far from being charmed, Lord Terrance was furious.

Lady Terrance edged behind Belle, while Earnest, smart dog, scrambled under the side table and tucked in his tail.

Belle told her fluttering heart to settle and held her arms out to her side, like a one-woman fortress.

* * * *

Rufus Marlesbury pocketed his key and raised an eyebrow at Lady Belle's display of foolish bravery. So she wanted a fight? He edged closer, hoping to intimidate her.

The move brought him within the sphere of her enticing lilac scent that he recalled clearly from last night. Standing this close, with more than lantern light to see by, he admired her long, curly eyelashes and luscious lips. It was deuced hard to hate a girl who looked this adorable.

She lifted her chin as if daring him to do his worst.

Her bravery incited a fervent desire to kiss her, something he had tried and failed to do last night. With his mother hiding behind the lady, now was hardly the moment for a second attempt. He stifled his unruly emotions and searched for his common sense. It had been there a moment ago.

To gain perspective, he focused on the room's other occupants. Under the table beside the door, Earnest caught his attention first. The disobedient pup was alive and well. A surge of pleasure swelled his chest. He squashed the urge to hug Belle and thank her for bringing his wolfhound home.

Could that be why she had come? He shook off that overly optimistic thought. Dark waters stirred this woman's mercenary heart. Her deplorable behavior last spring had resulted in her being ostracized by society.

"Cousin." Phillip's dulcet tone coming from across the room drew his attention. "Well met."

The splendidly dressed young gentleman looked as if he had presented himself for a night at Whites instead of a casual country stay. Aside from always outshining Rufus, Phillip could be deuced nosy, able to ferret out any covert activity. During their childhood, Phillip inevitably discovered whatever furtive goings-on his cousin was involved in and then blabbed about it at inappropriate moments.

Rufus wanted to groan. He was on a highly secret mission to uncover his father's murderer, so this was the worst time for Phillip to be here. Worse, he had brought his choleric mother with him.

Rufus tipped his head, biting the urge to suggest they both return to London, and said, "Good morning, Phillip. Aunt."

"Terrance," Mrs. Jones said, and sniffed in disdain. "I see your household is as well managed as ever. I suppose I need not be surprised that your hands on the reins are not as effective as my dearly departed brother's."

He ground his teeth to curb the urge to verbally react to that slight.

His mother came to his rescue by moving to the chaise across from Mrs. Jones. "Belle, come sit beside me. Susie, you too. It seems so graceless to carry on a discussion while on our feet."

"No more than locking your son out," Rufus said in a sour voice.

"Nonsense, dear," his mother said. "You are here. So how could that be, and so fast, if I had locked you out?"

"It helped that the servants know who covers their wages," he muttered under his breath.

* * * *

Belle gave Lord Terrance a startled look before she followed his mother to the chaise. He had spoken in a tongue-in-cheek manner that hinted at a sense of humor. He was unpredictable—one moment stern and forbidding, and the next tolerant and humorous. And last night, before he realized who she was, he had been so tender that she had been tempted to kiss him.

Was he a traitorous villain, as the villagers she had met at the Briar Inn insisted, or merely a too-proud, aloof gentleman? Either way, getting to know Rufus Marlesbury, the Earl of Terrance, might prove to be as dangerous as freeing the dark spirit haunting Clearview.

The moment she took her seat, Earnest came over to lie heavily across her feet. Lord Terrance aimed his disapproving frown at both of them, and the puppy hid his head under his paws and whined.

Belle scratched the wolfhound's ear. Earnest might belong to his lordship, but in her opinion, Lord Terrance had no understanding or appreciation of his pet's discerning behavior or finer characteristics. Which explained why the dog had run away. She had half a mind to keep the hound. After all, it was an established custom that finders were keepers.

She straightened from petting the dog to encounter Lord Terrance's narrow-eyed gaze. Had he gleaned her thieving intentions?

If only she could read him as easily as he read her. Unfortunately, her extra senses worked to their own agenda. Though his brooding gaze did suggest that his incensed feelings toward her from last night had altered somewhat. Then he had been angry enough to slander her name and throw words that had steamed her ears. Now his anger seemed more personal, intense, and, dare she believe it, passionate.

Lady Terrance touched her hand.

Realizing she had missed something, she said, "Oh, I beg your pardon. I was woolgathering."

"No wonder, my child," Lady Terrance said. "After your terrible experiences last night, and then with that falling icicle, your nerves must be stretched thin."

"What icicle?" Lord Terrance asked and took a seat near Belle.

"One crashed from the eaves and almost pierced the poor girl," his mother said.

"You did not faint?" Mrs. Jones's query sounded like an accusation.

Belle hid her smile. The straight-laced woman would not be appreciative of her humor. "I *was* startled, Mrs. Jones."

"A proper young lady would have been overcome."

"She was being brave," Lady Terrance said. "I fear, Rufus, we have no option but to invite her to recuperate in our home. After all, she almost died on our doorstep."

The countess obviously held no qualms about playing on her son's guilt. Belle glanced at Lord Terrance to gauge his reaction and caught him staring back at her with a deeply thoughtful look. Her heart skipped a beat in alarm, and, flustered by his brooding glance, she looked away.

"Mama has you there," Susie said, her smile suggesting she enjoyed her brother's predicament as she took her place beside her mother. "It will be fun to have Lady Belle visit."

"Yes, marvelous idea," Phillip said. "When mother suggested we come to the country, I feared I would be bored."

"It is our Christian duty to visit relatives during the festive season," Mrs. Jones said. "And I was sure Terrance would have no objection to me visiting his country home, even if I am no longer welcome to live in his London townhouse."

Rufus kept mum about that well-deserved accusation. After his father's murder, he had needed to do a thorough search of his townhouse from top to bottom, and he could not do so with his aunt poking her nose into every room he ransacked for clues. The fact that they did not get along had merely given him the perfect excuse to offer her alternate accommodations.

"And it was you, Phillip," she continued, "who reminded me that Constance might need my company during this first winter without my brother. Though I will not tolerate talk of ghosts while I am in residence."

"Well said, aunt," Lord Terrance said, and then looked startled that they were in agreement. "On that note, I, too, extend my invitation to Lady Belle to stay at Clearview Manor, *if you agree* there will be no more talk of spirits or mysterious happenings with my family."

Everyone's attention swung to Belle, and she turned to Lady Terrance. After all, her hostess had invited her to help with a haunting, not to pay a social call.

Giving a melodramatic sigh, her ladyship said, "Very well."

Belle hesitated longer, and Lord Terrance's challenging gaze relentlessly held hers captive. She disliked lying. If she gave him her word, she would keep it. But if she disagreed, Lord Terrance would show her the door.

She replayed his exact words, and that cheered her. He had said "no more talk" of otherworldly topics. Not that she must stop working to rid his house of its troubled spirit. Belle was more than happy to complete her task with no one else the wiser. In fact, it might work out better that way.

She nodded. "Agreed."

His eyebrow shot up as if in surprise and then as quickly, he smiled and nodded in approval.

Belle's extra senses surged to life, and a sense of "correctness" settled into the room. She had made the right decision. That sense of clarity was so strong she smiled.

Lord Terrance's gaze dropped to her lips and stayed there, as if he were enraptured by her smile. Then his aunt called his attention with a question.

Lady Terrance leaned toward Belle and whispered, "Well played, my dear. I assume you had your fingers crossed, too."

Susie smothered a laugh behind her hand. At Belle's surprised look, the young lady tilted her head toward her mother's back. Belle followed her lead and found Lady Terrance's fingers firmly crossed. Her ladyship's slippers were set at an odd angle that suggested the countess's toes also might be twisted.

"Since Phillip and my aunt seem to have already settled in," Lord

Terrance said, "it is time Lady Belle was shown to her quarters." He stood and extended his hand. "If you will allow me, it would be my pleasure to guide you."

"I am sure Felton is capable of doing that later, Rufus," his mother said. "I had hoped to speak with her more."

"She is travel-worn and should recuperate before you enlist her help to entertain you, Mama."

Without a word, Belle rose and allowed him to escort her out. As Earnest followed close beside her, Lord Terrance shot the dog a frowning look.

"I did not realize he belonged to you, my lord," she said. "You should have said something when we met last night."

"Ran over me, you mean."

Belle's cheeks warmed. "An accident. I explained that, but you refused to listen."

"All I heard were your intentions to upset my mother with talk of ghosts."

So, he had not forgiven her after all—not for taking his dog or invading his home. She suddenly understood that he intended to evict her. Escorting her had merely been a ruse to diplomatically remove her from his mother's side. Resigned, she paused by the front entrance.

Earnest stayed close, as if announcing he would go where she went.

Lord Terrance gave her an inquiring glance, and she said, "Is my maid still outside?"

"I sent her to unpack your bags. And I have ordered a cage to be brought up for the wounded owl once it is returned to you. My huntsman, who is good at attending to injured birds of prey, is currently tending it."

"You did all that?" And *before* his mother ever spoke on her behalf? Her heart was especially touched by his consideration for the owlet. What a complicated man.

"And Mr. MacBride and Mr. Winfield?" she said.

"Both had other matters to concern them. I saw to it that Mr. MacBride was adequately compensated for his troubles." He indicated the stairs. "Shall we?"

Still, she hesitated. "You said yesterday that . . ."

"That was yesterday." With a hand on her elbow, he urged her toward the stairs. "Today, you have stormed my castle and tamed my mother so that there will be no more talk of ghosts. You are a worthy opponent. One I plan to keep a close eye on in order to win this war."

Her startled gaze swept up and clashed with his frown. Even in anger, he made her heart skip. She did not want to spend her entire visit quarrelling.

They began the trek up to the first floor, and she said, "I am not playing a game, my lord, nor are we engaged in battle. You have nothing to fear from me. I am not your enemy."

At the landing halfway up to the above floor, Lord Terrance swung her around to face him. "You are the slyest of opponents," he said, eyes like flint. "One who battles from within rather than attacks from without. Never fear, I will ensure you are disarmed and rousted from my home before the week is out."

"You are completely mistaken in my character." She wanted to tell him that all she wanted to do was help his mother, but she knew he would not listen. "What possible harm could I mean to you or your family?"

"What harm do women always mean?"

She stared at him, confused. Before she could fathom his words, he pulled her closer with a firm hand on her back.

Mirroring her conflicted emotions, Earnest whined, then growled, and then whined again.

The shock of contact left Belle breathless. She stood with her palms pressed against his chest, a traitorous enjoyment creeping from her toes to her hairline. His hold forced her limbs against his hard legs. The heat of his breath brushed intimately against her mouth.

She knew she should give him a severe set-down, but all she wanted was to see his angry gaze melt with desire. Why would he not end her torment and kiss her? Mortified by that improper thought, Belle leaned away, but the dog was plastered against the backs of her knees. Some watchdog. She shoved him back, but Lord Terrance held her in place, as if to assert his mastery. To prove she was being released, not pulling away.

"How . . . how dare you, sir." The protest came far too late and sounded abysmally weak. In her mind, she heard Mrs. Jones say, *A proper young lady would be overcome by the experience.*

"I am a lady." She cursed her breathy voice, no longer certain the statement was even true. Did ladies dream of being ravished? "I am not a . . ."

"A Cyprian?" The word was a caress.

She should not know what that meant, but she had heard the word whispered as another form of harlot, a mistress, an illicit lover. "I have no idea what that means."

The tips of her ears singed with guilty heat even as he laughed with patent disbelief.

"My lady?" Mendal called from upstairs.

For once, Belle was grateful for Mendal's over-protectiveness.

"I am here," she called back. "Lord Terrance kindly showed me the way. Mendal can direct me now, my lord."

He bowed and released her with an annoying grin on his handsome face. "Till our next skirmish, Lady Belle," he said before leaving her standing alone on the landing.

There had been laughter in his tone, as if calling her a "Lady" was his private joke. *Beast.* Her hand clenched. What she would give for a ball of snow right now.

"Help him!" a man said in a harsh whisper.

Belle swung around, her pulse jumping. There was no one on the stairs but for her and Earnest, and the dog now cowered beside her. He shook so hard he was vibrating her right knee.

"Mendal?" she said, her neck hairs quivering, "did you see a man up there?"

Running footsteps brought her maid to the top of the stairs. "Are you speaking to me, my lady?"

Belle went up to the first floor to meet her. "Did you see a footman or some other man near here just now?"

"No, my lady. I have been standing over there by the door to our room waiting for you. No one came by. Is everything all right?"

Her skin prickling with unease, Belle shook her head. "No, Mendal. Everything is *not* all right with Clearview Manor."

Chapter Three

The next morning Rufus guided his mount, Goodwin, down a hill and toward the village. Although the official story said his father had died in a hunting accident, the late earl had been murdered. Even his mother was unaware of that.

The day after the murder, the Prince Regent had summoned Rufus to inform him of the findings of their initial investigation. He was told the investigator believed Rufus may have murdered his father. Rufus had sworn to his innocence, insisting he had only come upon his father's body that fateful night. He pleaded for, and was granted, a chance to clear his name. Temporarily. He had until the turn of the New Year, during which the royal investigation would be underway in London.

If evidence was uncovered to his culpability, he would be tried in the House of Lords and possibly face the hangman's noose. Rufus suspected that a runner or two had been on his trail since he left Westminster Abbey after that tension-filled meeting.

He shrugged off the thought. No time to worry about those who watched him. He needed to concentrate on his investigation. Having wasted more than five months exhausting every possible lead to the killer in London, Rufus had returned to the last place his father visited before his death, this sleepy village. But a fierce snowstorm had kept him housebound for a week, or at least until last night, when he had foolishly gone in search of Earnest. While stuck at home, he had spent his time doing a thorough search of his father's living quarters, which luckily were two doors away from his mother's rooms. Unfortunately, he had found no clue to a possible motive for his father's murder.

Today, he was keen to return to the hunt. Though the November sky was a brilliant chilling blue, his troubles trailed him like a snow-laden dark cloud. He would begin his investigation by acquainting himself with the local vicar, a man his father had appointed two years ago while Rufus was in Oxford for his final year. He would know everything about everyone in his parish. If Rufus made a favorable impression on him, the man could serve as his main source of insight into current life at Terrance Village.

Children's laughter drew him toward the churchyard. The moment Rufus entered the area, they quieted. Solemn eyes turned in his direction. Then they scattered. He looked behind him at what might have frightened them. No one was nearby but him. He swung back, scowling.

Within moments, the vicar stepped out the church door, one child hiding behind him. "Morning, my lord."

Rufus nodded as more parishioners exited. "Mr. Bedlow."

In every man's, woman's and child's gaze, dread seemed to lurk. As if they were astonished and dismayed by his presence. *Why?* They would not know he was suspected of murder. Now his father was gone, most of them owed him their living. He had every right to ride here, on his land, and pay his respects to the vicar.

"How unfortunate you missed the service," the vicar said with a genial smile as he approached him.

"Yes." Rufus was oddly tongue-tied. He sat on his horse, shoulders stiff, hands jerking the reins until Goodwin pranced.

Mr. Bedlow moved back as if afraid he might get trampled. Those gathered also shifted and eyed the horse with doubt. Rufus imagined the talk in their sitting rooms later. *Lord Terrance rode by the church. Sat his horse like a cow-handed youth and practically trampled the vicar.*

This was not the time for a private conversation. Wanting nothing more than to leave the lot of them to their gossip and speculation, he said, "Good day, vicar."

He tapped the gelding with his foot. The horse unexpectedly leaped into the air and took off at a gallop. He must have kicked harder than he thought. Rufus got the animal under control, but by then he was too far away and in too foul a temper to go back and apologize if he had frightened anyone.

The snow-covered hills lost their appeal, and his breakfast churned in his stomach as he went home. He spurred on his mount, his thoughts whipping him as fiercely as the wind.

Why do I let the villagers bother me? Befriending them is not part of my plan. He dismissed that needless worry. Nevertheless, by the time Rufus arrived at his stables, his temper still churned. The sight of Lady Belle looking serene and delightful in a green riding dress did not help.

He scowled at her. This was the worst time for visitors. Though he had accused her of being a distraction to his mother, he was the one in danger of being diverted from his purpose. Conceding he had a wild desire to kiss her at every meeting, he decided it would be prudent to keep her an arm's length away at all times.

With her attention fixed on the manor's upstairs window, she did not notice his return. He followed her gaze, and a quick check confirmed nothing but a fluttering curtain on a deserted upper floor.

Did she imagine a ghost lurked there instead of dust motes? The thought annoyed him, but since she had sworn to not share such silly speculations with his family, he let it slide.

Earnest stood nearby, wagging his tail, obviously eager for their outing. The hound had never shown such interest in going out with Rufus. Normally, the puppy was hard to locate except at meal times.

He dismounted and handed a sweating Goodwin to a stable boy. "Walk him before you rub him down."

With a wave, Rufus dismissed the groom waiting to help Lady Belle mount her horse. "I will assist her." He gave her a bow. "A fine morning to be outside. But it is not wise to ride alone. I can have another horse saddled and come with you."

"That is most generous of you, Lord Terrance." She gave him a wary glance. "However, I have already procured a riding companion."

Phillip, was his first thought. Had she given up seducing him in favor of his cousin? A sensible move, but it irked.

Discarding his recent injunction to keep his distance, he moved closer. To his dismay, unlike most females of his acquaintance whose charms declined on closer inspection, this lady's attraction increased. Her cheeks looked soft and touchable, her lips full and inviting, and her warm scent intoxicating. His cousin could not withstand such temptation.

"Phillip is hardly worthy of your interest," he said, trying to sound reasonable. "Although he is a splendid fellow, he is not plump in the pocket. As well, you would do better to set your sights on someone not burdened with a mother as controlling as his."

"I am not setting my sights on anyone." Her cheeks showed her blush to perfection. "Why do you always assume I am on the trail of a husband? Do I have that goal painted on my forehead? Is my conversation so laden with longing for a man's touch? Have I failed to show that I am pleased with my own company?"

"All women seek a mate. It is the law of nature." He was an expert on this subject. The female sex had been chasing him since he turned twelve.

"Not *my* nature, my lord." She sounded serious.

He coated his answer in disbelief. "Truly?"

She gave a curt nod. "I have ridden along that road, and the prospect has proven neither pleasant nor welcoming."

Was that a hint of bitterness? "But what would a well brought up young lady do otherwise, hmm?"

Absently, he gently brushed a lock of her chestnut hair off her shoulders. He could not help but linger on the dark, plush, silken cords meant to bind a man. His arm brushed her delicate collarbone, and his nerve endings reacted. Instinctively, he tightened his hold on her shoulder.

She shivered as if experiencing a mutual spark, and he smothered a triumphant grin. She might say she was uninterested in finding a mate, but her body disagreed. He wanted to show her the illogic of her stance. "If not marriage and children, what can you look forward to in life? You are wealthy enough that you would not need to take a menial position such as a governess or companion. What would you do with your days?"

She dislodged his touch. "I have plenty to occupy me."

She slipped away, and it was as if he had lost hold of something precious. "Such as?"

"You have forbidden me to speak of it."

Now he retreated, startled by her serious expression. Her gaze again flicked to the upstairs window. "Are you speaking of chasing after your silly imaginings?"

Her gazed hardened. *Wrong choice of words.* He was about to apologize when a more mischievous thought occurred.

"If marriage is truly out of your realm of interest"—he inched closer until her rapid breaths brushed against his throat like a warm wind—"I can suggest a more diverting pastime than frequenting mouldy old castles and desolate graveyards."

"Morning, Rufus."

He started and swung around, guilt riding him hard. Could Susie have overheard his impudent suggestion? He was unsure why he had even spoken so. Except Lady Belle seemed to stir his basest instincts.

Susie strode toward the stables wearing a dark blue riding habit with a black sash and sporting an innocent smile. "Are you coming with us?"

"You are riding with my sister?" he asked Belle.

"Yes, my lord." She signaled the groom to come closer.

"You look chipper to be out, Susie," he said. His sister had not looked so happy in a long while.

"I can hardly wait to ride Danielle." Susie's eyes were practically sparkling with excitement.

She was such a pretty girl. Why could she not dress to show herself to better advantage? "Your jacket is several years beyond the pale. And that skirt can garner no more comment than that it looks warm and serviceable. At least you are no longer in full black. Blue suits you," he told her.

She flushed darker, as if unhappy with his compliment.

"I only meant," he said, regretful that he had inadvertently hurt her, "that you can purchase any fripperies you desire. Make better use of local seamstresses."

"I like my dresses as they are," she said in a quiet voice and avoided his gaze.

Lady Belle was up to current fashion in a short white cloak over an emerald riding dress that came above her ankles and showed off her calf boots to advantage. While he spoke to Susie, she had mounted her horse and sat as if the two of them were made for each other.

Beside him, Susie's shoulders had slumped. Her gaze swung toward the house, as if she debated forgoing the ride and returning to the manor.

Lady Belle called to the groom to assist Susie to mount. She then drew abreast of his sister and, bending, whispered something in her ear. Immediately, Susie's back straightened, and his shy, dowdy sister looked every bit a lady. A few moments later, the two women cantered away.

Rufus returned to the house deep in thought. He might have misjudged their new guest. It appeared she could have a good influence on Susie. Lady Belle would have had at least two London Seasons, so she might be able to assist Susie prepare for her first.

He would watch his guest's actions over the next few days to see if she had outgrown her hoydenish ways. If she had, he would speak to his mother about Lady Belle joining them next spring in Town, as Susie's companion. Having someone closer to her age whose guidance she trusted might help bring his reclusive sister out of her shell. And might assist Lady Belle to see that there were more enjoyable aspects to life than make-believe ghosts and goblins.

With more optimism in his heart than had been there all morning, Rufus dashed up the steps and entered his home. Suddenly, he was hopeful that he would succeed in clearing his name so he could proudly present Susie at her first ball. And then he imagined leading the enticing Lady Belle onto the dance floor. For now, he had the house relatively to himself and a great opportunity to search for clues. He would begin in the library, another of his father's favorite haunts while at his country home.

* * * *

Earnest ran ahead to scout out the terrain, rouse birds into flight, and chase rabbits into warrens. The peaceful snow-draped countryside gave Belle time to calm her agitated emotions. Lord Terrance's touch on her hair and his breath on her skin had sped her heart rate and heated her cheeks. She had wanted to run her fingers across his face to see if he was as strong and tender as he looked.

Thankfully, she had broken away from his hypnotic gaze before she made a fool of herself. He would have laughed at her ardent response and said it was proof that she had come to Clearview Manor to seduce him. The arrogant earl was too aware of his effect on her. Belle had never been this attracted to any man before, not even her betrothed. She had known Jeffrey for over a year, and he had only kissed her on her cheek. Lord Terrance had attempted to kiss her on her lips on both their first and second meetings.

Fool that she was, she had been disappointed when Mendal interrupted them both times. Today, if Susie had been even a little late, Lord Terrance might have succeeded on his third attempt, and Belle worried she would have been complicit in the crime. What if he found a fourth opportunity and there was no rescue?

A delicious shiver spun through her.

"Are you cold, Lady Belle?" Susie asked. "Do you wish to return?"

The quietly spoken question startled her. They had ridden for a half hour without saying a word. Susie had been upset and Belle distracted, but it was bad manners to ignore her. "I am perfectly fine. Sorry to be so quiet."

Susie shook her head. "I like quiet."

The girl had lost the joy she had displayed when she first came outside. Lord Terrance's fierce glowers and sharp comments had completely dampened the young lady's enjoyment.

"Your brother can be foreboding," she said with sympathy.

Lady Susie looked off into the distance. "He means well."

"I am sure he does."

The day was bright and inviting. Having spent most of her life in gray, crowded London, Belle fell in love with the open countryside. Lady Susie, on the other hand, probably took this wide rolling landscape for granted.

"Thank you for this tour of your land," Belle said. "I am enjoying the ride."

As if recalling her role as guide, Susie launched into a list of all they rode past. In a monotone, she described whom each farm belonged to and the names of every hill and mere.

When Susie pointed to a stately home whose dilapidated appearance suggested a more interesting history than Lady Susie's clipped "Windhaven," conveyed, Belle had to break in. "You must love this village and everyone in it."

"I have never given the subject much thought."

"If you do not care to live here, surely you would spend more time in London?"

No response.

Belle's extra senses tingled, giving her an impression of light suppressed by a cloak of darkness. The image suggested that lurking beneath Susie's deceptively placid façade was a vibrant personality waiting for an opportunity to shine.

On this bright cold morning, Belle wanted to break into this lady's solitary world, one with apparently more bars and locks than the Tower of London. "I met a group of locals at the Briar Inn yesterday," she told the young woman. "They apparently breakfast together every Sunday to speak of local news and events."

"I rarely socialize," Susie said. "It is too tiresome."

"Not even dinner parties?"

Susie remained silent so long that Belle gave up hope of ever receiving a response. When her companion finally spoke, her voice was such a whisper that Belle had to lean in to hear.

"Papa did not encourage Mama and me to socialize without his supervision. He feared we would embarrass him. I obeyed his strictures."

"That sounds lonely."

"My rooms and plants are all the companionship I require."

If that were true, then Belle was honored to have Susie's company.

At the village, several people stopped to wish them good day. Susie avoided eye contact and, with head tilted away, spurred her horse forward. Belle thrived on the conversation, and Earnest loved the pets. But both had to abandon their socializing early in order to catch up with their guide.

They rode by a lane that led to a church and then followed a path through snowy fields. Earnest romped through the snow, barking. Soon they would be back at the stables, and Belle still had a sensitive topic to broach.

"May I confess something?" she asked.

Susie nodded. "I am good with secrets. Better than Mama."

Belle smiled as she visualized the countess's crossed toes and fingers. "Your mother is a dear, sweet woman and incorrigible. She expects me to disobey Lord Terrance's orders about—" she paused.

"Ghosts," Lady Susie whispered.

Belle nodded, knowing they treaded on forbidden ground. "Do you believe in them?"

"Mama does. She is afraid to sleep."

That was troubling. Did her son know?

"Once, late at night, I went to the library for a book," Susie said. "My mother's room was lit. Since then I have checked on several nights, and each time, the candles burn in her room. Occasionally, I hear her voice."

Where earlier, Susie's words had trickled out, now the floodgates had opened as she continued with, "Her maid tells me that Mama does not fall asleep till the sun comes up. That she has not slept through the night once since Rufus brought back Papa's remains and buried him behind the manor."

"I was afraid that might be the case," Belle said. "She requested my help to settle a restless spirit."

"Can you do so?" Susie gave her an inquiring look. Unlike her brother, Susie seemed more curious than scoffing.

"Perhaps. Although your mother expects me to disobey your brother's wishes, I intend to keep my word."

"You will not help Mama, then?" Concern framed her face.

Belle shook her head. "I did not say that. I simply do not intend to involve the countess in my activities. This news of her restlessness is worrisome, however. Ghosts are notorious for venturing out after midnight, which is when I must track it. If your mother is awake then, we must distract her from my activities."

Silence settled once more as Susie considered the matter. They rode into the stables, signaling an imminent end to their private conversation.

"Rufus will be displeased if he finds out you cling to your quest," Susie said and reined in.

"I will not to speak of ghosts to anyone, including you, from this point forward." Belle also drew her horse to a halt. "I will act as if I am merely paying a visit to Lady Terrance to appease my grandfather, who is worried about her."

"I met Lord Alford once, about ten years ago," Lady Susie said. "He was a kind man. He spoke about you at great length, especially to my father. Mama suspected that he wanted to set a match between the two of you, once you reached your majority."

Belle arched a brow in surprise at this comment. Susie was full of intriguing information. Belle wondered if her grandpapa still nursed a hope for a match between her and Lord Terrance, and if that was why he had encouraged her to come. If so, then Lord Terrance's fear about her presence in his home might be closer to the truth than Belle cared to admit.

She accepted a groom's help to dismount.

The stable hands moved away, and she and Susie walked toward the house. Despite being far from anyone's earshot, Susie still whispered, "We did not know about your special abilities then."

"At that time, neither did I. My ability only manifested after I came of age. I suspect your father would not approve of me now, any more than your brother does."

"Rufus believes nothing odd is going on in our home."

Belle stopped and faced her companion. "And you?"

Lady Susie absently petted Earnest's head as the dog sat between them. "Most of my time is spent in my chambers, and nothing odd ever happens there." She sounded as if she regretted her peaceful existence. "I know something troubles Mama, though, and if you can alleviate her concerns, it would ease my mind greatly. I do not need to see a specter or hear strange sounds to believe something is wrong with Clearview. The house feels wrong. It has been so since my father died. My brother would say it is a manifestation of our grief. But then he does not believe in anything he cannot see, touch, smell, hear, or taste."

"He has a point," Belle said. "Much of what I do seems illusory to most people."

Keeping Lord Terrance's strictures in mind, she did not add that while she had waited for Susie earlier, she had sensed that someone watched her from a third floor window. And the icicle that fell on the exact spot where Mr. Winfield and she had stood had been real enough.

All indications were that a spirit did haunt Clearview Manor, and Belle intended to contact that spirit. When she succeeded, she would try to discover what kept it earthbound. Susie might be able to help with that discovery.

"It has been my experience," Belle said, "that if something monumental worries a person while they are alive, that worry can linger in a place they consider their home. Do you know of anything that your father was concerned about before his death?"

Susie shook her head. "My father never confided in me. Rufus might know."

Belle sighed. "Unfortunately, he is the one person I cannot ask. Nor your mother. And you and I shall speak no more of what your brother calls my 'silly imaginings.' Now, shall we go in for breakfast?"

"Yes, I am famished. As for my brother, I know how to behave around him. The same way I did with Papa. While in his presence, I behave as he expects me to, and I avoid him the remainder of the time. Then he does not bother me."

Belle gave the young girl a startled look. "Is that what you want? For people to not bother you?"

"Of course. It is best not to be bothered by those who cannot accept me as I am."

"That is a rather lonely life."

"Safe," her new friend replied.

"Tedious."

"Dependable."

"Dull as ditch water."

Susie laughed and held up her hand for peace. "You win. At least in this war of words. But my way works well. I have not had to go for a Season. Every time Papa broached the subject, I had a megrim. So off he would return to London and leave Mama and me in peace."

"And both of you missed the excitement of balls and musicals." Belle saw no wisdom in Susie's course.

"We have books to entertain us. In the last year I have traveled to Paris and China and India in my mind. As for Mama, she did not want for company. Many locals call her friend. The baker, you have met. There was also a Mr. Darby, the local blacksmith. But he died recently."

Belle already knew about the blacksmith. A Sunday morning breakfaster at the Briar Inn had mentioned his name. Darby had been well-loved by the locals, and they deeply mourned his sudden death.

"It is strange," Susie said as they climbed the front steps, "but ever since Papa died, Mama has not visited with anyone." She visibly shuddered. "If Papa had found out about Mama's friendships, the house would have shook with his temper. I loved him dearly, but . . ."

"It is best not to dwell on the matter," Belle said.

Earnest, having run ahead, now lay by the front door. The wolfhound, with his gaze trained expectantly on her for some reason, reminded her of Lord Terrance.

"What about your brother?" Belle asked. "While you and your mother were entertaining yourselves, who looked out for him?" Her question surprised her because Lord Terrance had never evoked sympathy in her before.

"Rufus?" Lady Susie said, sounding equally surprised. "Why does he need looking after? He can take care of himself."

"No need for a mother's hug or a sister's embrace, you mean?" The words came forth with more passion than Belle had intended. She took a breath to formulate her thoughts and find a way to explain where her emotion came from. "I lost my parents and my sister to whooping cough when I was five. Though I love my grandpapa, I know how it feels to be lonely."

"I had heard about your loss," Lady Susie said. "You have my deepest sympathies."

Belle nodded acceptance. "It was a terrible time. Even though I was young then, I remember their pain, the horrific whooping sound my sister made as she attempted to take in a simple breath. Mama seemed so weak, and even Papa, whom I always pictured as robust and powerful, was confined to bed for days on end. Grandpapa would not let me near them, so every day I waited and listened to their coughs."

She paused as a familiar heaviness settled in her chest. "I am sorry to go on so about my past."

"Pray, do not be embarrassed. I would like to hear the rest. Finish the tale. It will help."

Oddly, Belle felt that Susie spoke the truth, and she nodded. "The worst day of my life was when I could no longer hear my sister's whoop. Grandpapa came to tell me Ellen had died. Then Mama passed away. A day later, Papa was gone. Life was never the same."

Susie touched Belle's arm, and Belle treasured that slight contact. She had never spoken of that terrible time to anyone before, and now that she had, she did feel better for it.

"When your mother embraced me at Clearview's doorstep, I had never felt so welcomed or wanted since I was a child. My grandfather loves me dearly, but he does not show his emotions with physical gestures. Although your brother has a mother and a sister, if you do not share such gestures with him, he must feel as alone as I do."

"I hope during your stay you will consider me your sister." Compassion shone from Susie's gaze. "But you are mistaken in one thing. Rufus is much like Papa. He does not need comfort."

Help him. That was the phrase she heard on the staircase yesterday. Could this be what Lord Terrance needed help with? "Everyone needs comfort," she said thoughtfully.

Susie did not respond to her comment, but said instead, "We shall seal this new relationship by calling each other by our first names. I hope you feel at ease to call me Susie."

Belle nodded. "Please call me Belle."

Susie reached for the front door handle, and inspiration suddenly struck Belle. "Wait."

This lonely existence of mother and daughter, one separated from friends while the other was cut off from normal human contact, was unhealthy. Sad thoughts and depressed emotions encouraged trouble spirits to linger, made them unwilling to leave those who loved and still grieved them. Also, spirits tended to make an appearance between midnight and three in the morning. So she could both discourage the nightly hauntings and improve the occupants' moods if they found a way to effectively distract the countess after midnight.

"I have an idea of how to help your mother," she told her new friend.

Susie gave her a questioning look. "What would that be?

"I noticed this morning that you have a billiard table. Do you and your mother play?"

"Yes."

"Then I suggest we hold some nightly games. But let us keep this between us. I promised your brother no more talk of ghosts, so we cannot tell him the reason for the timing of these particular games."

The feasibility of secret midnight games and possible repercussions played across Susie's face as her emotions fought a battle between protecting her privacy and helping her mother. The moment her decision was made, Belle sensed Susie's response had swung in her direction.

Belle's excitement built, and her cheeks heated with her excitement. If this worked, it would certainly be fun, and that was something she had not enjoyed in many months. More importantly, raising Lady Terrance's spirits by engaging her interest would aid in ridding the darker spirit haunting the woman. They just had to find a way to do so without Lord Terrance finding out.

Chapter Four

Later that night, Belle lay in bed and let Earnest warm her feet through the blankets. Mendal's objections to a dog on the bed were forgotten the moment her maid departed. The owl, whom Belle had named Lady Sefton—after the one benefactress Belle had left following her disastrous second Season—was secure within her bamboo cage and glared at Earnest with studied insolence.

When Belle's bedside clock ticked two in the morning, she sat up. Earnest jumped off the bed, tail wagging. Under the dying hearth's dim light, she tied on her slippers and shrugged a warm woolen dressing gown over her nightdress. With Earnest by her side and a candle in hand, she ventured into the corridor.

On the landing by the stairs, she waited, as arranged, and wondered if Susie would come. The girl had skipped dinner so Belle had missed the chance to confirm their rendezvous.

The house was eerily silent. Time ticked by. The entry hall below was unoccupied, the servants long since gone to bed. Earnest sighed heavily and slumped onto the wooden floor.

After several minutes, Belle's back ached from standing, so she stepped down two stairs and rested her bottom on the landing. Earnest shifted to lie against her back and gave another loud sigh.

She appreciated his warmth next to the cold floorboards. Her comfortable bed beckoned her to snuggle beneath its still warm covers. *Should I give up?* She rubbed her arms and legs. With lack of movement, the night was chilly, even indoors.

Suddenly, the air stirred, and Belle's special senses snapped to attention.

Earnest growled low and deep.

Had a door opened? She leaned over the dog to peer to the left. No one lurked along that corridor. Yet Belle was certain she and Earnest were being watched. By the ghost?

Suppressing a shiver, she stood and used her "other sight" to check around her. No shimmer. No shadow. Not even a sound. Yet the warning sensation remained.

Earnest, also on his feet, stayed stuck to her hip like a third leg. Not that there was any reason to be afraid. From all the countess had relayed to Belle's grandfather, though an ethereal entity hovered near her bedroom ceiling each night, it neither approached nor disturbed an item.

Belle suspected that the spirit was the lady's recently deceased husband. As such, it might be entirely nonthreatening, but its visits had to stop. She had been summoned to Clearview to ensure that outcome.

She inched toward the left corridor where the presence was strongest. Earnest whined and stepped on her dressing gown. She pulled free. She deepened her breathing, calmed her thoughts from their frantic rush of worries until all she thought about was the corridor, the shadows extending from her candle, each step she took, each breath she released. Her pulse slowed to a soft *thump-thump, thump-thump*. The air shifted from merely cold to bone-chilling, and her ears popped.

"Who's there?" she whispered. A breeze grazed her cheek, and she sensed the rush of intense turmoil. A roar of anger whipped through the peaceful corridor. *Find him!*

Belle reeled in shock, trying to make sense of the ghost's message. *Find whom?* And why? "I mean you no harm." Brave words when the ghost was apparently not the one in danger. "Will you speak with me? Whom do you seek?"

"Belle," a soft voice said from behind her.

She swung around. Susie stood with flickering candle in shaky hand.

"You came." Belle's heart still thundered. The air returned to a normal winter-coolness. Earnest shook himself and gave a loud snuffle. A glance back showed her ghostly visitor had gone.

"Whom were you talking to?" Susie asked.

Belle remembered Lord Terrance's stipulation about ghostly topics with his family members. "No one. I was worried you had changed your mind."

"Almost did." Her nightcap secured under her chin in a fine bow, Susie looked as if she might still run away. She checked over her shoulder.

Belle took a deep breath and sported a mask of gaiety, hoping that would draw the real feeling to her. "Is this not exciting? Far better than hiding in your room, surely?"

"Not if we get caught," Susie said in a fierce whisper. "If Rufus discovers us, I will never hear the end. His lectures can run for days."

"We are on a sacred mission." Belle's mood lightened at the thought of outfoxing Rufus Marlesbury. That was the best part of her plan. "Heroines must never give consideration to possible retribution. Do your books not say so?"

"They do, but those characters never had a brother like Rufus. Be assured, he will give us his 'consideration to possible retribution' when he catches us."

Earnest whined as if in support of Susie's concerns.

Belle rolled her eyes at her faint-hearted companions. "*If* he catches us. Come, we have one more to gather for our party."

She took Susie's cold hand and tugged the girl toward her mother's chamber.

Susie pulled back. "Belle, Rufus's rooms are across the hall from Mama's. My heart beats so loudly, he will hear it if we go any closer."

Earnest lay down and covered his head with his paws.

"Faint heart never won fair lady," she whispered before urging them toward the countess's doorway. "You go in first, Susie. She might scream if she sees me at this time of night."

Susie eased open her mother's door and peered in.

"Well?" Belle practically mouthed the word.

"No light in here, but her bedroom door is ajar. There seems to be a candle lit there."

All three entered, and Belle eased shut the door behind her. "Earnest and I will wait here while you speak with your mother."

To Belle's night sensitive eyes, the room seemed filled with dainty chairs and knickknacks poised to crash at a dog's sniff. She took a firm grip on the wolfhound's scruff before he thought to run wild in here.

Susie scratched on her mother's bedroom door and then entered to announce herself. After a moment of conversation, the countess appeared, dressed in a silk dressing gown.

"My dear Belle, what a wonderful plan." Lady Terrance rushed across the room and hugged her. Belle returned the embrace, loving the warm human contact after her chilly supernatural encounter.

Behind her mother, Susie looked pleased and rather proud.

"We must be very quiet," Belle said when the countess released her. Then added with a mischievous grin, "And do not forget your change purse."

Soon, like three young girls out for a lark with their dog—with skirts raised, candles shaking and smothered giggles—they tiptoed below stairs. Belle entered the games room first, while the countess, Susie and Earnest cowered behind the door.

The large room, with balcony curtains drawn back, was moonlit and silent. There were antlers on one wall, a tapestry on another, and several comfortable chairs positioned around the hearth. The most striking object, however, was the large rectangular slate table with three ivory balls on its green baize top. It fairly shouted for players to pot all but the cue ball into one of six pockets.

"It is safe to come in," Belle told her companions.

"Good," her ladyship said and followed her in.

Susie and Earnest shuffled in last.

"I shall fetch the cue," her ladyship said.

Belle lit candles and soon had the room ablaze and scented with paraffin and beeswax.

Susie remained motionless by the door. Belle left her to come to terms with joining this party. If she were to truly turn her back on solitude, she must do so voluntarily, or at the first sign of trouble, she might retreat.

Belle used a candle and some tinder to light the hearth's coals. By the time she turned around, Susie hunted inside a sideboard.

"What do you look for?" She was thrilled to see her new friend actively participating.

"Port," Susie said. "I have always wondered why Rufus finds it so appealing."

The grin on Susie's face was infectious. If she would steal her brother's drink, then she had indeed taken the first crucial step to overcoming her dread of wrongdoing.

"Good girl." Her mother emptied her change purse on the billiard table in a jingle of coins.

Belle did the same, and Susie added her booty to the pile. They separated the coins into three equal portions and then set the rules for the bets.

The countess won the right to start.

"If we are to drink on top of gamble," Belle said, "we will need sustenance."

"A grand suggestion," the countess said. "Be a dear and fetch us some of that roast duck cook prepared for supper. I was not hungry earlier, but now I would love a bite. Susie, let us practice. I have no intention of letting Belle return home with more coins than with which she came. Alford would rub it in with every letter we exchange."

Belle's smile stretched from ear to ear as she made her way to the kitchen, Earnest at her heels. While she remained at Clearview, she intended to ensure the countess did not spend another night alone while wide-awake and worried.

By the stairs, her glance flew to where she had encountered the ghost. That brief brush suggested the spirit haunting Clearview was not benign. The icicle crash now made sense. The ghost, in her brief contact, had given the impression that it not only churned with fury, but was also on the hunt.

"Just my luck. I have to deal with a spirit as contentious as his son," she whispered to the dog.

Earnest whined as he paced between a door to the left and her. He was restless to get to that bone she had promised. "All right, lead the way to the food."

She followed him to the kitchen. Her thoughts, though, lingered on the late Lord Terrance's ghost because Belle carried some guilt about his death.

On the day he died, she had been at a card party and had a vivid vision of a pistol aimed at him. Certain that death stalked him, Belle became panicked, determined to go to his rescue. Unable to locate Mendal, she had left a message for her maid and asked Lord Fitzgerald, a gentleman closely allied to the Terrances, to escort her to their London home, post haste.

With her thoughts centered on the imminent danger to Lord Terrance, she had not noticed, until after they entered the carriage, that Fitzgerald was deeply in his cups. His alcohol-imbued breath soon suffocated the confined space. If that were not bad enough, the gentleman then proceeded to mistake her innocent request for his escort and introduction to the Terrances as a cover to a liaison.

When the vehicle finally stopped, Belle, having fended off the letch for the entire horrifying ride, rushed to escape. He drunkenly stumbled after her. Then, in a desperate bid to keep from falling, he had grabbed at her gown, and it tore from bodice to waist. That horrendous ripping of satin and sarsenet still haunted her.

From his front windows, Rufus Marlesbury had witnessed the entire sordid display. She shuddered at the memory. He had a right to his low opinion of her. On the surface, that scene must have looked damning.

Unfortunately, his solution to the problem of unwanted drunken guests on his front steps had been to send her home, thankfully alone, in a hackney. Talk of her escapade could not as easily be resolved, as it spread like wildfire within the Beau Monde.

As Belle dealt with those repercussions, her grandfather brought more bad news. The Earl of Terrance had indeed died the night before. But of a hunting accident, not murder.

Smarting from embarrassment, Belle's doubts about her so-called "ability" had plagued her for weeks afterwards. Or it had until she arrived at Clearview, and Lord Terrance had accused her of being a charlatan. Since then, she felt compelled to defend her talent and was proud of every sign of its manifestation.

On reflection, her encounter tonight attested that her ability was real enough. "For if the late Lord Terrance's death was simply an accident, Earnest, why is his spirit so restless?" That begged two more questions.

Was my vision at that card party right? Had Lord Terrance's father been murdered?

They arrived in the kitchen, and ghosts and deaths were apparently the last things on the dog's mind as he sniffed out the larder. Belle proceeded to pile a platter with roast duck and bread and cheese. Then she procured a meaty wing for her four-legged friend, whom she deemed a more worthy escort than his two-legged master.

In the end, the tray was heavier than expected. Carrying it and the candlestick proved difficult. She debated how to manage the task when Earnest's attention swung toward the door.

A moment later, footsteps sounded down the corridor. Had her pilfering woken the housekeeper? Or, heaven forbid, Lord Terrance?

Neither option was palatable, so Belle ducked under the kitchen table. Luckily, it had a cloth that hung low enough to cover her presence.

Earnest! He sat too far away to reach and pull in.

The door swung open, and the intruder came into sight. A male wearing expensive slippers and a magnificent Chinese dressing gown, if the embroidered hem was any indication. Belle shivered in excitement at seeing his lordship in his night attire.

"What have we here?" the man asked.

Not Lord Terrance. Where Lord Terrance's sarcastic tones could send shivers up her skin, this gentleman's subtle voice merely intrigued. Her hopes came crashing down, and a contrary part of her lamented her bad luck.

Earnest, on the other hand, wagged his tail in welcome.

"Earnest," the man said, "did you pack that tray yourself?"

It was Mr. Phillip Jones, Lord Terrance's cousin. *Drat!*

He bent beside Earnest, and Belle edged back.

Mr. Jones ruffled the dog's fur. He then lifted the tablecloth and stared at her. "Good evening, Lady Belle."

"Good evening, Mr. Jones."

The muscle movements of his cheeks suggested he suppressed laughter. "One might almost say good morning. It is but a few hours before the sun is due to rise." He shook his head, as if confused. "I thought young ladies did not arise until several hours after sunrise. Are country customs different?"

Belle shifted uncomfortably. How to explain her presence and not give away her partners in crime? "Yes, well, my appetite flared suddenly, and I thought to come here for a bite to eat."

His eyebrow rose, as if he considered her words, then he raised his head as if to study the mound of food. When he glanced at her next, her cheeks heated.

"With something for Earnest, too, no doubt," he said. "He does have a big appetite."

The dog obligingly licked his chops.

Again the eyebrow lift before he silently held out a hand. She accepted his help and scrambled out from beneath the table.

Once she was on her feet, his gaze thoroughly appraised her. As she did him. Her senses flared. This man was more than the dandy he portrayed. Keen intelligence burned behind his inquisitive gaze.

Curiosity replaced Belle's embarrassment. "If you do not mind my inquiring, sir, why are you here?"

Immediately, a curtain of ennui descended. A handkerchief appeared in his hand, and he waved it about the room. "As with you, Lady Belle, I came because my appetite plagued me."

As succinctly as those words were pronounced, she sensed them to be a blatant lie. Her inner sight showed him upstairs, hidden by the wall, watching her cross the floor below, and then he deliberately followed her downstairs. *Why?*

The door burst open, and Susie ran into the kitchen. "Belle, you have been an age. Mama thought you might be lost."

Her words died under her cousin's quizzing eyebrow.

"Good evening, Suz," Mr. Jones said. "We missed you at supper. Aunt said you were indisposed. Glad to see you recovered."

"Oh, Phillip," Susie said in a weak voice.

The girl was retreating, and Belle refused to allow that. Not after she had fought so hard to get Susie to drop her guard. "You have caught us, right and proper, Mr. Jones. We might as well admit all. We—the countess, Susie, and I—plan a game of billiards for tonight. Would you care to join us?"

He swung around, and his gaze again pierced her. "I did not realize ladies played the game."

"Oh!" Susie said, "you cannot mean for us all to play, Belle? He is my cousin, but he is a stranger to you. It would be most inappropriate, after dark, and you in your nightgown."

"Dressing gown." Belle tightened her belt in emphasis. "Besides, I am already in his company—after dark." She turned to the gentleman. "It would be more appropriate with Susie and the countess as my chaperones, do you not think so, Mr. Jones?"

"Your logic is exemplary," he said, with a quiet laugh. "Besides, Suz, it is not as if I have any blunt to attract Lady Belle's attention. So, if you are worried about my virtue, you need not be. I am perfectly safe in her company."

He gave an exquisite bow, and Belle responded with a deep curtsy, loving his absurd sense of humor. He might be a rogue, but she liked him.

"You are both hopeless," Susie said. "What will Rufus say when he finds out? And he will. He always does. What if he insists you marry Phillip?"

"Well," Belle said, "Mr. Jones will no longer be poor, I will have a husband who tolerates my impish behavior, and you will have a new relative who is also a friend." She patted Mr. Jones's arm. "But you need not worry about that, sir. From what little I have seen of Lord Terrance and his family, I am certain he will not discover us. He would never guess his mother and sister have any interests outside reading and sleeping."

"You are mistaken, Belle," Susie said. "Rufus knows Mama and me quite well."

"How could that be, Susie," Belle asked in a gentle voice, "when neither of you spend more than a few minutes with him?"

While Susie pondered that, Belle handed Mr. Jones the platter of food and took the candlestick. "Shall we?"

He bowed and gallantly held open the door. Belle rather liked Mr. Jones, even if he was a liar.

To her mind, there were at least three types of men. There were *Unprincipled Cads* like Lord Fitzgerald, who took advantage of innocent women caught in unusual circumstances. Then there were *Men In Disguise,* like Mr. Jones, who might have a perfectly good reason for hiding their true selves, and she hoped that time and closer acquaintance would help unmask him. Lastly, there were *Incomprehensible Mysteries,* like Lord Terrance, who had a fiery temper and a scorching appeal. But approaching too closely might get her burned.

I wonder into which of those categories Jeffrey fit? Then she added a fourth. *Cowardly Cold Fish.*

Earnest led the way back to the games room. He wore a proud grin on his long face as he checked back, which he did frequently, to ensure Belle and her friends followed close.

As they passed the stairs, Belle wondered if either of the Lord Terrances, alive and dead, might indeed get wind of her game.

* * * *

The next morning at breakfast, Rufus was alone in the dining room but for his aunt. He listlessly picked at his warm and delicious eggs and bacon rashers. Other than the servants, apparently he and his aunt were the only members of his household who had bothered to wake with the dawn of a new day.

Hair pulled back and dressed in a mobcap and black gown, Mrs. Jones appeared a somber matron. The only good thing about her company at table was that she sat at the other end.

Too far away to berate me, thank heaven.

His gaze shifted to the door. It remained shut. Hours kept at Clearview were different than in Town, but he recalled country people waking earlier, not later.

The butler, Felton, entered the room and bent beside him to speak. "Mr. Nightingale has arrived, my lord."

Rufus nodded. "Show him into the study."

Mr. Nightingale, the Agent in Chief of the family's Cheshire holdings, had sent Rufus regular reports to the London townhouse. Busy ferreting out the events that led to his father's death, Rufus had neglected them. Now, back at Clearview, he had taken the opportunity to read the man's missives thoroughly, and what he discovered did not please him.

This was his first interview with Nightingale, and he had better present a more congenial aspect than the tone of his reports had conveyed. In writing, he came across as rude and presumptuous, and he had intimated that Rufus was more interested in his Town activities to the detriment of his assets.

His father would have never tolerated anyone so ill-mannered to stay in his employ. Rufus, too, was ready to discharge the man out-of-hand, but then remembered how he must have seemed to the vicar yesterday and decided to hear Nightingale out. Everyone deserved a second chance.

He stood and pushed away his half-eaten breakfast. "By your leave," he said to his aunt, who barely nodded.

He had reached the door when she spoke. "Where are you off to, Terrance?"

The clipped tones and unfamiliar address stopped him in his tracks. In all his years, she had always called him "boy." It was only since the death of his father that she addressed him by name. The formal address gave him little pleasure, since each time she said "Terrance," it still sounded like "boy."

"I meet with Mr. Nightingale on business, aunt."

"I will accompany you then." She put aside her letters.

"Not necessary." Bad enough he had to breakfast under a cold shower. He did not need one while he berated Nightingale.

"Since your dear mother is hardly capable of holding two thoughts at the same moment without confusing issues," she said, "I often assisted my brother with estate business. It took his mind off such pedantic details. Although this is my holiday, as you are my brother's son, I will help you, as I did him."

"That will not be necessary." He ground his teeth at the insults poured on his mother's head, and she not here to defend herself. For that matter, where was she? "I will take care of my own business."

"A sign of maturity is knowing when to ask for help."

Rufus mastered his temper. How did Phillip tolerate her? But his cousin did, and seemed to care a great deal for his mother. For his sake, Rufus softened his tone.

"If I need help, I shall be sure to ask. Good day." He shut the door with a firm click before she thought to follow.

But his offended emotions could not be shut out as easily. *How dare she suggest that I am incapable of handling the estate? Had she voiced this doubt to Father? Was that why he held such a low opinion of me?*

Rufus entered his study still seething. His agent was walking around the room, looking at all the books strewn on the floor and tables. Rufus had spent his morning alone searching for clues to his father's activities. He had gone through every book in his father's study, looking for a secret note or a hidden safe in the paneling. He had found nothing.

His agent's arms were crossed; his face was pinched the way Rufus's aunt's face often looked before she lectured him about a misconduct.

Rufus's back stiffened in rejection of any lecture on his behavior from this agent. The moment the man spotted Rufus, he stood to attention, his posture showing respect, but his eyes condemned his master.

"Good day, Mr. Nightingale. I am glad you could accommodate my request for this meeting."

"I am at your service." His stance was stiff, eyes sullen.

"Be seated." Rufus reclined in his chair behind the desk.

The man walked over to the chair and perched on the edge of his seat.

"I have gone through your reports." Rufus tossed the pages across his desk. With a flutter and crinkle, they scattered across the wide surface.

Mr. Nightingale's neck stretched, and his mouth thinned.

"The farms' profits are down," Rufus said. "Have decreased for a good number of years. The local mill has needed repair for the last three years. Our boot industry, which thrives elsewhere in Cheshire, shows a loss in Terrance Village. Your records show funds from the estate were drained on a regular basis. It is a wonder I have any left to pay your wages."

Stony silence greeted him as Nightingale's lips tightened so much they formed a straight line.

Rufus drummed fingers on his chair arm, and when the man remained silent, he said, "I am grateful for my father's investments in shipbuilding and income from overseas trading. They appear to be better run. Now, tell me, Mr. Nightingale, why I should retain you as my man of business when your records indicate your talents are abysmal? I wonder if you are capable of handling your position."

The man's mouth opened and closed several times. His eyes, which had widened with Rufus's every word, shut along with his lips. He then stood and marched toward the door, stopped and appeared to almost turn, then opened the door and departed without a word, quietly shutting the door.

As confrontations went, this one had been startlingly peaceful. Rufus had just gathered the scattered paper when a violent scream rang through the halls. Then there was a moment of silence before Mr. Nightingale re-entered the study.

"My lord," the man said in a clipped tone, "you have grievously harmed me. I shall not forget this. Mark my words, I shall not forget this injustice. My resignation will be on your desk by this afternoon. Good morning!"

The door slammed on his second exit, shaking the house.

Rufus stared in astonishment, and then his lips twitched, and a laugh burst out. Mr. Nightingale had shown the presence of mind to leave the room before he vented his temper. And he had stood up for himself and spoken his mind. All admirable traits.

Rufus stood and hurried to halt Nightingale's imminent departure. After all, second chances often required a deeper second look.

As he stalked toward the door, he heard a scraping behind him. He swung around. All was quiet, but now that he could see the room from this angle, he realized he had made a royal mess. One of the servants would have to put everything back on the shelves. What had he heard? Perhaps a stack of books had tipped over. It was hard to tell among all the chaos.

He turned back to follow after Nightingale and had his hand on the door when he heard the scraping sound again, followed by a soft wooden tap. This time when he looked back, he saw what had moved. His father's portrait was tilted sideways and looked as if it was about to fall.

He rushed toward it, having to jump over a pile of books to get to the wall before the portrait crashed. He straightened the frame, checked that it was level, and released it. It immediately tilted. With a frown, he took down the portrait and looked behind it. The hook and string were in place. He then wiggled the nails on the wall. They seemed secure, so he placed the portrait back. This time it stayed in place. With a satisfied nod, he hurried to the door, hoping he had not missed Mr. Nightingale because of the delay. As he left the room, he heard scraping again. He shivered at the sound and increased his stride, refusing to look back.

Chapter Five

With fingers crossed that she was not too late for breakfast, Belle descended the stairs with Earnest. A scream brought her to a startled halt. A neatly dressed young man stood outside the study door. Had the sound come from him?

His flushed face seemed to indicate this was the case.

Before she could inquire after his well-being, he went into the study. Within a few seconds, however, he was out and marching double time toward the front doors.

Earnest growled. The young gentleman moved at a swift clip, but he was not fast enough to beat Earnest. The dog leaped forward and pounced on his quarry. Once felled, the Irish wolfhound stood proudly over his prey, teeth bared.

Belle ran over, grabbed Earnest's scruff, and gasped, "So sorry, good sir. He probably thought you wanted to play when you ran from the study. I hope he did not hurt you."

She tugged the dog from the stranger's back. At her firm, "Sit," the hound sat, as docile as a dove from heaven.

As she helped the young man up, she took note of his appearance. His brown jacket was clean, and his white linen shirt and brown breeches pressed. His neck cloth was tied neatly, if not expertly. Unlike his humble attire, what rocked her back on her heels were the gentleman's emotions.

He seethed with overwhelming anger and hurt. Overshadowing that was a helpless sense of devastation.

"Sir, what ails you?" she asked with concern.

"I have been grievously injured." He sounded close to tears.

Belle, in a bid to divert and disarm his fury, said, "Earnest did not mean to attack you."

He glanced past her toward the study, and in her mind a silent, black-and-white vision formed of Lord Terrance, strung from the ceiling by a rope wrapped round his neck. His eyes bulged, his tongue was blue and gray, and his legs dangled.

She fought the urge to race into the study to check on his lordship. True visions of real events always came as a cacophony of color, texture and sound. She would have seen details about the rope, a toppled chair, and heavy breathing. This mind picture was a daydream. She *must* believe that.

Also, Lord Terrance's presence, alive and well, throbbed from nearby. She would swear to it. His essence was unmistakable. She had not been able to shake that essence of him since she stepped foot into his home.

But where had the image come from? Even as she asked the question, she knew the answer. It was a fantasy of the man who stood before her. It was up to her to draw him back from that abyss.

"He is still rather young," she said. At the man's startled look, Belle indicated the dog. Still trying to draw the gentleman from the emotional cliff he straddled, she added, "His name is Earnest. As I said, he did not mean you harm. Or does the winter gloom trouble you, sir? Such foul weather can make anyone feel indisposed."

He blinked rapidly, a definite sign that her wandering speech had distracted him. The image of Lord Terrance strung up faded. Encouraged, Belle kept up her nonstop one-way, inconsequential chatter. "I believe that light is important to a sound soul. I was about to take the dog outside for that very reason. Some light, fresh air, and a bit of exercise. Would you care to join us, sir?"

He straightened his jacket, as if suddenly aware that he spoke with a lady. "How can you invite me when you do not know who I am . . . I could be a murderer, for aught you know."

"But you have such an innocent countenance." She smiled mischievously.

He hesitated. Then the lines of tension smoothed, and a smile tugged at his lips. "You are funning me."

"I only wish to take your mind off Earnest's bad behavior."

He shot a glance toward the dog and then back to the study door. When he finally focused on her, his shoulders relaxed, and he stood tall and in control of his emotions. He gave her a credible bow. "I am Mr. Nightingale. I am Lord Terrance's agent." The smile wavered. "Or I was, until this morning."

"How do you do, Mr. Nightingale." She curtsied, ignoring the tremor in his last words. "I am Lady Belle Marchant. Well, I am happy to hear your good news. You must be thrilled."

He gazed at her in confusion. "What do you mean, my lady?"

"Why, if you have finished your employment with Lord Terrance, then it must mean you are off to a new adventure. No doubt to better and brighter things."

He stared at her, open-mouthed, and then burst out laughing. "That is exactly right. My world has not ended. It has expanded to allow room for more opportunities. Why, you have described my future to perfection."

"Lady Belle." The call came in clipped tones.

Both she and Mr. Nightingale swung around.

Lord Terrance stood by his open study door. He looked angry, but then when did he not? Belle was pleased no cord hung off his neck and that his eyes were still in their sockets. In truth, he looked exceptionally handsome in a black serge spencer jacket that covered his wide shoulders. Beneath it, he had on a white shirt, a beautifully cut waistcoat with silver buckles, and black drill trousers that outlined long legs to perfection. To cap off the outfit, a cravat overflowed the high starched points of his collar, oriental style.

Mr. Nightingale stiffened, obviously not as impressed as Belle by his lordship's excellent physique or dashing apparel. He moved closer to and a little in front of her, as if in a protective gesture.

"Good morning, my lord," she said, and looked for the Irish wolfhound. "I was about to take Earnest for a walk."

As if to call her a liar, Earnest had disappeared.

"Nightingale, did we miss something in our discussion?" Lord Terrance asked.

"No, my lord," he said. "I believe all that needed was said. Good day."

Still, Mr. Nightingale hesitated. His expression reminded Belle of the ones that Earnest sported in Lord Terrance's presence—a flash of hope, followed by dismay.

Belle reached out and squeezed Mr. Nightingale's hand, and he started. The light returned to his eyes, and he bowed. "Until we meet again, my lady."

"That is highly unlikely, Nightingale," Lord Terrance said.

Belle was surprised to find him suddenly by her side, his hand on her elbow. When had he moved closer?

"You have work to do," he said and gestured to the butler to come with the gentleman's jacket.

Mouth shut tight, Mr. Nightingale shrugged into his coat and hat. "I shall be back with the letter of which we spoke."

"If I want a letter from my staff, I shall ask for one. What I want from you, Nightingale, is your proposal for removing my Cheshire holdings out of the abysmal condition they are in. It will list every farm's and every business's particulars and their immediate intentions for improving their business this coming year. All of that information is to be outlined in detail. When I am satisfied with your submission, then we will discuss your future in my employ. Good day, sir."

Felton gently propelled the young man, who seemed to have lost his power of speech, out the door. Then he quietly removed himself from the entryway, leaving Belle and Lord Terrance alone.

Belle withdrew her arm from his lordship's grasp, thinking to also quietly remove herself from the line of danger. "I am off to breakfast."

"Not so fast," Lord Terrance said tersely. "Must you flirt with every man you meet?"

She stared at him, appalled, "I did no such thing."

"You took Nightingale's hand."

"I merely commiserated with him. He was under the impression he had been summarily discharged. Do you plan to do that to the poor man?"

"Whom I employee or dismiss is my concern." He took a breath, and she suspected he silently counted to ten. She wished she had vanished like Earnest had the moment Lord Terrance appeared. But she had been so relieved he had not been hung that she had stayed rooted.

"I do not wish to argue with you," he finally said.

"Then why do you do so?"

He clenched his jaw. "May we have a private word?" His open palm indicated the study door.

Her heart dropped to her belly. Why? Had he found out about her midnight game with his mother and sister? His face gave nothing away. Had a servant seen her last night? Or reported on the shrunken larder contents? Or had Phillip told the tale?

No matter. With chin up, she entered the study, ready to do battle.

He closed the door and indicated that she should sit. She frowned at the untidy appearance of the room. Perhaps he was having the servants rearrange the shelves in a new order. She took the seat before his desk. Instead of moving behind the desk, he leaned in front of it, looming over her.

"Did you have a pleasant night?" he asked.

Belle's conscience pricked. To gain some upper ground, she focused her extra senses on him. If she could read his mood, she could turn the course of this conversation onto safer channels. But while her extra senses could see past most people's dissembling to the truth in their hearts, she had the hardest time sensing this man's true feelings.

He gave her his whole attention. His blue eyes showed a lively curiosity, and his chiseled face displayed naught but calm seas ahead. Past his blandness, she sensed nothing. She feared she could stare from daybreak to twilight, and her recalcitrant senses would remain as silent as the oceans deep as to what emotions he felt.

His mouth relaxed into a gentle smile. "Do I pass inspection?"

She pretended to examine the intricate inlay of his mahogany desk.

If she were not careful, he would read her better than she could him.

"Was the bed lumpy?" he asked.

The absurd question drew her attention back to him.

"Did the fire go out too soon?" he persisted. "Did you toss and turn all night and dream about your lost betrothed?"

Heat seared Belle's face. Did he accuse her of lusting after Jeffrey while in bed? *What impertinence!*

"I merely wondered at your late rising." He leaned forward, voice deep and evocative. "It seems to me that you are not the type of woman to lay about unless troubled by sleeplessness."

She wiped her damp palms on her gown. Their gazes were locked, and she could not have looked away if Mr. Nightingale barged in with his strangler's rope. And why must they discuss beds? Since he had brought up the subject, she could not help but visualize herself there, but not alone. She swallowed painfully, able to count her heartbeats, they beat so loudly.

Jeffrey had never made her feel this aware of him or of herself.

In Lord Terrance's company, every part of her vibrated with tension. His closeness brought a whiff of fresh baked bread and strawberry jam, overlaid with an intoxicating male aroma. He had probably already breakfasted.

Immediately, her unruly mind took her to bed where Lord Terrance fed her tender, flaky pieces of bread overflowing with sweet, red jam. She was bewitched into licking those droplets off his fingers, and . . .

She could almost taste those sweet, tart, imaginary berries. Belle abruptly stood and strolled around the cluttered room. A tilted frame drew her to it. Licking her dry lips, she absently lifted her skirts to step over a pile of books on the floor in order to reach it. All the while, her confused mind straddled the solid reality of Lord Terrance following her with her more lurid fantasies. She straightened the frame, frowning at the tingling the frame left in her fingertips. Odd.

Deciding that focusing on the decadent bedroom scene playing in her mind would be her undoing, she abruptly turned to return to the desk. Not prepared for her sudden spin, he stopped short and stood far too close. Must he look quite so tempting in reality as well as in her fantasy? Why could he not have a chicken neck with leathery skin and a pale cast rather than that muscled column leading to such a handsome countenance?

"You have not spoken a word, Belle," he said. "May I call you that?" His hand brushed her cheek, and her nerve endings, already on high alert, spiked. "Since you are friends with my mother, it seems a shame for us to be on formal terms."

His touch reminded her of when he had regained consciousness after the carriage accident. He had asked her to kiss him then, to confirm that he was still alive.

She had almost obliged. She wanted to oblige now.

Breathe, she commanded. Her chest expanded, eager for the air.

His thumb brushed her lips, stirring tingling sensations along every point of contact, while his gaze followed the rise of her chest, as if that was where he really wanted to touch.

"Were you cross with that young man who left, my lord?" she asked, desperate to change the subject from beds and intimate forms of address.

"Rufus," he said, rolling the "r."

Her stomach flip-flopped. "Since we but met a few days ago, it is too soon to address each other by given names."

"Is it not better to be friends than enemies?" he asked in a bantering tone.

She once again had to force herself to breathe. "It is you who insists I am your enemy."

Had she leaned her face into his touch? Had he noticed? The delighted look in his eyes suggested he had not only noticed but also thoroughly approved.

His thumb meandered along the line of her chin. "Time would pass much easier if we did not argue constantly. We should make a pact."

"A pact?"

"Hmm. While you are here, we should agree to not disagree."

"I do not wish to disagree with you, my lord. I merely asked a question about Mr. Nightingale, which, by the by, you have yet to answer."

"You taunted my actions with him." He withdrew his playful touch and raised his head.

She had sparked his temper. *Good!* An angry Rufus was a less tempting Rufus. *Drat*. Now she thought of him as Rufus.

"My business with Nightingale does not concern you," he said. "And you took his side."

"I took no one's side."

"You laughed with him." Angry lines formed on his forehead as his frown returned.

An angry Rufus might be safer, but she missed the playful one.

"I should warn you that you waste your time with him," he said before she could respond. "That young man will not have a successful future, especially if he carries on as he apparently has. Nor does he possess a station that should warrant your attention."

"My lord, you mistake my meaning." Her irritation rose to meet his. "You have mistaken my words and actions since the moment we met. You assume you know what I feel or wish for without asking me. And even when you do ask, you do not believe my answer. It is most unfair."

"I agree," he said. "Which is why I propose this pact."

She gave him a narrow-eyed glare. She did not trust him. He liked to taunt her, and every time they were close, her extra senses deserted their post, and her common sense played hide and seek.

"What sort of pact?" she asked.

He brushed a lock of her hair off her shoulders. "My father believed that only strict discipline overcomes bad habits."

"I do not have any bad habits," she said.

"Then what would you call your penchant for argument?"

"I am not arguing."

"Good, then you agree."

"To what?"

"Our pact. Kindly pay attention," he said in a patient voice, but she picked up an undertone of deviltry in it. "I will explain the rules of our agreement as clearly as I can."

"Pray, do so," she said cautiously.

He moved forward again, and Belle realized there was no more room to retreat. Her back was literally against the wall, though he had not cut off all lines of escape. She could still slide sideways and rush for the door. Only the challenge in his gaze kept her in place.

She would not allow Rufus Marlesbury to frighten her as he did half the villagers.

His was playing with her hair now, his fingertips brushing her scalp and wreaking havoc on her restraint. It took supreme concentration to not snuggle into that tender palm. "What type of pact are you offering?"

"What would be a good deterrent to your disagreeing with me?"

"I am not overly fond of drinking chocolate." She scrunched her face, as if the taste of that delicious drink already soured her mouth. "I suppose that every time we disagree, you could make me drink it."

He threw back his head and laughed. "Good try. You would have driven my father to distraction. When he asked my sister that question, she honestly admitted that she would hate to relinquish even one of her plants." The thought seemed to sober him. He shook off whatever made him melancholy. "It matters not. Susie has all the plants her heart desires now."

He lifted her chin with a finger and grinned. "Your words have given me an idea."

She distrusted that complacent tone and eyed him warily. "What words?"

"You insist that you are always circumspect. Although I doubt your sincerity—"

He ignored her unladylike snort.

"—I will accept your word as truth."

"It . . . it is the truth." She sensed a trap. *Now* her extra senses come to life? *Useless things.* "I try my best to always act circumspect."

"Then it is plain what we must agree upon."

"Plain for you. I am totally at sea as to your meaning, my lord."

"Why, it is simple. To discourage you from arguing with me, every time you do, you must pay penance by doing something that is *not* circumspect."

She let out her breath in relief. For a moment she worried he was leading the conversation someplace she could not control. Actually, his deterrent was no more abhorrent than drinking hot chocolate, but he need not know that. She had spoken the truth when she said she always *tried to* behave well. It was simply that circumstances sometimes forced her to misbehave.

"Agreed." She held out her hand without a qualm of doubt. "Shall we shake on it, like gentlemen."

He took her hand in his. "We will agree as would a lady and a gentleman." She had not put on her gloves yet, and he bestowed a light kiss on the back of her naked hand. Shivers sped up her arm.

When he released her, she scrambled sideways to escape, no longer concerned about how the action might be perceived. Once clear of his presence, her breathing returned to normal, and she made a quick twirl, glad of her freedom.

She had come out of that encounter unscathed. He obviously did not know about the billiards game, or he would have mentioned it. And his injunction that she not argue would be easy to keep because she had no wish to do so anyway. He was the argumentative one, always questioning her motives.

"Well, my lord," she said, "if there is naught else you wish to say to me, I shall see if cook has some strawberry jam, um, I mean eggs and toast for breakfast. I find my appetite has returned."

He leaned against the wall, arms folded, appearing long, lean, and dangerous.

Her body trembled, acknowledging he was a tremendous temptation. But one she intended to withstand. His smug expression only added to her determination.

"Good day, then." She walked toward the door.

"Do you not want to ask what the discipline will be?"

"Discipline?" Had she agreed to one?

"When you disagree with me."

A snippet of their conversation returned. "Well, I must simply do something *not* circumspect."

"Yes." He pushed away from the wall, and his slow approach seemed to take an eternity. "But what will that be?"

"I can choose what that will be," she said, "if the circumstance ever arises. But I have no intention of arguing, so we need not worry about the specifics."

"We must absolutely know the specifics." He once again stood too close. "How else can it deter you if the repercussion is not precisely defined?"

She sighed. The man was persistent with details. In any case, it did not matter, for how hard could the repercussion be? "Very well. I shall—"

He wagged a finger. "After your last hot chocolate suggestion, I shall set the mark for a punishment appropriate to the crime."

She swallowed the lump in her throat, but then consoled herself with the reminder that Lord Terrance was a respectable man. What he disliked about her was his supposition that she did not act properly, so whatever he chose could not be that hard to follow.

"What did you have in mind, my lord?"

"By your own words, you deny that you came to Clearview to trap me into marriage, but purport, instead, to be here on a ridiculous ghost-hunting expedition."

"I came here only because your mother said she was concerned about a haunting at Clearview," she said. "You think too much of yourself if you consider I would travel cross country just to appeal to your . . . your . . . Well, I did not. I am not interested in any man in that way." She waved her hand at him in an effort to convey what "that way" meant. "After my experience with Jeffrey, I find the whole concept of marriage, or social interaction merely to lead to that vaunted state of nuptial bliss, unappealing."

"Excellent. Then you should find this entirely abhorrent."

Without warning, Lord Terrance's lips descended on hers. His mouth teased her lips with a dance so seductive her mouth participated before receiving conscious consent. The kiss enticed rather than offended. His arms wrapped around her waist and pulled her so close and so high, her toes barely touched the ground. She had to lean against him for support as her mind whirled out of control.

His right hand descended to mold her to him in such an intimate manner that it rivaled the liberties he took with her mouth.

All of a sudden, she was set back on her feet as abruptly as she had been swooped up. She staggered and grabbed a chair back for support. Her breathing came out fast and unsteady.

Lord Terrance seemed in a similar state of unrest. His eyes had grown wide, and his face, no longer smiling, wore a shocked expression. He took a deep breath, and then another, which seemed to steady him.

She did the same, hoping for a similar result.

His gaze immediately fell to her bosom, and her breath caught in her throat. She turned to face the window. This could not be happening. She wrapped her arms around herself. Jeffrey had never kissed her like that. If he had, instead of being half relieved to be free when he asked her to cry off, she would have denied his request.

"Well, that should act as a sufficient deterrent," Lord Terrance said.

"Deterrent?" she repeated, unable to follow his thought process.

His breath brushed her neck. "We discussed punishment if you disagreed with me. Do you not recall the conversation?"

His teasing propped her flagging temper. He seemed completely recovered. *So quickly?*

His vile words during the snowstorm swam into her head.

You are not at all to my taste, my dear. In friendship, I prefer my women honest and well-behaved. In lovemaking, my preference runs to companions who sport a lighter shade of hair and more generous curves than you appear to possess.

Heat flared into her cheeks, followed by hurt, and then a wave of temper. Had his kiss been a game then? One he played with someone he deemed a loose woman? If so, the villagers' title of "Lord Terror" did not suit. He should be "Lord Torment."

I cannot let him see that he has more of an effect on me than I have on him.

She took a deep, searing breath that hurt on its passage in and out. "Now that I think on it," she said, glad her voice came out strong and clear, "it seems unfair that only I must be disciplined if we disagree. What is to be your punishment if you begin our argument?"

She turned to face him and then regretted it. He stood so close, their lips almost touched. She paced the room's length, stepping around piles of books.

"I believe I have the right to choose the consequence of that," she said. "Now what would you most dislike, hmm?" She touched a leather bound book about crop rotations and dairy farming on a table.

"I am not too keen on kisses," he said.

She made the mistake of glancing at him and saw a suggestive glint in his eyes. "I think not," she replied and looked away. "I suspect you hold the same abhorrence to them that I do to hot chocolate."

His laughter filled the room.

Belle ignored the enchanting sound, her mind busy with possibilities. The villagers were frightened of him. He had obviously never attempted to make friends with them. "I know, it shall be a visit with one of your tenants."

Her words silenced his amusement, and he said, "Why would that act as a deterrent? It is my duty to speak with my tenants."

"I said visit with, not merely speak with. If you begin an argument with me, you will invite yourself to a meal at a tenant's home, and you may not speak about work, your role in their lives, or their farm."

"You wish me to sup with commoners?" he asked in shock.

Hah! Now she had him. With a smug smile to rival his earlier version, Belle walked over to tap him on his shoulder. "I do believe I have discovered the best deterrent to your arguing with me."

"And how will you ensure I follow through?"

"You are a gentleman. I shall accept your word."

"No," he said. "If I am to visit with my tenants, then you must accompany me to ensure I do not lapse and talk of estate business."

She shrugged. "Very well. Unlike yourself, I do not object to dinner with farm workers. They do not call me 'Lord Terror.'"

"Lord what?" he asked, looking stunned and perhaps a little hurt.

She shut her mouth too late. In crowing about her victory, she had let a secret slip out. When she made to move away, he held her in place.

"Tell me what you meant," he ordered.

"Nothing of import. No more than a nickname, my lord."

"By whom?"

"I may have heard a villager use it, but I do not recall who it was. Pray, blame my bad temper for mentioning it." She pulled out of his hold and ran to the door. When the cold, metal handle pressed against her palm, she glanced back. Lord Terrance stood motionless, his face troubled.

* * * *

Rufus let Belle leave the study without protest. *Lord Terror, indeed.*

He had been foolish enough to tease her a little, and she retaliated thus. What game did she play? First she claimed his mother believed in ghosts, and now she intimated the villagers were terrified of him.

Standing by the window, he glared at the white landscape. The open country reminded him of his ride to the church yesterday and the children's reaction to his arrival. Even as that scene appeared to substantiate Belle's position, he shook his head in denial.

They were children. They should be afraid of strangers.

Their parents too? a discontented voice rejoined, and he recalled the faces of all the adults who had watched him with trepidation from behind the vicar.

But Belle could not possibly know how the villagers feel toward me. She only arrived the day before yesterday and spent one morning at the Briar Inn. Hardly time to become knowledgeable about the villagers' viewpoints.

At the tail end of that logical reasoning, a sense of calm descended over his racing thoughts. He breathed deeply, and his tense shoulders loosened and dropped. His neighbors and tenants did not even know him well enough to dislike him. He had lived away from Cheshire since he had turned eighteen. First, he had been at Oxford and then in London. On the rare occasions he had come home to visit Mama and Susie during the past five years, he had had little contact with anyone from Terrance Village. And if they were, for some reason, concerned about his behavior, he would show them they were mistaken. Once the villagers become better acquainted with the man he had become, they would have no cause to fear him.

He also needed to question some of villagers about his father's last movements. Find out who he had seen, where he had gone, and what, if anything, had been on his mind during those final days before his death.

With the reminder that this village was where his father had spent his last peaceful moments before he returned to London and met with a villain's bullet, the deep sense of sorrow that Rufus had lived with since finding his father's body returned. With a heavy heart, he rang for the butler.

Chapter Six

Within a half hour after Lady Belle revealed that the villagers' nickname for him was Lord Terror, Rufus was mounted and eager to face the people whom he apparently terrified. He gave Goodwin free rein to gallop across the rolling countryside under the bright morning sun.

He did not slow to a canter until the Parkers' farm came into view. Nightingale's records said this dairy farm's production had deteriorated in the last four years. Once it had been renowned for the best cheese for a hundred miles. These days, the farm barely made enough to cover their taxes.

The farm was now a drain on his estate. A note written in his father's hand suggested that this spring the Parkers must be given notice to leave and new tenants obtained. It was a duty Rufus did not look forward to, yet it behooved him to see to the estate's prosperity for the benefit of all.

Laughter, intermingled with shouted words, drew him on. He reined in Goodwin near the edge of a wood that bordered the farm and looked at the farmyard where four children played: a boy of about nine, another probably a year younger, a girl of around six, and the youngest no more than three. When the younger boy argued with his older sibling, the elder boy stood on his toes, as if adding a few inches would gain him a degree more respect and authority.

Rufus shifted on his mount. It was not so easy to gain respect. He had adequate height, an honorable title, and enough wealth to buy this farm a hundred times over, yet none of it garnered him any more respect than the boy's brother paid his older brother. Fear, certainly. Obedience, no question. But respect? Unlikely.

The younger brother flicked the elder boy's cap off his proudly tilted head, and a friendly wrestling match ensued. They both tumbled into the snow. The girls, full of giggles, buried the boys with handfuls of white powder.

Goodwin neighed, unhappy at standing still so long.

The youngest girl looked up. Her gaze rounded on Rufus, and her arms came to rest at her side. Her sister's glance shifted from the boys to the little one, still and silent beside her, and from there to Rufus.

Not wanting to frighten them, yet too far away to greet with words, Rufus tipped his hat and with a gentle nudge, urged Goodwin to lift one foreleg and bend the other in a bow.

The little tot of three moved forward, her gaze fastened on Rufus's horse. He had captured her interest, and with luck, her respect. Before he could respond, the elder girl shouted a warning, and in a blink, they were all gone.

Disappointed that he had spoilt the Parker children's game, Rufus rode toward the farm. This would be their last winter here. He wanted to ask what they would need to enjoy a good Christmas. He dismounted and knocked on the farmhouse door.

No response. Were the children alone and too frightened to answer? He waited a moment and knocked again.

"This is your landlord, Rufus Marlesbury. Is anyone home?"

Silence. He returned to his horse with a mental note to check here on the way home. On the farm's outskirts, before he turned onto the main road, he glanced back.

The children and a slender woman, likely the mother, watched him. When he slowed, they all scurried into the house.

Nightingale must have warned them they were soon to be evicted. And fool that he was, Rufus had announced himself when he knocked, and so they hid.

Lord Terror.

The errant thought surfaced unbidden. He shook it off and rode on through the empty fields of snow.

Shortly, the church spire rose on the horizon, and he patted Goodwin. "This time, we will both be on our best behavior."

At the churchyard, he dismounted, tied Goodwin to a tree, and walked inside. Most of what he remembered of this place had faded into the mists of childhood memories. He did recall with clarity the stained glass windows on opposing walls. The way the multicolored, reflected light played across people's faces or shoes, and its dance along the aisle as the hour advanced—all had fascinated a boy more interested in movement than sermons.

Mr. Bedlow stepped out of a back room. "My lord! How wonderful that you have come for another visit. I hope you are able to stay longer this time."

"Good morning, vicar. I do wish to have a word."

"Of course, of course. How keeps your mother, by the by?"

"She is well. Thank you for inquiring."

"My wife would be pleased to pour us tea while we talk."

"If you have no objections, I prefer that we speak here."

The thirteenth century church's arched ceilings, wide pews, and finely detailed cross, resting high above the altar, made it a private place. Less chance of an eavesdropper.

Rufus sat on a bench while Mr. Bedlow stood. The short, round man seemed at ease. The vicar's relaxed smile of welcome was an encouraging sight after the Parkers' cold reception.

"Your mother seemed dispirited when I came by last week, my lord," Mr. Bedlow said. "Talked a great deal about your father. It would do her good to consider the living more."

Rufus thanked him for that sage advice, which he too held, and made a note to speak with his mother on the matter. "I actually came to ask you about my father. The week before he died, he returned to Clearview. Did you see him then?"

Mr. Bedlow took a seat beside him. "Why, no, my lord. He was in Cheshire, but he did not come to see me, and I did not feel I should intrude without an invitation."

"Do you know with whom he met?"

"That information did not reach my ears, my lord. I could ask my wife." He spread his hands wide. "Oft times she tells me who sees whom and goes where, and the information slides in and out of my ears without pause."

Rufus nodded. "I would appreciate any help you can give me on the matter. But please keep this conversation confidential. No one must know I inquire. Not even your wife. If you question her, I request you do so discreetly."

"As you say, my lord. What do you wish to discover?"

"What I seek will announce itself soon enough." He stood and shook the vicar's hand.

Mr. Bedlow accompanied him to the door. "Will you be at service next Sunday?"

"If time permits," Rufus said before exiting the church.

The vicar followed him. "I only ask, because your dear mother has not come to church since your father died. It cannot be healthy to be away from regular service for so long." He glanced back to the church, then returned his gaze to Rufus. "Without the good Lord's guidance, our fears can sometimes overtake our senses."

Rufus understood him all too well. So, the rumor of a spirit haunting the manor had spread to the village. He would check with Ellison to ensure the tale had not ignited from the servant quarters. Then again, Belle had announced her suspicions about ghosts in front of that family she had been with during their first stormy meeting. The story had likely spread from there.

As for the vicar's suggestion, he had no great hopes that a sermon would shake any ideas his mother harbored about spirits. Once a notion found its way into her head, it rarely departed. Still, it could not hurt for his mother to socialize again. If she were to meet some local gentry, the interaction might distract her from maudlin thoughts.

"I will speak with my mother," he said and left.

His next stop, the Briar Inn, was a local favorite according to Ellison. Villagers gathered in the taproom to converse. A perfect place to ferret out information.

On his arrival, a postboy took his horse.

The innkeeper greeted him at the door. "My lord, what a great pleasure to have you in my humble inn. How may I serve you? Shall I show you to a private parlor?"

"I shall sup in the common room." Rufus left the man staring after him in astonishment.

He found the chamber lightly sprinkled with men from the village. He chose a table near the far end where a lack of windows gave it relative privacy.

A maid came by to ask his drinking pleasure, though her coy smile offered more than ale or whiskey.

Rufus gave her a coin and settled for whiskey. He sat for a time to allow his neighbor's curiosity to subside, then motioned to the innkeeper.

The portly man hurried over, eager to please.

"Who among here knows best what goes on in the village?" Rufus asked.

The man turned to study his customers and then pointed out one who nursed his drink beside a group of men. He was unshaven, unwashed, and his clothes appeared unchanged in months.

"Name's Brindle, my lord, Harry Brindle," the innkeeper said. "Spends all his time chattin' with folks. Wife died of influenza. Spent every penny to see to her needs and then for 'er funeral. Lost his farm when he could no longer pay the levy to your father. Harry sent his two mites to his sister's place in Yorkshire. Not much work here, as these are hard times in Terrance. I let him clean up the place. Widow Harken lets him sleep in her barn, if he tidies it." He gave Rufus a knowing look. "He would trade a word or two for a small coin or a tankard of ale."

Rufus asked that the man be sent over.

The innkeeper spoke to Brindle. Despite being in dire straights, the man appeared to take a great deal of convincing. At one point, he made a run for the door, but the innkeeper caught the back of his coat and made the signal for cash with his fingers. Brindle still looked unconvinced.

Rufus took out a shilling, then tossed it and caught it.

The man's eyes widened. Finally, with the innkeeper's

encouragement, Mr. Brindle reluctantly approached.

"Mor'n, milord." Harry Brindle doffed his hat.

"Sit." Rufus indicated the chair opposite him, then almost regretted it. A foul odor wafted from the man. They might as well have held this conversation inside the barn.

Brindle scraped back his chair and sat at its tip, woolen hat scrunched between both hands.

"Good morning, Mr. Brindle," Rufus said. Although his attention remained focused on his guest, he noticed that the taproom descended into an arena of silence. He could almost picture every ear trained to catch each word he and Brindle spoke.

Brindle's gaze swung to the door, and in a bid to ease the man's tension, Rufus mentioned the weather. "Glad the snow finally stopped. You fared it well?"

Brindle's gaze returned to Rufus and then dropped to the table. "Well's could be 'xpected, milord."

Rufus motioned to the innkeeper, and the man hurried over.

His guest ordered ale, and Rufus paid for it and waited.

Once the drink arrived, Brindle abandoned his cap on his lap and grabbed the sweating mug with large, coarse hands. He downed the contents. Dribbles slid along the sides of his mouth while he swallowed in rapid succession. He returned his empty mug to the scarred wooden tabletop.

Rufus ordered the mug be replenished. Slowly, he sipped his own whiskey, enjoying its sharp, dry bite. As the chatter about the room rose, the man's tight shoulders loosened.

"The innkeeper tells me you are an avid source of village gossip," Rufus said. At his guest's blank stare, he rephrased. "You know a lot about what happens around the village?"

"I knows some, milord."

"Do you remember the last time my father came to Terrance?"

"All knew whenever the Black Ter, um, his late lordship, were here."

The man's gaze swung to the doorway as if he were considering bolting for the exit. Brindle's fear and his hesitation over Rufus's father's name would have to wait for later consideration. He must be careful, or he would lose the man's cooperation.

"Do you remember what my father did the last time he visited?"

Brindle's attention returned to him, and a light appeared in his dull brown eyes. He straightened his shoulders, and his face changed from slack and lifeless to alert, with a hint of optimism. The man lifted his mug and emptied the remnants. Though his hands still shook, this time

Rufus suspected it was more from excitement than fear. With care, Brindle laid the empty mug down with a soft *thunk*.

He leaned forward, bringing with him a nauseating odor of stale sweat and horse droppings.

Holding his breath, Rufus also leaned forward.

"I might knows something about something, milord."

Rufus reclined and let his breath gush out in relief. Before the day ended, he might know who killed his father. He hid his excitement behind a bland face, like the ones Phillip wore in polite circles. A flick of his finger again brought the innkeeper to replenish his guest's mug.

Once they were alone, he placed a shilling on the table. Brindle's hand sneaked out to grab the prize, and Rufus covered the man's hand. "First, tell me what you know."

Brindle would have withdrawn, but Rufus held him in place.

Fear returned to his companion's eyes. "Heard that before he left, someone had him raging."

"Who?"

Brindle shook his head. "That never made sense to me, milord. There was no cause for his lordship to be angry at this man. He never hurt no one, I swear. Anyways, it makes no never mind now. Your da's enemy is dead."

Rufus sat back in surprise and disappointment. Brindle secreted his win inside the recesses of his coat and took a swallow of his drink.

"Who was it?" Rufus asked.

"The old blacksmith, o'course," he said. "Heard Mr. Darby even went to London Town when he found out the earl left the village. Had matters to discuss with him, he said. They both died there. Your da shot through the head, and poor ol' Darby strangled. They said by footpads, but them runners never caught no thieves."

Rufus brought out another shilling and kept it visible within his fingers' grip.

"Who else knows this?"

Brindle licked his lips and moved his hands nervously over his coat. A commotion by the doorway caught both their attention. Phillip, Mr. Winfield, and a stranger entered the taproom. His cousin hailed him from across the floor and came over.

Dash it!

Brindle made himself scarce before the newcomers made it halfway to their table.

"Rufus, why did you not wait for me?" Phillip asked. "Luckily, I met Winfield in the village, and he suggested you might have come here." He looked around the establishment and wrinkled his nose. "What draws you to this place, old man? And why no private parlor?"

Rufus ground his teeth. He wanted to go in search of Brindle. Instead, he sighed with resignation and settled his attention on his cousin. "If I had known you wished to join me, I would have waited. Would you gentlemen care to have a seat?"

Phillip moved toward the chair recently vacated by Brindle and then paused. "What is that stench?"

His nostrils waved like a flag as he sniffed in every direction for the offending odor. Unable to find the source, he brought out his lace-edged handkerchief and waved it.

An effervescence of violets wafted toward Rufus, who could not decide which scent he detested more—Brindle's or his cousin's. "Sit, Phillip."

His cousin complied as Winfield snagged an empty chair.

"Where has your man gone to?" his cousin asked Winfield.

"Yes," Rufus said, looking for the stranger who had been with him.

"My farmhand," Winfield told Rufus. "Gone on a scouting trip. I am in need of more staff. So, Terrance, I see the bucolic splendor of village life has not worn off on you yet."

"It has its moments." He sipped his drink, his attention returning to his cousin. Phillip leaned his silver handled cane against the wall. Why was he in Terrance? This tiny backwater village, in the middle of nowhere, was not his usual haunt.

He was excellently turned out, of course. The brim of his hat had a graceful curl. Even Brummell would envy the cut of his waistcoat. Next to him, Winfield appeared like a local squire with presumptions toward fashionable dress. Then again, compared to his cousin, Rufus doubted he fared better than Winfield.

"Do you find country life a touch slow, Mr. Jones?" Winfield asked Phillip.

"Better than expected."

"How so? Are there amusements at Clearview?"

"There are amusements, and then there are amusements."

Phillip wore such a mysterious look it annoyed Rufus. What did his cousin hint at? His mother and sister had been indisposed for days. Breakfast alone with his aunt had left Rufus sadly flat. And his only encounter with Belle had ended in a fight.

Could Phillip refer to Belle's company? When could they have had time to converse?

He straightened in his chair to ask, but Winfield looked at him and said, "I take your mother to still be in mourning, Terrance. If not, my mama would love to pay her respects and meet your houseguest. I told her how charming Lady Belle is." He switched his gaze back to Phillip. "Do you not agree she is charming, Jones?"

"Charming," Phillip said with heartfelt agreement, his smile reappearing.

His cousin's manner suggested he knew Belle better than Rufus did, and his knowing smile churned a hot, unpleasant burning in Rufus's chest. If Phillip were not his cousin and as close to him as a brother, he would have been tempted to wipe that smile off his face with a well-aimed fist. *But how could Phillip possibly know Belle better than me? He had only just met her, while, in London, she had practically disrobed on my front doorstep.*

"It is noon," he said for a change of subject. It did not do to think of Belle disrobed. He was far too distracted by her already. "Are you two gentlemen up to testing the inn's fare?"

"Tip-top idea," his cousin said. "Seems an age since I breakfasted."

"Hardly an age, since you had not yet made an appearance at breakfast when I left. Country hours are earlier than in Town."

Phillip laughed. "Did you sit with Mama? Her wish for an early rise is my reason to keep Town hours in the country."

Their conversation continued as they set to a leisurely luncheon of oxtail soup and then Cornish hens done to a nicety and stuffed with savory onions, rice, and juniper berries.

Between courses, Winfield left for a short while to give his servant further instructions. Phillip, too, stood. As he delicately put it, he had personal needs to see to. Both men returned shortly to finish the excellent fare.

For the last course, the innkeeper brought steaming lemon patties fresh from the oven. A gift, he said, for his lordship and his guests from Mr. MacBride, the local baker.

Rufus sent his compliments to MacBride for the mouth-watering pastries.

While Phillip and Winfield played whist, Rufus excused himself to deal with some tedious tenant business. As he hoped, neither gentleman showed any interest in the subject.

Once outside, he made straight for the stables. Aside from speaking to the new blacksmith, he also wanted to find Brindle. The man had been helpful, and if he continued to be so, then as reward, he would gain more than a few shillings. Rufus would give him a new job at Clearview's stables, and that might reunite him with his children.

A postboy ran over to inquire after his lordship's wishes. Rufus sent him off to find the blacksmith.

Inside the stables, he strolled along the wide, straw-laid center aisle, surprised by the many empty stalls.

Terrance Village was a crossroads stop, so the inn should have boasted more than a paltry dozen horses. Near the back, lamps were unlit and the area dark.

Out of curiosity, Rufus peered into each empty enclosed stall to see if it had been recently used. Many had a barren look, as if they had lain empty for a long while. At the last stall, he paused, disturbed by a sense of unease.

"My lord." A tall man hurried from a side corridor. He wore a leather apron and carried steel tongs. "I am Mr. Langley, the blacksmith. How may I serve you?"

"Good day." Rufus tossed the postboy a six-pence. The boy caught the coin and ran off with a wide grin. Rufus rested his riding crop on the railing and leaned against the wooden structure. "How do you like your new position, Mr. Langley?"

"Very well, sir. Shall we go outside where it is lighter?"

As they walked, he said, "Did you know the old blacksmith?"

"I never met Mr. Darby. When I came to the village to apply for this post, the position was vacant."

Once they stepped outside, Rufus squinted into the bright sunlight. "Since your arrival, have you noticed anything unusual?"

"Such as what, my lord?"

"Anyone behave out of the ordinary? Blast, I have left my riding crop."

"I can fetch it," Mr. Langley said.

"Unnecessary." Rufus sprinted back to the last stall. Crop in hand, he was about to turn away when he again sensed something out of place. That scent. The stalls were clean and appeared unused except for this one, where a long wooden handle stood upright. This stall had a foul but familiar odor. He leaned over the railing for a better look, and in the shadows, saw a man's leg.

Chapter Seven

"Bring light!" Rufus shouted.

An ostler grabbed a lantern and ran to him. Rufus scaled the railing and knelt to examine the body of Brindle. A pitchfork had been stabbed into his chest. Poor bugger.

"Send a runner to fetch the magistrate."

He ordered a gathering crowd to stay back, and, leaving the blacksmith in charge, he joined Phillip and Winfield outside.

The innkeeper scampered into the stables to view the body and then back out with his estimation of events.

Brindle must have had too much to drink. He often chose to sleep it off in the stables if too tired to walk back to Widow Harken's place. In his drunken state, he could have tripped while scaling the railing, fallen, and accidentally impaled himself.

Rufus listened to the scenario, but found it hard to believe. Though he had bought Brindle several drinks, and the man had drunk them fast, he had not seemed drunk. He had been quick and accurate at grabbing the coin off the table, and he had left without a stagger.

Then again, in the darkness, he might not have seen that pitchfork. He could have tripped, but why had a pitchfork been left in an empty stall? And why had no one heard him cry out?

The stable was a busy place, with ostlers and postboys and even the blacksmith attending to chores. Assistance came quickly enough when he called for light.

"Well, that is quite a lot of excitement for today," Phillip said. "Cannot complain it is dull in the country any longer."

Winfield's farmhand joined them. The man wore dark breeches, a brown wool coat, and boots that looked like Hessians. Rich for a farm lad, but they were likely Winfield's castoffs. What caught and held Rufus's attention was that the boots were covered in dirt and sawdust.

"Were you near the stables?" Rufus asked him. "Did you see or hear anything unusual?"

"I was in the kitchen, my lord, speaking to the cook about working for Windhaven. Mr. Winfield had heard good things about her culinary abilities and asked me to speak with her."

"Brindle's next of kin will need to be notified," Winfield said. "I shall see to it."

"Not necessary," Rufus said. "The man has two children. I shall ensure they are contacted and taken care of."

"You realize he is no longer your concern, do you not?" Winfield asked. "Your father turned him out a year ago. No one blames you."

The casual comment struck Rufus hard, especially if the drinks he had bought Mr. Brindle really had contributed to his death.

"Blames him?" Phillip said. "What an odd thought to cross your mind, Winfield. Rufus could hardly know the man."

"My apologies, Terrance." Winfield bowed, and then his gaze returned to study Rufus with an intense curiosity. "Were you not with Brindle when we arrived? That would make you the last person he spoke with. Was anyone else with you when you stumbled across the corpse? Odd place for an earl to frequent—the back end of a barn. Did you have business there?"

Did Winfield suggest he had murdered Brindle? Outrage strangled the words of protest in his throat. Tight-lipped, he stepped back. He refused to dignify either offensive accusation with a response. Who was Winfield to question him? He was nothing but a . . .

"Sir," Phillip said, in a bored tone, "where my cousin frequents, and with whom, is of no concern to us." He yawned and tapped his lace handkerchief across his mouth. "This day's amusements have worn thin. Shall we return to the manor, Rufus? A game of billiards might liven up the afternoon. I recently learned a new shot I want to demonstrate."

Rufus nodded, glad to be rid of the upstart Winfield, and followed his cousin toward their horses, which were tied to a post by the inn's front doors. They mounted and left, ignoring the blatant curiosity written across Winfield's face.

On the ride back to Clearview, Phillip remained silent, apparently lost in thought. It gave Rufus time to consider all he had learned and lost that morning. The one man who could give him information about his father's movements was dead. It had been difficult to get Brindle to trust him. Yet, having done so might have sentenced him to death.

He took his aggravation out by urging his mount into a gallop across the packed snow. Goodwin took to the command with alacrity. They flew across the track, racing like the North wind. He arrived at the outskirts of the Parker farm in a fraction of the time it had taken him to ride to the village from here. His fury spent, Rufus finally slowed Goodwin and belatedly thought to check on his cousin. To his surprise, his fastidious cousin had kept pace and slowed within moments of him.

"Good ride, Cousin," Phillip said as they trotted the horses to cool them down.

Rufus nodded but did not respond. His thoughts were still struggling with odd pieces of information that refused to fit together. Why had

Brindle been so afraid to speak to him? Could Belle have spoken the truth when she said the villagers viewed him as *Lord Terror*?

What had Brindle almost called Rufus's father? The Black something. Could he have been about to say *Black Terror*?

His back stiffened in rejection of the unfair insult to his father, but then his mind replayed childhood scenes from his servants' and tenants' perspective.

While his father had been strict with Rufus and his sister, who were aware his actions were based on familial feelings, the tenants and the villagers could not rely on any such support or loyalty. They were expendable, as Brindle had been when his father gave the man's farm to another because Brindle hit hard times. Just as Rufus planned to do with the Parkers.

"Wonder what that is about?" Phillip nodded at the nearby farm.

The Parker children had spotted him and once again ran inside.

"They hide from Lord Terror," he said, a cold certainty settling in the pit of his stomach.

"Ah." Phillip laughed. "A children's game. Are we the terrors, then? Shall we race down, shouting? Give them a good show?"

Rufus shook his head, his heart heavy. "They do not need more than what my father and I have given them."

* * * *

After breakfast, Belle went for a long walk with Earnest. Her conscience pricked at her because she had obviously hurt his lordship by blurting that the villagers called him "Lord Terror." The walk proved refreshing, but her guilt clung to her like a barnacle.

Once back at the manor, she sent the dog to the kitchen for his mid-day meal and asked the butler about the household's whereabouts. Felton informed her that Lord Terrance and his cousin were riding. Lady Terrance and her daughter were in their rooms while Mrs. Jones was in the library.

Belle decided to seek out Susie. She wanted to check on the shy young woman after her first late-night adventure.

"Belle!" With a warm hug, Susie ushered her inside. "My maid has gone to fetch my breakfast. Would you join me? I can easily ask her to double the portion.

Belle gladly accepted.

Susie's sitting room had a feminine air that suited her. Shades of pink and cream and laces and frills abounded. Plants trailed or climbed, and books of various shapes and sizes lay scattered on every available surface. Despite the general clutter, every shelf and table was dusted, and the windows sparkled.

Susie cleared a settee of books and papers. "Have a seat."

As she did, a maid brought in the tea tray, and Susie asked her to fetch another cup and more sandwiches. Once the maid returned with the requested items, Susie poured tea for the both of them.

"It is nice to see you smiling," Belle said.

"I am so because of you," her friend replied. "Before you came, I had little joy. I want this delight to go on forever."

"And why should it not?"

"Happiness is an elusive thing," Susie said in a quiet voice, her brightness dimming. "When you think you have a handle on it, it slips away. Much like your ghosts, I suspect."

"It need not be that way." Belle picked up her cup of tea and took a sip before adding, "Joy comes from our hearts, not someone else's actions."

Susie sipped as she thought that through. "Then if I am elated that you have come to visit us, it has nothing to do with you visiting with us?"

"Precisely," Belle said. "The visitor could as easily have been a servant, a neighbor, a stranger. Now, may I ask a question?"

Susie giggled. "It would give me joy to answer it."

"Do you know what troubled your father most recently?"

Her humor died, and she looked at her fingers, gripping each other. "If you had known my father, you would not ask such a thing."

Belle raised an eyebrow in surprise.

"*Everything* upset Father," Susie explained. "He expected those around him to act as he wished. Woe betided all who strayed from that narrow path."

"He was difficult," Belle said with sympathy. "But did anything in particular trouble him prior to his passing?"

Susie remained silent with her gaze lowered for such a long time that Belle wondered if her questions had pushed her new friend too far.

"He came to see us in the spring," Susie said in a quiet voice. "Unusual for him. Once Parliament began, we did not normally see him again until the fall."

"Do you know the purpose of his last visit?"

Susie shook her head. "I hid in my rooms. Out of sight, out of mind. But . . ."

"But what?"

She glanced away, and her voice shook as she replied, "I did not know that would be my last chance to see him again."

Belle touched her hand in comfort. "Thank you for confiding in me. I am sorry to have pressed you."

Susie nodded and sniffed. "I am fine, Belle. Do not concern yourself. My relationship with my father was never good. I only wish I could tell him that I did love him despite that."

Belle nodded in consolation.

"Will you tell him for me?" Susie asked abruptly.

That surprised her. To this point, Susie had never admitted to truly believing in the existence of an afterlife.

At her half-hopeful, half-terrified look, Belle shook her head. "I do not need to. He has heard it from your heart."

Susie sucked in her breath sharply and then laughed. "Yes, you are correct. For no matter how often I misbehaved or he punished me, I could never hate him. Every night when he was here, I hugged him good-night. Even when he had been particularly cruel, like the time he took away my plants. Each time before I released him, he always hugged me back."

"I am not in the least surprised," Belle said, and decided it was time for a change of subject. "Now, tell me about these wonderful plants. I recognize some but not all."

The ensuing discussion showcased the young lady's knowledge and confidence. Belle was amazed by her expertise and heretofore hidden passion for all things green. Once one worked past her layer of shyness, Susie showed a depth of interest and vivacity that might astonish even her brother.

A long while later, a knock interrupted a fascinating discussion on the symbolism of flowers.

Susie went to answer the door. "Mama!"

"Good morning, Susie," Lady Terrance said. "Felton tells me Belle is here. I must have a word with her. May I come in?"

"Of course, come in, come in."

"Good morning, Lady Terrance." Belle stood and curtsied.

"What a glorious morning this is," the countess said. "Have you two breakfasted?"

The mantle clock, draped by ivy, began to strike. After two bells, it stopped.

"Mama, you slept in. I shall order more sandwiches to assuage your appetite until dinner. And hot tea for all of us."

"Thank you, dear." Lady Terrance took Susie's empty seat.

Susie returned from speaking to her maid to clear a chair for herself. "I meant to speak with Belle about last night, but once we started talking about plans, I forgot all about the billiards game. Are we to have another tonight?"

"Too many late nights might tip your brother to our mischief," Belle said. "He already questioned my late rising."

"Besides," Lady Terrance said, "we shall be too busy."

"Busy?" Belle said. "Doing what?"

"Why, ghost hunting, of course."

"Oh, Mama," Susie said. "I get the shivers every time you mention ghosts."

"I promised Lord Terrance I would not speak of such things in your presence," Belle gently reminded the countess. "I would not wish us to anger him."

"Pish posh," her hostess said. "Everything I do angers Rufus these days. I pay him no mind. Until he calls me Mama again, instead of *Madam*, I shall not listen to one of his reproaches. In any event, I had my fingers crossed. Did you not? Although we find your company enjoyable, my dearest Belle, cleansing the house is the main reason you came, is it not?"

Put so bluntly, Belle had a hard time formulating an argument against her ladyship's stated goal. Especially since she had planned to do as the woman requested tonight—but alone. A curtain fluttering on the third floor window had given Belle an idea of where the ghost might be lurking.

"Mama, we should not push Belle on the matter," Susie said.

"Surely, if she wants to search for a spirit, my love, I can encourage her. Would she have posted herself here so promptly, otherwise?"

"Lady Terrance." Belle marshaled her defenses. "I would love to help. You have been a most hospitable hostess. However, I did promise your son that we would not *discuss* this."

She held up her hand to forestall any beseeching. "I did not say that I would not aid you. Merely, that we would not talk about the subject. Please allow me to deal with, shall we say, 'our problem.' Meantime, why do we not take this opportunity to become better acquainted? Grandpapa spoke fondly of you, and I have looked forward to meeting you."

The Countess of Terrance looked ready to argue, but her daughter broke in first. "Belle is quite right, Mama. The very idea of ghosts frightens me. I would much rather plan another billiards party."

"Please, your ladyship," Belle said. "Trust me to see to your needs as far as your house troubles go. I will not let you down." She glanced at Susie, who stood wringing her hands. "It would be best not to speak of this matter again."

The countess glanced from Belle to Susie and back. "Yes, I see your point." She took Belle's hand and pulled her close to speak in her ear. "My husband was unhappy in life, Belle, and I fear he is as troubled in death. I want him to find the peace I could never give him."

The lady choked on her last words.

Belle squeezed her hand in sympathy. "You have my word that I will do the best I can for him," Belle responded softly.

"Are you whispering about Father?" Susie's eyes filled.

With a distracted sigh, Lady Terrance released her grip on Belle and sat back. "We were wondering how to outwit Rufus in order to have the next billiards tournament."

"Yes!" Susie clapped, and her teary face cleared up.

"What is all the excitement?" Lord Terrance asked from the open doorway. Phillip Jones, dapper as usual, was at his side. "Is this a private celebration, or may anyone join?"

While Lord Terrance seemed subdued and troubled, his cousin looked as if he were a cat who had spotted a mouse.

"Here you all are." Mrs. Jones moved into the room past her son and nephew. "I have been downstairs for hours. A shocking way to treat guests, Constance. I had to settle for a book of sermons I found in the library. Though that I found it at all was a surprise considering the shocking state of that room. There are books strewn everywhere." She gave a forced little laugh. "If I believed in such things, I would say a ghost had been in there inflicting havoc on the shelves. But I have it on your butler's authority that the mess was created entirely by your son. Though I cannot imagine what he was looking for that would require flinging so many volumes onto the floor."

"Rufus is very fond of books," his mother said in a placid tone, entirely missing Mrs. Jones's insult toward her son's reading habits.

"In any case," Mrs. Jones continued, "reading the sermons was enlightening. Each of you might gain insight from such a worthwhile occupation, if you would but open the cover of that good book. The pages were unsoiled from use."

"Good day, mother." Phillip laid a light kiss on her cheek that halted her flow of recrimination.

So many people crowding into the room made Belle feel cramped. She stood and walked over to the window, and a strange sense of calmness invaded her mind. All quieted, and the voices receded.

Belle leaned against the windowpane, allowing its coolness to seep through her dress. She took a deep breath, and her mind wandered to a straw-laden room with stalls.

The place was overrun with boys and men who moved horses around, joked about their girls, made plans for a dance this coming weekend. The room was packed with human chatter, neighs and stomps of horses, and then a waft of hay.

A stooped man, who stank of stale sweat and wore soiled clothes, walked into a secluded area where light did not reach. His belly was full with warm food, and he climbed the railing while he licked his lips and savored the last drops of ale that lingered there. He fingered a silver coin as he made plans to buy a doll for a little girl and a smart cap for a young boy.

Someone whispered his name. *Brindle.*

Surprised, he hid the coin inside a hidden seam on his coat and faced the person. They talked, he denied he had taken any coins, or said anything to anyone. Then, in his mind, a picture of Rufus Marlesbury flashed once. From behind him, a cloth was pressed over his mouth. A searing pain erupted in his stomach, but his cry was smothered.

Belle acted for him and screamed. Then all went black.

* * * *

When Belle opened her eyes, Lord Terrance loomed over her. They could have been back in the snowstorm, only this time it was she who had been thrown off the horse, and he nursed her.

"You were hurt," she said and touched the back of his head. "I meant to inquire about it, but since we inevitably argued every time we met, the thought slipped my mind."

"What is the matter with your head, Rufus?" Lady Terrance asked. "I did not know you had been hurt."

"I am fine," he said. "It is the young lady on Susie's settee that we should be concerned about, not my old injury."

Lord Terrance held her hand and sat on the seat's edge, effectively imprisoning her.

"What happened?" she asked.

"You screamed," Susie said. "Did you see a gho . . ."

"No, she did not," Lord Terrance snapped, then dropped Belle's hand and stood.

"No, I did not," Belle said, missing his touch. She swung her legs to the floor and raised herself. The room wavered. She touched her forehead, where it throbbed as it always did after a vision. This time she was bedeviled by the added worry of why a dead man's last thoughts were of Lord Terrance. "I was lightheaded, that is all. Pray, do not be concerned."

"Why did you scream?" Susie asked.

"I . . . I thought I saw a spider," she fabricated. With so many plants here, surely that could not be so far from the truth.

"A spider!" Susie swung around to look at her plants and books with suspicion. "Where? Where did you see it?"

"With this much greenery," Mrs. Jones said, "it is no wonder there are crawling things about. Terrance, you should order the servants to clear this room of rubbish. It cannot be healthy for a young girl to live in such an unkempt chamber."

"Rufus, you would not do such a shameful thing," Susie said. "You said I could have whatever I wished in my room."

"I promised that no one would hurt you again, Susie." He put an arm around her shoulder and drew her close for a hug. "But if there is a spider here, it behooves us, and especially you, to root it out before it bites you or multiplies."

"I will not allow my plants or books to be taken away."

Belle realized she had upset Susie, and she felt abominable about it. This was the young woman's only sanctum, the one place where she felt safe. "It was probably a shadow that startled me."

"Children should not raise their voices to their elders," Mrs. Jones said before anyone could respond.

Susie's mouth pinched into a thin line, and high spots of color painted her cheeks. At any moment, Belle expected her to blow like a kettle.

"I feel a megrim coming on." Lady Terrance pressed a hand on her forehead.

"Mother," Phillip Jones said, "this is hardly the time for domestic details."

"I am sorry I made a fuss," Belle said. "I am fine now."

"If you are sure it was not a spider?" Lord Terrance said.

"I am sure."

"In that case," he said, "shall we adjourn to our respective rooms to rest and prepare for the evening? That should help put this episode behind us."

They withdrew en mass from Susie's quarters. Once out the door, Belle placed a hand on Lord Terrance. "My lord, may I have a word in private?"

"My dear Lady Belle, for you, I always have time."

She did not care for his suggestive tone or his accompanying smile. Lord Terrance this friendly was a bad sign. With everyone gone to their rooms she had all the privacy she needed, but as she eyed the man's handsome visage, she suddenly realized the danger in that wish.

"I believe I made a mistake." She backed away. "As you said, it is best to get ready for dinner."

"Wait. If something worries you, I hope you feel you can discuss it with me." A serious cast replaced his mischievous one. "In lieu of your grandfather, I am at your disposal."

Now, Belle was touched. His eyes looked kind and sincere, but could she trust him? If only she could get a glimpse of his intent. She peered into his face, to see past his façade to the man beneath. As had happened in his study yesterday, she sensed nothing from Lord Terrance, and the effort to see past the face he presented to the world made her head throb.

"Do you not trust me?" he asked.

"How can I, when I cannot know what is in your heart?"

"What do you imagine is in my heart?" His eyes smiled.

"Where were you earlier today, my lord?" she asked, ignoring his question.

That killed his humor. "Why do my whereabouts matter?"

"Were you near a stable?"

He folded his arms, and his expression turned stony. "Where I spend my time is of no concern to you."

She stepped closer. "Did you see a man dressed in shabby clothes who reeked of barn? Someone named Brindle?"

His expression hardened. "So, that distasteful news has already spread to the manor. Of what concern is this matter to you?"

"Tell me your connection to that man," Belle said and touched his arm. "It is important that I know."

He stepped back, dislodging her touch. "We had this discussion before. What I do, and with whom I do it, is my business. Your question suggests you listen to kitchen gossip, and that, my lady, is a sad example to display before my mother and sister. I can only hope you have not seen fit to spread such tales." Without warning, he gripped her arms and pulled her close. "Did you? Speak to my mother and sister of any of this?"

"No, I did not." She pulled free and brushed her arms where the strength of his grip already brought forth a stain of red. She adjusted her shawl to cover the marks before he noticed them. He would think he had hurt her when in fact her skin easily showed the slightest of bruises. Despite his disagreeable attitude, her instincts insisted that Lord Terrance was incapable of murder. But how could she trust her special senses when they refused to show her his heart? It would help to know about his connection to the murdered man.

"You came into Susie's room with your cousin," she said, more to herself than him. "He might tell me what I seek."

The suggestion seemed to enrage him. "You have become friendly with my cousin? Did you not take my earlier words seriously? I assure you that Phillip receives less than a hundred pounds a year, most of which is directed back into his mother's coffers. He would make you an unworthy match."

Belle's mouth opened wide in shock. She wanted to blast him with words for once again insulting her character. Then she shut her mouth as a better plan came to mind.

"Why, Lord Terrance, I do believe you have begun an argument. That means you owe me a visit to one of your tenants." Murder and visions momentarily forgotten, she rubbed her hands in jubilation. "Since I won, I shall pick the family with whom you must dine."

He looked stunned by her audacity to call him on his own wager. He recovered quickly enough, however, and laughed out loud. "Why, you are absolutely correct."

He moved closer. She retreated to the stair rail.

He followed and looked over into the entryway where a servant crossed the floor with a broom in hand. "This discussion requires privacy and a history lesson."

He took her hand and drew her toward the stairs going up. Belle resisted, but he kept a firm grip on her hand as he raced upstairs. She had to pick up her skirts to keep from tripping. When they arrived on the third floor, he turned and swung her onto the landing.

She glanced at the darkened corridor with trepidation. This was where she suspected the ghost loitered. The race upstairs had her breathing deep as she asked, "My lord, why have you brought me here?"

"For privacy and that lesson I spoke of." With a teasing smile, he drew her along a corridor that turned and turned again until she was lost. Her grip on his hand tightened, and he returned the gesture, raising her fingers for a light kiss.

Her hand tingled, and she forgot her fears. When he held her so tenderly, she felt safe and secure, as if nothing could ever hurt her. They arrived at a long narrow portrait gallery, and his gaze swept the walls with a careless glance.

"Lady Belle, may I introduce on this wall, all the monarchs from our honored past and across from them, my lowly ancestors who served them so loyally."

Belle did not care for this gallery at all. The only light came from a half-open curtain far down the passageway. She instinctively moved closer to Lord Terrance and eyed the portraits with unease. "I do not like it here."

"But this explains why your calling me on my wager is ridiculous. All these men were lords of the manor, as I am now. We have a duty to care for our tenants. Our role is to ensure their safety and security, not to become their bosom bows."

"Supping with your tenants is not allowed?"

"It would be unseemly. They would be tongue-tied in my presence, making them more ill at ease than myself."

"I beg to disagree," Belle said. "It will be your role to ensure they are not discomfited, my lord."

He frowned. "So you insist on going on with our wager?"

"I do." Belle withdrew her hand from his grip and crossed her arms. The row of Terrance men who lined the wall behind her might disapprove as much as the one who stood before her, but she had won the bet fair and square.

He placed his hands firmly by her waist and tugged her closer, drawing her wandering attention back to him. "Then I am forced to remind you that you began our argument when you questioned my whereabouts."

"That was not an argument." Belle forgot the portraits, her attention focused entirely on his lordship.

"Time to pay up." He had brought her so close they touched, toe-to-toe, bosom to chest.

Her breath caught in a startled gasp as his lips descended. Rethinking her position, she put a finger against his mouth. "Very well, I will concede that we both lost. Shall we call a truce? Neither one of us need pay. This once."

He nibbled her finger. She quickly pulled back.

"No," he said. "A pact is a pact. So, my part of the price for our argument is to swallow my dignity and spend an interminable time conversing with people with whom I have nothing in common?"

She nodded cautiously. Could his nibble on her finger count as her part of the pact?

He looked away as if to consider the proposal. When his attention returned, his shoulders relaxed, and his eyes held a tenderness that suggested he would not press her on her payment.

Belle breathed a sigh of relief. "Thank you, my lord."

"You are most welcome," he said. Then claimed her mouth with his.

As before in his study, his lips played gently against hers, but when she gasped in surprise, he laid siege to the open invitation, his desire strong and urgent. His hands molded her to him until their bodies and legs became intimately entwined.

Belle moved her head aside, and he continued his sensuous assault along the side of her face, within the folds of her ear, and along the curve of her neck. At the cleft of her bosom, his hand aided his assault by unveiling her flesh so his lips could continue their exploration unhindered.

Her flesh burned and melted where his mouth nuzzled and nipped. A groan escaped. To her shame, it was one that pleaded for more of this uncontrollable ache he generated.

Instead, breathing heavy, he stepped away. "You can drive a man mad, Belle. I almost forgot that you are an innocent."

Belle reached behind her and stumbled until she could steady herself against a wall. A hard frame pushed painfully into her back, but she ignored the discomfort.

As she stared at him, his gleaming eyes tempted her with more than a mere kiss in a dark hallway.

Belle sorely felt the lack of womanly wisdom. Her governess's counsel on how to behave with men had comprised no more than the proper way to curtsey, how to flutter one's fan to signal the wish for another dance, or the right time of day to accept callers. There had been no hint about what to do if a man enraptured her as Rufus Marlesbury had, or what dangers that look in his eyes posed to a maiden.

Common sense warned her this wager with his lordship was most unwise, and the sooner she curtailed it, the better.

"Would you care to rescind our wager now?" Though he spoke negligently, his wild eyes and clenched hands suggested it took supreme control to keep his distance. His self-control offered her no comfort, for she wanted to fling herself back into his embrace.

He crossed his arms, fists still curled tightly. "If you keep losing, I shall have to offer for you before the week is out."

"What do you mean?" Her words were a breathy gasp as her body still raged at the loss of his touch. Why must they stand apart?

He shrugged. "All you need do is go downstairs, and everyone will know you have been thoroughly compromised. Your lips are swollen red, your face is flushed, and your dress"—his gaze slid there and lingered—"reveals your delectable assets to advantage. If your game is to trap me into marriage, this is your perfect opportunity."

Shame doused her desire, and Belle swung around to face the wall. His description made her feel vulnerable, more so than when he had held her. She readjusted her gown and shift, both of which had let her down. And her shawl was a puddle on the floor. She let the useless thing lie there.

"Still here?" he asked. "Why not run screaming that the lord of the manor has ravished you?"

She ignored his taunt and focused on the gold embossed frame that had bit into her back. The golden frame contrasted sharply against the deep crimson patterned wallpaper. Inside the frame was the portrait of Lord Terrance's father. Her thoughts, which a moment ago had swirled like a hurricane, settled with unease.

"As I have already told you, my lord," she said in a calm tone that belied her worry that both father and son might be listening, "I am not interested in acquiring a husband."

"Why not?"

By the breath that brushed her neck, he was close. Her hard won composure crumbled, and she hugged herself to hold onto what little remained.

"You are still a young lady, gently born," he said. "Your manners are presentable and your features comely." He curled a lock of her hair with a finger and tugged it. "And despite your denials, you do enjoy the pleasures a man can give you. It makes no sense to turn away from a married life."

"I would never trick a man into marriage."

"If you wish to be courted, London is the place to find eligible men to fill your delicate ears with Byron's words." His finger traced her ear lobe. "And bestow soft kisses on your hand." He raised her hand to match action to word. "Instead, you are in Cheshire, in the dead of winter. What is a reasonable man to make of your intentions?"

She snatched her hand away. "Even if I were back in London, I would not moon over a man who cooed sonnets in my ear." She moved along the passageway, away from the overwhelming temptation to lean back, to let him pleasure her. "But that is neither here nor there. I came here at your mother's behest."

"Ah, yes, the ghost."

"You do not believe in such things." She traced the line of another frame.

"No, I do not."

She faced him then, chin high, eyes firm. "Well, my lord, that answers your question, for I do believe in things not seen by ordinary people. What you consider mere children's tales or old women's superstitions has a deep root in my everyday life. As for seeking a husband, experience has taught me that there are few—no why not confess the truth. There are *no* eligible men in our society who would overlook such 'irrational' beliefs in their wives. So, rest assured, I am not in your home to catch your interest. I am here to catch a ghost."

Chapter Eight

Belle held up a hand when Lord Terrance would have spoken. "Until this moment, I have kept my promise to not speak of such things, but understand this. Though I may not speak of them, I still believe in them."

He grazed her cheek with his knuckles, beginning a tremble in her again. "Life would be simpler if you tried not to." There was a disturbing thread of sadness in his voice. "By holding to this stubborn stance, you seal yourself to a life of empty nights and lonely days. Is that what you want?"

"That is the life I live. It is not of my choosing."

He shook his head. "It is most entirely of your choosing." This time, a note of steel threaded his words. He tipped her chin up. "Close your mind to the dead and focus on the living. You said you learned from experience that men would not want a superstitious wife. I say you missed the lesson entirely. Put aside these foolish fantasies and begin to live your life."

"By denying who I am?" She dislodged his grip.

He shook his head, looking frustrated. "Think not only about your future, but of the man who may wish to marry you."

What did he mean? Did he hint that he might wish to marry her if she denied her beliefs? She dashed away that false hope. She was certain he spoke of Jeffrey.

"I have it on the best of authority that Jeffrey already plans to ask Lady Delaney to be his wife. What I believe or not will make scant difference to him."

She made to walk away, but he gently pulled her back. "And is he the only man who may wish to marry you?"

"I will not marry a man who does not understand me. If he asked me to be other than what I am, how, then, can he truly care for me?"

"You are being deliberately stubborn. I cannot believe your grandfather is willing to allow you to throw away your future like this."

"My grandfather loves me and believes in who I am." *As you do not.* She smiled to mask her hurt. "This brings us to the real matter at hand."

"That is?"

"Since I have now paid my penalty, it is time you paid your debt."

His face assumed a bland mask. "You will hold me to it?"

"You gave your word." She did not care how awkward he might feel. She would not let him slip out of his payment after he had so skillfully extracted his tormenting kiss.

"Very well. To show my good sportsmanship, I will even advise you to pick anyone but the Parkers."

"Why not the Parkers?" she asked.

"You would find it difficult to obtain an invitation. They run inside their home the moment they see me come."

"As you said, the choice is mine. I will make arrangements and let you know when, where, and with whom we will sup."

He gave an elaborate bow. "May I escort you downstairs?"

Belle shook her head, more at the thought of him touching her than a rejection of his escort. "I wish to have a closer study of these portraits. Alone."

He hesitated and then said, "Dinner is at eight."

She was not ready to face anyone else for the rest of the day, so she pretended to study a portrait of King Charles. "I remember."

His departing footsteps were the loneliest sounds Belle ever recalled hearing.

She remained in the gallery long after Lord Terrance left. The memory of their impassioned embrace would not leave her as easily as he had. How was she to sit across from him at dinner and see his strong hands expertly wield his knife and fork and not imagine them caressing her? How could she watch his sensuous lips brush his wine glass, and not remember how he had taken possession of her mouth? She picked up her fallen shawl, hugged herself, and wandered the shadowy hallway, drawn toward the light by the far window.

Was he right? Would people know that she had been ravished? She could not bear to let that happen. No one must suspect the effect Rufus Marlesbury had on her. After the many pitying looks directed her way because of her broken engagement, she had promised herself to never let people see her as weak.

It grew late; the winter sun sat low over the empty hills and fields. She should return below before it grew too dark to negotiate the corridors. She straightened with resolve.

She would skip dinner, since her appetite was gone anyway. Lord Terrance might deduce why she wished seclusion, might even laugh at her timidity. His enjoyment of her fears did not matter. Before she next faced him, she must compose herself, be rid of these troublesome sensations he had generated. Mendal could relay the message that Belle had a megrim.

She turned away from the window only to discover the long corridor ahead was bathed in darkness. She had tarried too long. Using touch to orient herself, she went back the way she came.

She vaguely recalled the path. The rise and fall of each frame against her palm marked her progress. She turned left and then right. The stairs should be coming up soon.

She turned a corner and stopped in dismay. Although no light signified where she stood, a familiarity brought a sinking sensation. Lord Terrance had kissed her here. How could she have come back to this spot when she had walked the other way?

Her palm touched a heavy picture frame, and shock spiked through her arm, into her body, and erupted out of her back. At that moment of contact, a spirit's overwhelming anger eclipsed her wants and needs.

She swung around to see who had used her as a portal. The darkness remained. Belle hugged herself to control her shaking. Air cooled by degrees, and her shawl proved inadequate yet again. Once back in her room, she would get rid of it. It reminded her too much of how easily Lord Terrance had disrobed her.

But she had to regain her room before she could do that, and she was no longer alone.

Belle took a shaky breath and prepared to reason with this restless spirit. "Whatever you seek, I can help."

The coldness circled her, and she followed its advance until she no longer knew which direction she faced. Controlling her panic, she let her purpose for coming to Clearview rule her response.

"I mean you no harm. Her ladyship summoned me to help."

"You desire my son," a harsh voice said.

Heat suffused Belle's cheeks. Did she wear her emotions on her sleeve? And then another thought surfaced. His words confirmed the spirit haunting Clearview was indeed the late Earl of Terrance, Rufus Marlesbury's father.

The ghost must have seen her kissing his son, and now it berated her on her behavior. Obviously both father and son found her an unsuitable match. She refused to take umbrage. It might surprise them both that she agreed wholeheartedly.

"I will not take any action to have him. I came to help you, and the moment I do so, I will leave Clearview. You have my word, my lord. You need not worry on behalf of your son. Indeed, you should be proud of him. You and Lady Terrance have raised a wonderful man."

Her words seemed to still the spirit. She sensed him at her right side, and she turned to seek its presence only to confront a wall. That overwhelming agitation was gone, however, and in its place, peace invaded the corridor.

"Is that why you stay at this manor house?" Belle paused and thought about the man's death and her last vision. "How did you die, my lord? Did someone deliberately harm you?"

A bitingly cold wind whipped her backwards and made her swallow her next question. She would have tumbled to the ground had she not grabbed a heavy portrait for balance. It tipped sideways under her weight.

Suddenly, all went calm again. The portrait under hand shifted back into position. Belle let it go in fright and backed away.

The cold air warmed marginally, and she sensed that her supernatural visitor had departed as abruptly as he had appeared. Now that the spirit was gone, another worry surfaced. When she first touched the late Lord Terrance's portrait, and the spirit had used the contact to enter her body, she had feared it would take her over. There were terrifying accounts of such possessions.

At the idea of such an invasion of her body, her legs buckled, and she sank to the cold floor. Her skin grew chilled, as if she was caught in a wild snowstorm. Though she had encountered spirits before, none had frightened her as this one did, even after it left her.

Shivering uncontrollably, she replayed her conversation with Lord Terrance. He had told her that she had chosen her life. Could he have a point? Simply because she could sense such supernatural disturbances, must she deal with them too?

He had suggested that if she but chose differently, put aside her fantasies, she could live as a passionate woman. Could she do as he asked? Close her mind to this aspect of her life? Find a husband, have children, claim a chance to be cherished and loved and enthralled by a man's desire, as she was whenever Lord Terrance touched her?

Surely that was a more favorable existence than to cower in the dark, live a shadowed existence, and act as if she were part of her society, yet remain excluded from it in all the ways that mattered?

She took a deep breath, and then another, and willed her body to be calm and her mind to be rational. One encounter with the ghost of Clearview, and she was ready to bolt home. If this entity visited Lady Terrance nightly, no wonder she slept so little and seemed so fragile.

Her ladyship could not even seek out her son for comfort and advice, for he did not believe in such things. After months of solitude and anxiety, she had sought aid from an outside source, and by doing so, had widened the rift within her family. How could Belle leave now, reject her ability to help the countess, a woman who had been as kind to her as a mother?

With a sigh she stood. Her legs still trembled, but she was

determined to not run away. Nor was she foolish enough to believe that if she dealt with this one ghost, she could snuff out her talent as one did candlelight.

She had resigned herself to a lonely future. Yet, with one kiss, his lordship had made her rethink her decision. That must not happen again. It did not signify how much her body craved another lifestyle. It simply meant that she lived in a society that refused to accommodate both her heart's desires and her special calling. One must give way to the other.

This time, when Belle strode along the corridor on her way toward the stairs, she pushed open curtains to let in the late afternoon sun to light her way.

All thoughts of Lord Terrance were pushed aside, and she focused, instead, on his father. The late earl had died last spring in London. The public report said it had been a hunting accident. Moment by moment, Belle became certain that it had been murder. Why else would his spirit remain at Clearview? Obviously, he could not rest as long as his murderer walked free. Did he seek to protect the rest of his family from this villain, or was vengeance his sole purpose?

Most curious of all, why was he at Clearview? Why not roam Richmond Park where his body was discovered? His remains had been brought here, so that might be the link. Or did the man or woman responsible for his death reside in this house?

She pulled her shawl tighter and made her way downstairs. By the time she reached her bedroom door, she knew what she must do. To release this troubled spirit from his earthly worries, she must discover what distressed him. And if the ghost refused to tell her, his human family must do so. Avoiding people was no longer an option. Not tonight. Not tomorrow. Not until she laid the ghost of Clearview Manor to rest.

* * * *

The moment Belle entered her room, Mendal looked over at her and gasped. Her maid had always been very observant. Belle felt shattered, both by Lord Terrance's torrid kiss and then her terrifying encounter with the ghost. Her lips were sore, and she was sure her gown was askew, perhaps even torn, for she felt a cool breeze at her lower back, and her skin was so chilly she probably looked like a ghost. She wiped her cheek and realized she was also crying. Her maid was no fool.

Earnest, less observant, barked in welcome and came over with his tail wagging.

She held up her hand to forestall her maid's questions. "I need you to do something for me, Mendal."

"Anything, my lady." There were tears in her eyes now.

"I am physically unharmed, Mendal," she said. "Breathe easy on that score." *But I need time to recover in private.*

Belle sent her maid to the servant's quarters to procure information about the Parkers. Where did they live? Who lived in their household? What was their current circumstance?

"And Mendal."

"Yes, my lady?"

She gave her the shawl. "Burn this."

Mendal was gone a good hour, bless the thoughtful woman. During that time, Belle washed her face, brought normalcy to her scattered hair, and sponged herself clean, relishing the feel of cool, clean water as it wiped away all signs of her fevered emotions. She then put on her leather glove and took out the owl to feed her. Once the bird was returned to its cage, Belle sat on the floor and buried her face in Earnest's fur for a prolonged hug. That last act especially helped her recover a semblance of serenity.

On her return, Mendal laid a piece of paper with the Parkers' directions on the night table and hurried to ready Belle for dinner. As she slipped a white cambric muslin dress over Belle's head, Mendal spoke about the Parkers.

They had fallen on hard times, the maid said, and were likely to be thrown out of their home by spring. The husband was away in London seeking work. The wife had recently recovered from an illness. She had four adorable little ones who were always well-behaved in church, though they were rarely seen in school anymore. The local vicar checked on the family often, especially this winter.

Belle's gown fell elegantly over her stays and slip. The material was light yet warm. It had a demi train and long sleeves. Far better than anything the Parkers could afford. Pinched below her bosom, it showed off her figure. Belle's chest squeezed tight as she imagined what Mrs. Parker's figure must look like after her recent sickness.

With a critical eye, she viewed the trim of scalloped lace that was broad over her bosom and narrow by her shoulders and murmured, "It will do his lordship good to see the condition his tenants live in. I hope he squirms."

Mendal draped a warm, violet Pomona wrap over Belle's arms. It perfectly matched her eyes. "Can they afford to feed two more, my lady?"

"We will feed them," she said. "Tell the housekeeper that I will need a banquet for seven prepared and packed, ready to be delivered to the Parkers by three and thirty sharp. I shall go first to prepare them for Lord Terrance's later appearance."

"Is this truly wise, my lady?" Mendal asked.

Belle understood the meaning beneath her maid's words. What she meant was, *is it wise to go there alone with his lordship?* That did not bother Belle. The entire Parker family would be her chaperones. No more kisses in dark corridors.

"I go for a meal with a widow and her small children, Mendal." She waved the directions at her maid. "According to this, they are quite close by, so it will be a short journey there and back. I will also have Earnest for protection."

Mendal gave the wolfhound a skeptical look, and the dog chose that moment to bear his teeth at the owl. The bird leaped onto the cage's side and hooted at him.

"I am sorry, my lady. Your grandfather sent me to care for you, and I must do so to the best of my conscience. If you insist on going to this dinner, then I will accompany you."

"But Mendal . . ."

"Your mother passed away long ago, but she could not love you more than I. I will accompany you, my lady, if I have to walk all the way there and back."

Belle stared at Mendal, her lower lip trembling. Then she hugged her maid tight, and all the tears she had bottled up since Lord Terrance left her on the third floor, spilled.

It took them another half hour to repair her face so no trace of Belle's emotions showed. Belle was determined that no hint of the lady whose composure Rufus had shattered would be visible tonight.

"I wish to wear my mother's gold earrings and necklace."

"They will go splendidly with that gown," Mendal said and wiped away an errant tear of her own.

Fashionably late at twenty minutes past six, Belle descended the stairs. Her slippers made little noise on the thick red carpet. The idea of besting Lord Terrance at his own game made her tremble with conflicting emotions. If she succeeded, she could suggest they forget their wager and thus end what had turned into a dangerous game.

If that happened, her innocence would be safe, yet she would never experience another of his embraces. He was right on one count. She did enjoy his touch, and the thought of never experiencing that surge of passion his kisses evoked made her inconsolably sad. Yet, if she failed, she might lose her chastity and honor before she ever cleansed the manor of its resident ghost.

Flushed from the direction of her thoughts, she fanned herself mid-stairs and prayed for courage.

* * * *

Rufus waited impatiently in the drawing room for Belle. His glance was rooted to the closed doors. If she did not arrive soon, they would have to go in without her. At least her maid had not come to say her mistress had a headache. He had half expected that to happen, and he was prepared to scale the stairs and barge into her chamber to verify if the message was true or merely an excuse to avoid him.

Since their kiss in the gallery, images plagued him of Belle under his bed linen, in his arms, and entwined around his body. Common sense advised him that none of those things must ever come to pass. The truth of that put him in a foul temper with the servants, his family, but most especially, himself.

For years Rufus had successfully avoided the parson's mousetrap. By dallying with Belle, he now threw his plans to marry a suitable wife to the winds. Yet, to have one more taste of Belle, he was ready to lay down his neck and let the trap snap.

Of course, he must not do as his heart dictated. Belle was the most unsuitable of brides. Worse, he now suspected she would refuse him if he were to be so foolish as to offer. She was convinced only someone who believed as she did in that folderol about ghosts could truly and completely love her.

"Rufus, come sit by me." His mother tapped the seat beside her. "You have been glued to that wall for the last hour and begin to resemble a sconce."

"In case your eyes deceive you, Madam, I am no longer a child who needs instructions on how to behave."

"You were never that, Rufus," she said with an easy laugh. "You were always so intent on behaving properly that it is a wonder you were ever considered a child."

"As he should have been," Mrs. Jones said. "Though obviously, it seems to be more trial for him to behave properly than it is for my dear Phillip."

Phillip, who sat in a chair beside his mother, received a fond caress on his cheek, which he withstood with a pleasant if empty-headed expression.

Rufus grunted with impatience at his cousin's tolerance.

"Do sit," Phillip said. "I suspect that wall is sound and does not need your stalwart support." His handkerchief appeared in his hand, and he dabbed the perfumed cloth on his face. "Shame to waste all that effort on concrete and mortar."

"Is it not time to eat soon?" Susie asked. "I wonder what keeps Belle?"

Rufus spared a look at his sister. She was better turned out tonight than usual. She wore a pretty, white half-mourning dress with a black ribbon border. Her eyes were bright and cheerful. Not at all the normally reticent Susie.

He had hoped Belle would bring his sister out more, and she seemed to have achieved that effect. If only Belle did not harbor such strange thoughts about spirits, he could wholeheartedly welcome her as a companion for his sister.

His gaze moved back to the doorway. What kept Belle? Had he pushed their wager too far? Even if he had, he knew she had enjoyed his kisses, and he would not allow her to convince herself otherwise. "I will see what keeps her."

"Best send Felton," his aunt said. "It would not look right to approach her yourself. Might give her the impression that you have an interest."

"What nonsense," his mother said. "Rufus, interested in my Belle? She is far too sensible for him. Now, Phillip would make a perfect match."

Rufus's neck burned with outrage. Was his mother truly insane? Phillip was entirely wrong for Belle. He would bore her after an evening in his company, let alone a lifetime. She needed someone strong and passionate to match her spirit.

"I beg to differ, dear Constance," Mrs. Jones said. "Phillip has his sights set on a Miss Warwick. She is a lovely, well-behaved young lady who is due to have her come-out next spring. Completely unspoiled. Her grandfather is a duke, and her father is in direct line to inherit." She tapped her son on his knee. "Unlike some," her gaze flicked to Rufus, "Phillip has learned it is better not to chase after ladies of low caliber."

Phillip's lips had thinned into a narrow line of displeasure. Rufus waited for him to set his mother straight, but he said not a word. His cousin looked as if he were fighting a demon of his own. It made Rufus curious about this "lady of low caliber" that his cousin had learned not to chase.

"There is nothing wrong with Belle's caliber," Susie said, with outrage. "She is a perfect lady and the granddaughter of a marquess."

"To argue when you know nothing of what you speak," Mrs. Jones said, "shows lack of breeding."

Rufus strode out the door. His aunt's words about Belle's

unsuitability matched his recent thoughts too closely for comfort. He did not care about her unsuitability. He intended to drag her downstairs if he had to dress her himself.

Belle standing naked and still as he pulled her underskirts over her legs sent his desire soaring. He squirmed where his undershirt was tightly wrapped between his legs. After returning from his encounter with Belle, Rufus had soaked for a half hour in a cold bath, but it had done little to completely subdue his arousal.

Eventually, Ellison, with a remarkably stoic face, had suggested that the long linen shirt be wrapped in such a manner as to protect his master from any embarrassing reveal later.

Cursing Ellison, Rufus swished his hips to loosen the tight hold before taking the first step up. Then he saw her.

Dressed in a low-cut silk gown and a violet wrap that made his fantasies seem tame, Belle stood hesitantly halfway up the stairs. The ladies of the Ton wore gowns more revealing than hers, but even dressed in a burlap bag, Belle could snatch his breath away. It took a while to find his words, and when they came, they were more clipped than he would have preferred. "We waited dinner on your appearance."

"I am sorry to have kept you, my lord."

She descended, placing one delicate satin-slippered foot ahead of the other. With skirts held up, her every step showed glimpses of a luscious ankle.

He silently thanked Ellison for his forethought and held out his arm. "May I escort you in?"

She slipped her hand around his elbow, as if she belonged beside him. He covered her fingers, proud to claim this lady as his, if only for the short transit from entryway to drawing room. All too soon, her hand slipped away as she went to greet Susie.

"I am so glad you could join us tonight," his sister said.

Rufus noted that a sparkle she had lacked for many a year was present in Susie's eyes. Until now, unbeknownst to him, a quietness had invaded his sister that he now realized was one more of a lack of spirit than of peace.

Belle had managed to breathe life back into Susie. He glanced over at his mother, who also looked animated. *And my mother.*

Felton entered. "Dinner is served, my lord."

Conversation during the meal swirled from the latest happenings in London, as told by Phillip, and the arrangements that would be needed if Susie were to have a Season next spring. The latter subject made his sister irritable since she denied any liking for the project.

"Any young lady would be thrilled to have a Season in Town," her aunt said. "I can assure you that you will not find a worthwhile candidate in this backwater village."

"There is nothing backwater about Terrance," the countess said. "I have been quite happy here. This society is a match to any you will find in London. The most interesting people reside in Terrance."

"If you mean the baker, I beg to differ, Constance," Henrietta Jones said. "Although he may bake a loaf worthy of the prince himself, he is not a suitable companion for a countess, and I should hope you have better expectations for the daughter of an earl than for her to marry some village bumpkin."

"I did not suppose any such thing," Lady Terrance said, her face as pink as her steak. "I merely meant there are suitable companions in this village, too."

"Poppycock," Mrs. Jones said. "You have rusticated in the countryside too long. If you had come to London as your husband wished, you would know that only by attending the best parties and gatherings can Susie's needs be met. However, since we are all aware of your preference for the country, I would be happy to chaperone Susie on your behalf."

"Oh!" Susie gasped and turned a horrified look on Rufus.

He took pity on her plight. Susie cared for society as much as his mother. It would be difficult enough for her to be among strangers and on her best behavior without his aunt at her side, constantly finding fault.

"I hoped to approach Lady Belle privately on this subject," he said. "She would make an admirable companion for Susie."

Belle looked surprised. And no wonder. Since her arrival he had done naught but decry her behavior. If she agreed, it would gave them a chance to continue the fascinating and frustrating conversation they had left off on the third floor.

"You could offer Susie your knowledge and companionship," he said, "making the London entertainments more enjoyable for both of you."

Henrietta Jones responded to Rufus's gambit first. "Out of the question. Lady Belle is not . . . I do not believe . . ." She stopped, obviously not wishing to insult Belle to her face.

Rufus hid a smile at leaving his aunt speechless.

"Capital idea," Phillip said. "Hope both of you stunning ladies will save a dance for me at every ball you attend. And we might find time to play a game or two of . . . well . . . whist."

Susie giggled. The countess, having taken a sip of wine, sputtered.

Belle kept her eyes focused on her plate, but her lips twitched, and her cheeks seemed inordinately bright.

Rufus studied all of them through narrowed eyes. He remembered his cousin's comment earlier at the inn, and now he watched the foursome's sly glances and recounted his family members' unusual vivacity, and suddenly, all of it fell into place. Something was up. And it had nothing to do with a game of whist. Worse, they had not included him in their secret machinations. Appetite lost, Rufus toyed with his meat. When had he become the outsider within his family? That reminded him that, if he did not find a way to clear his name soon, he would become the outsider in a much more stark fashion. *Was it only six weeks to the New Year?* And Belle's suitability became immaterial, because he certainly would not be in a position to court her or any other woman. And he would be leaving his family, their livelihood, and his tenants in dire straights without him here to look after their welfare.

Tomorrow, he must return to the village inn to seek out another source of information besides Brindle. Someone else might know about his father's movements during his last visit to Cheshire. Hopefully, the discovery of a new informant would not result in another murder. But unfortunate as Brindle's death was, Rufus suspected it was a clear sign that his search had taken him closer to his father's murderer. It was the only ray of hope he had found to cling to in months.

Chapter Nine

"You honor me with your invitation, my lord," Belle said, bringing Rufus's attention back to the dinner conversation.

Seated beside his mother, she appeared to belong at this table, as if she were as much a member of his family as Susie. He could not imagine another female who could fit in so well.

How absurd, he immediately chided himself. His wife would belong in his home more than a guest. Yet, Belle seemed a perfect fit for Clearview.

"As much as I would enjoy Susie's company," Belle said, "I do not plan to participate in the upcoming social events in Town."

Her words broke into his thoughts like a knife slicing through meat.

"But you must," Susie said.

His sister snatched the words out of Rufus's dry mouth. What did she mean she did not intend to participate? Even as he asked himself the question, he knew why. Well, her ghost hunting be damned. He would not let her leave him.

"Say you will come," Susie said. "I could not bear to go if I did not have you by my side to offer me your wise counsel."

"Hmph!" her aunt said from across the table.

"What I mean is," Susie said, "Belle is more my age, and she has experienced the Season in Town, so she would be able to advise me on the best way to behave."

"Child, you have no more sense than a worm out in the rain," her aunt said.

"You might be right, Henrietta." Lady Terrance placed her glass on the table. "I have been away from Town too long. If anyone is to escort the girls, it should be I."

"Oh, mother, do you truly mean that?" Susie smiled brilliantly and clapped her hands.

Rufus's heart did a jig. Despite all his father's pleadings, his mother had not left Clearview in years. Rufus had not believed she would ever return to society.

Awestruck, he glanced at Belle. This change was because of her, and he knew it. He no longer cared what secret she shared with his family. In a few days, she had accomplished what he and his father had been unable to contrive in years. No wonder he loved her.

His fork clattered against his plate at the thought.

"Rufus," his mother said, a note of trepidation in her tone, "do you not approve of my coming?"

"I thoroughly approve, Mama," he said.

She blinked, as if shocked by his answer, and then she smiled. "This Season is important for Susie's future. And Belle, well, she does not have a mother to guide her, and it would make me proud if she would allow me to act in that regard."

"My lady." Belle's eyes were filled with tears that threatened to overflow. "I would be honored to have you play such a beloved role."

His aunt seemed ready to argue, so Rufus rushed to forestall her comments. Belle had impulsively agreed to come along, and he did not intend to let her wriggle out of her commitment.

"Then it is settled. We shall all attend the next Season."

Now that he had admitted that he loved Belle, Rufus was determined to win her—heart, mind and soul. He was also certain he could make her forget all about ghosts and spirits and any other supernatural imaginings. As he considered ways he might accomplish that task, he shifted in his chair and again gave thanks to Ellison.

But despite the discomfort, he felt more cheerful than he had been in months. Rufus held up his glass to toast the coming year, but deep inside, worry and unease rumbled. Would he even be with his family next year to make a toast to their health, or would he be standing before the House of Lords to plead for his life and praying that his family would not pay the price for his failure to catch his father's killer?

* * * *

Later that night, Belle and Susie gathered in the countess's room until it was time to start their billiards game. However, hour after hour, Lord Terrance kept Phillip Jones busy in the games room doing exactly what Belle and Susie and the countess wished to do. Finally, disheartened, they disbanded to their respective chambers.

Belle lay awake, replaying all that had happened at the dinner table. Lord Terrance had gazed at her as if she were a roast duck set before him for his pleasure. Then, somehow, he had tricked her into agreeing to accompany his family to London despite her adamant stance that she no longer wished to find a husband. She had backed away from her promise when she later met with Susie and Lady Terrance, but both women refused to listen.

A warm, heavy lump beside her feet, Earnest shifted and yawned. Her restlessness kept the tired dog awake. She turned over, her mind racing like a mouse inside a wall.

A few days ago she had been perfectly content to spend her life caring for her grandfather and answering the call of her gift. Yet, what had once served as an achievable dream, now seemed lonely and deprived, all because Rufus Marlesbury had held her in his arms and stirred desires that were better left dormant. She punched her pillow. Why did he have to poke his handsome nose into her life?

She could not tolerate another Season where patronesses bestowed disdainful glances. And to be present while he paid court to the *Ton* ladies while she became a veritable wallflower—*Oh, it was insupportable.*

Earnest sat up and whined. The owl fluttered inside her bamboo cage and hooted.

"Sorry," Belle said, knowing she caused their restlessness, and lay on her back.

She took a deep breath and exhaled slowly. At least there had been one happy moment this evening. Before coming upstairs, she had managed to have a private word with Lord Terrance about their visit to the Parkers.

The astonishment on his face was well worth her losses this day. Her triumph tasted sweeter than the gooseberry cream she had for dessert. She closed her eyes. Then her eyes snapped open. What if Mrs. Parker refused Belle's plans for her dinner party?

* * * *

Three hours before Lord Terrance was to join her, Belle and Mendal arrived at the Parkers' farm. She had to ensure Mrs. Parker would not only acquiesce to the evening's plans, but was well enough to do so.

Four children who played in the snow ran to meet the one-horse cart on which she had driven over. Earnest jumped out to bark and run around the two boys and two girls. Mendal's research had uncovered the children's ages. They ranged from a nine-year-old boy to a little girl of three.

"Good afternoon," Belle said. "My name is Lady Belle Marchant, and this is my maid Mendal. I am staying at the manor." She raised a hand when the eldest boy would have spoken. "Wait. Do not introduce yourselves. If I can guess one thing that each of you are thinking, I shall win your name and a kiss on the cheek."

The children laughed.

"You will not win anything from me then," the tallest boy said and confidently petted Earnest.

Descending from the cart, Belle studied him. A tall lanky boy, he scrunched up his mouth, eyes, and nose, defying her to read his thoughts. She did not even try, for Mendal had learned the eldest Parker child greatly favored desserts. Already his nose twitched as he slit an eye open to follow the waft of apples, raisins, and lemon rising from the

Christmas pudding.

"Pudding," she said.

He stomped his foot, but being an honorable gentleman, he leaned over and pecked her cheek. "Steven, my lady."

Earnest jumped up and licked both their faces.

"You were not part of the game," Steven said to the dog. "You stole those kisses."

Belle moved on to the next eldest, a girl. By the time she won a wholehearted hug and a kiss from three-year-old Margaret, Mrs. Parker came out to greet them.

She looked as if she had hastily dressed and appeared too thin in a brown dress that had seen many a good year's wear. Her long face had dark circles beneath her sunken eyes, and her light brown hair hung limp about her shoulders. Belle suspected she was not yet completely recovered from her illness.

"Good afternoon, Mrs. Parker." Belle introduced Mendal.

"Good afternoon, my lady. Mrs. Mendal." Her hostess curtsied and wrapped her threadbare shawl tighter.

Belle said that she had heard they were a family in need during this blessed holiday season, and she had wanted to do her Christian duty and bring them some food.

"How very kind," Mrs. Parker said.

Belle recruited the two boys to carry the provisions. As the boys ran back and forth from the cart to the house, Earnest, ever helpful, followed them in and out.

"But there's so much," Mrs. Parker said.

"It is Lady Terrance who is generous with this gift," Belle said. "When I advised her I planned to visit one of her tenants, she insisted I take as much as I could possibly carry."

Belle took out a picnic basket and flipped off the top. "She even had cook bake us a meat pie."

"We could not eat so much in one meal, my lady." She glanced at Belle and Mendal, and after a moment of hesitation, said, "Would you care to join us for supper?"

"We would love to." One hurdle crossed. One to go.

"Do not worry about the amount of food," Mendal said. "In this cold weather, it should keep for as long as you need."

"I suppose." Mrs. Parker snagged Steven as he ran by. "These ladies will stay for supper, Steven, so please untie their horse and give it some feed in the barn."

They walked toward the house, and Belle took the woman's arm, ostensibly in a companionable hold, but in reality to ensure the frail woman did not trip on the icy pathway.

"With Christmas less than a month away, will you decorate your house?" Belle asked.

"As my husband is away, we do not plan a celebration."

"It seems to me that is the perfect reason to have a celebration," Belle said. "If he returns early, it would be to a cheerful home, and if he cannot make it back in time for the holiday, the decorations might raise our spirits."

"I suppose. We shall have to see."

Belle sensed a lack of enthusiasm. In her drained state, the poor thing probably worried as much about the work it would take to dismantle the decorations after Christmas, as it would be to put them up now.

"They have not begun to decorate the manor either," she said, hoping to give Mrs. Parker an easy way out. "Are such things not the custom in Cheshire?"

"The villagers used to decorate the streets and homes and hold festivals," Mrs. Parker said. "There used to be a Christmas dance at the manor. That was a long time ago, of course, when I was a youth. We do not bother with such entertainments these days."

Belle helped Mendal unpack the various hampers onto the large kitchen table.

As Mendal had warned, the hearth was meagerly filled with coal. Belle had a large barrel of coal on her cart for just this need. She sent the boys to unload it. Once a hearty fire blazed, Steven hung a half-done roast there to finish cooking.

Earnest sat before the fire, pretending to guard the roast. Belle suspected both the fire's warmth and the succulent meat had drawn him to his position.

Mrs. Parker wanted to help with preparations, but Belle insisted that she sit and watch, for this was meant as a treat for the mother, not her guests. After a halfhearted protest, her tired hostess complied.

"Tell me about the Christmas celebrations in Terrance Village," she said to bring Mrs. Parker into the conversation.

"His late lordship was not much for socializing with villagers," Mrs. Parker said. "Though his good wife, when they were first married, loved it. Lady Terrance was a great one to chat with all and sundry. Since her husband disapproved of her behavior, as the years passed, they socialized less with us."

"But Lady Terrance still visited the villagers?" Belle asked.

"Oh yes. But she would wait until his lordship left for Parliament. However, since her husband died, she has stopped speaking with us altogether. At first, we thought she mourned, but she still does not come to visit."

Belle had her suspicions about the change in the countess's behavior. The nightly visits by her dead husband might keep her housebound as surely as if he were alive and residing there.

"Lady Terrance's son is home now," Mrs. Parker said, "but if you will pardon my bluntness, my lady, he has little time or patience for his tenants."

"Surely that cannot be," Belle said. "I understood him to care deeply about his new responsibilities as earl, and those would certainly include all who work for him."

"Then why does he plan to discharge Mr. Nightingale?" Mrs. Parker asked. "His agent was loyal to the Terrances. Yet, he is to be let go with no more thought than his lordship would give to flicking dust off his fancy boots."

"I must admit I know little of that matter," Belle said. "Has anyone asked Lord Terrance about Mr. Nightingale?"

"Question Lord Terror?" The moment she spoke, Mrs. Parker went deathly pale.

"Please, do not worry," Belle said. "He will not hear from me that you called him that name."

"Thank you, Lady Belle," Mrs. Parker said with a relieved sigh. "It has been most harrowing of late. First, Mr. Darby's death and then Mr. Brindle's."

The latter name rang a warning bell. "Where did they die?"

"Mr. Brindle passed in the village, just the other day," Mrs. Parker said. "Mr. Darby died in London Town, about six months ago."

Belle frowned at the information. That time period was too coincidental.

"We had problems with the farm about then," Mrs. Parker said, "and all my attention was focused on helping my husband." She gave Belle a side-glance filled with unease. "We suspect Lord Terrance plans to evict us, as his father did Mr. Brindle."

The lady's shoulders drooped.

Belle and Mendal exchanged a glance, Belle's filled with worry and Mendal's holding an "I told you this was a bad idea" gleam. Still, Belle was determined to cheer this household before she must confess that the man they held in such fear would shortly arrive for dinner.

As the hour progressed, her heart hammered faster. Impending doom approached, and she did not know how to stop it.

Unaware of their guests' tension, as they prepared dinner, the children sang and shared jokes. Scents of a well-done roast, potatoes and sausage rolls, cheese biscuits, and mince tarts infused the home.

Shelving her worries, Belle told the children a tale about Christmas pudding. She carefully laid out the thirteen ingredients, meant to represent Christ and His Disciples. Then every family member took turns stirring the pudding with a wooden spoon from east to west, in honor of the Three Kings.

To the children's delight, Belle reenacted the Medieval silver coin custom. She fetched the silver from her reticule, washed it, and with much ceremony, hand waving, and sound effects, plopped the coin into the pudding.

The children cheered.

As each child stirred the pudding, she told them how this age-old custom was said to bring wealth, health, and happiness to whoever found the coin. Even Mrs. Parker was invited to stir to add her good wishes to the family's future.

After clearing the table, Mendal spread a festive cloth overtop.

"Where I live," Belle said to the children, "our servants cover the whole house in greenery to remind us spring is near."

Mrs. Parker looked around her home and then caught the children's hopeful gazes. Belle was pleased to see more color on the mother's face. Either from the heat of cooking or their merriment of company, Mrs. Parker seemed to have improved in both spirit and body.

"Well," the mother said, "it might make the place lively."

The children gave her a warm hug and rushed out the door before their mother could change her mind.

"We will not be long," Belle said.

"I will watch the buns in the range," Mendal said.

"I can do that," Mrs. Parker said. "I have done so little."

"You have done the most marvelous thing of all." Belle took the woman's hands. "You have given me a wonderful chance to spend time with your children. I grew up as an only child, and being here has shown me I would love to have a family."

"No doubt you will soon," Mrs. Parker said.

Belle kept her thoughts on her self-imposed, lonely future private and gave her hostess a hug. "Thank you for inviting us into your home. I hope you never regret it."

"How could I?" Mrs. Parker spread her arms to indicate the room filled with scents of baking and counters and table overflowing with food. "We cannot eat half of what you have brought us today."

"Never fear, Mrs. Parker, I am sure we will find enough appetites to do justice to this food. Now, I had better be off before I lose sight of the children."

In the space of a half-hour, they returned to the cottage with their haul. The three eldest children carried armfuls of ivy and boughs of evergreens, while Belle carefully carted a sackcloth full of the prickly holly with its bright red berries. Three-year-old Margaret carried a shawl-wrapped bundle of mistletoe, which they had found growing on a willow.

They set to trimming the cottage. The children enjoyed strewing the branches of holly and ivy about the room and over chairs and tables while Belle placed several atop pictures and on tall shelves. She saved the mistletoe for last and then stood on a stool by the doorway and asked Margaret to pass her the plant.

"Do you know where the practice of hanging these over doorways came from, Margaret?"

"No." The child looked up at her with wide, curious eyes.

"Do you know who the Druids are?"

"My lady," Mendal said, "I hardly think that is an appropriate story for children."

"I do not mind," Mrs. Parker said. "They hear much worse in school. And now I am curious about the tale."

"Me too," Margaret said.

Belle hid her smile. "This practice stretches back to ancient Druids who believed these plants possessed mystical powers. The plants were said to bring good luck to the household and . . ." She paused to lean down from the stool and whisper, "Ward off evil spirits."

The older children had joined the youngest and now listened wide-eyed. Just then someone pounded on the front door, and they screamed. Earnest, brave dog that he was, scooted under the kitchen table. Belle exchanged a nervous and guilty look with Mendal.

"I wonder who that could be?" Mrs. Parker stood and leaned on the table, as if unsteady.

"Spirits from the manor house," Steven said.

Margaret screeched and ran to hide behind her mother.

"I suspect it is only Mr. Bedlow come to check on us," her mother said. "The vicar is a kind man," she said to Belle. "He has looked in on us most every week since my husband left."

Earnest ventured out from under the table to pad over to the doorway and sniff. Though his tail wagged, he gave a whine.

Belle descended from the stool. Like Earnest, she had her suspicions about which spirit demanded entry.

"I shall see who it is." She shifted the stool aside and opened the door.

"Good evening, Lady Belle." Lord Terrance tipped his hat. He had dressed formally, no doubt hoping to make her realize the folly of her suggestion that he dine with his tenants.

Two could play this game. She gave him a deep curtsy.

"It is Lord Terror," Steven said in a loud whisper.

On rising, Belle cringed. If she had heard that proclamation, so must have Lord Terrance. She stepped aside and waited for Mrs. Parker to come to the door. This was, after all, her home. She would not invite in the woman's enemy.

"How may I help you, my lord?" Mrs. Parker appeared paler than she had when Belle first arrived.

Belle put her arm around the woman's shaking shoulders, and Rufus's eyebrow shot up at that show of allegiance.

Did he realize yet that she had lied when she said she had garnered him an invitation here? In fact, in the course of preparing dinner, she had changed her mind about having him visit, but it was too late to stop this carriage wreck.

"Lady Belle." Lord Terrance pinned her with a narrow, assessing gaze. "When my mother informed me that you had come to visit one of our tenants, and that it was with Mrs. Parker and her lovely family, I simply had to come to see for myself."

Clever man!

"Your home smells heavenly, Mrs. Parker." He then smiled so wide that he took Belle's breath away.

He seemed to have a similar effect on Mrs. Parker, for she stood speechless.

Lord Terrance shifted on his feet, and though he easily topped everyone in the room, he made a show of craning his neck to see into the house. His body's movement plainly suggested that he wished to enter.

Mrs. Parker's shoulders sagged beneath Belle's arm, and her recently revived spirit evaporated like steam from a pie.

"Come in, my lord," Mrs. Parker said, sounding as if she were inviting the devil inside.

* * * *

Rufus handed the eldest lad his hat and coat and took time to study the room. The hearth had holly strewn over the mantle. Their red berries and deep green, angular leaves gave a bright festive air to the place.

Greenery adorned walls, hung off curtains, pictures, on the back of chairs and an old sofa.

To the left was the kitchen and dining area. A floral cloth covered the large kitchen table, and spread out over it, inside bowls and plates made of wood or tin, was every imaginable Christmas treat from his younger days. A center porcelain platter, worn and chipped, contained a well-done roast. The air hung steamy and warm from hours of cooking, and a scent of mouth-watering white fish lingered.

All four children crowded in front of their mother, as though to guard her. Belle stood by the partially open front door with her overprotective maid and his disloyal dog beside her, as if all three considered making a run for it.

Catching his challenging look, Belle's chin rose, and she shut the door and used her foot to ostensibly push the dog away. As if that gesture could fool him into believing that she had not stolen his dog's loyalty. The dog put lie to action by leaning against her legs the minute she released him.

He could not remember Earnest ever acting this attached to anyone in his family, certainly never to him. Not that he blamed the hound. Everyone at Clearview, except his aunt, responded to Belle's irresistible pull, most of all himself. He had profound sympathy with the dog's plight.

As he regarded her, he could not understand how she could look so charming while wearing a plain brown dress done up to her neck, with the sleeves sporting no more than the merest ruffle. For all that she was covered from neck to toe, Rufus was as enchanted by her appearance as if she wore the most revealing of gowns, regally embroidered. With effort, he shifted his focus to his hostess.

"I see I arrived in time to interrupt your meal, Mrs. Parker. You have set a most inviting table."

"Thank you, my lord. Lady Belle has been generous to us."

He gave Belle a side-glance. "Once one catches her attention, she is most assuredly generous with her bounty. How to keep her attention is another matter."

Mrs. Parker glanced with concern from him to Belle.

"The reason I am here is that she had promised to have dinner with us tonight and entertain us with a song."

Belle's eyes widened, but he ignored her silent accusation.

"Then I discovered she had made plans to come here."

"If you must leave us, we understand," Mrs. Parker said to Belle. "We never expected you to really dine with us."

Rufus's gaze settled on the two extra place settings.

Mrs. Parker, her face shifting from shocked to mortified, snatched up the plates and utensils and put them away.

He suppressed a frustrated sigh. He wanted this farm wife to invite him to stay, not throw all her uninvited guests out. Where would be the fun in that?

"Where is the good Mr. Parker?" he asked, for a change in subject. "Still in the village pub?"

"Mr. Parker has gone to London." Belle finally moved away from the door. "He seeks work, as the farm did not do as well as they had hoped this summer."

Mrs. Parker's face, which a moment ago had been beet red with embarrassment, now turned as pale as the fish soup on the table. "He will make the payments this year, my lord." She touched a chair, and her hand shook until she gripped its edge. "He is working very hard and hopes to cover our debt by springtime."

Rufus raised his hand. "I have no wish to discuss business tonight."

He glanced about the room to give Mrs. Parker time to compose herself. Then he waved a careless hand as Phillip often did, minus the handkerchief. "Your husband may see my agent about that issue."

"But I heard you planned to discharge him," Belle said.

He did not trust the light of battle in her eyes. "Business must wait another day." He was keenly aware of the rules of their engagement. Time for a frontal assault. "Since I am denied your entertainment at the manor, Lady Belle, I shall settle for Mrs. Parker's and her family's company."

The mother's mouth hung open, as if he had asked to permanently move in with the family instead of merely for one evening's meal. He folded his arms and waited with a polite smile.

"Oh," Mrs. Parker said. "My lord, er, would you care to join us for dinner?"

He bowed deeply. "Why, thank you for your gracious invitation, Mrs. Parker. I would be delighted to join you."

Mrs. Parker looked as if she would faint, and Belle squeezed her shoulders as if in a reminder that the woman and her family would not be facing their greatest terror over the dinner table alone.

He hid a sudden spurt of enjoyment that bubbled in his chest behind a bland smile. This might prove to be an amusing evening after all, instead of the awkward punishment that Belle had intended.

Chapter Ten

Mrs. Parker set out extra plates, and then Rufus held out a chair for her at one end of the table. Once she was seated, he held out one for Belle, and then another beside her for her maid, before he took his place at the head of the table.

The eldest boy then gestured to his brother to emulate Rufus's action. Together, they pulled the bench out on the other side of the table and waited for their sisters to sit. The girls gave the boys a surprised look, and then, skirts held in one hand, they sat quite prettily, no doubt mimicking Belle.

Once all were seated, Belle said a quick prayer. Rufus was surprised at how much he enjoyed the formality of the proceedings. Though everyone in his family sat for supper together, they rarely said grace. That blessing brought a surprising touch of peace to the meal.

"You missed the pudding stirrings, my lord," Steven said, then glanced at him with obvious apprehension.

Anger replaced his enjoyment. What had he done to produce such fear in a child so young?

His expression must have reflected his temper because Steven ducked his head.

"He meant no harm in his words, my lord," Mrs. Parker said.

Rufus's gaze fell with equal astonishment on his hostess, who appeared as terrified as her offspring. His chest tightened, and he frowned with a fierce effort to control himself. What could he say in his defense, and why should he say anything? He had been everything polite since he entered their home. He had doffed his hat and smiled benevolently and even complimented Mrs. Parker on the decorations. He had done nothing to warrant this reaction.

"His lordship is not angry with you, Steven," Belle said. All turned toward her in surprise, including Rufus. "He merely enjoys making funny faces sometimes."

Little Margaret giggled. "Like this?" She scrunched her face into a mighty angry pose.

"Margaret, no!" her mother said in a panicked voice.

Rufus could not take his eyes off Margaret. *Do I really look like that?*

Suddenly conscious of his countenance, he schooled his features into a bland mask. "Thank you, Miss Margaret. That is a good impression. You deserve a reward for such a brilliant display. Name your price, and it is yours."

Mrs. Parker gasped. All the children looked at Margaret, who gazed at him with a sweet smile as she filled her mouth with a piece of meat pie.

Her brothers and sister whispered suggestions. Margaret chewed her food as she listened, but at the end, she shook her head. "I want a doll with red hair and yellow ribbons."

Her mother gave a nervous sputter. "I am sorry, my lord. Ever since the Benson's child was given a doll like that, my Margaret has had her heart set on getting one. I have explained that in life you cannot always have what you most desire. Once she is older, she will understand better how life truly is."

"I am in complete sympathy with both of you, Margaret and Mrs. Parker," Rufus said. "Although I have held your view on life for many years, recently I, too, have had a difficult time releasing what my heart desires."

He looked at Belle, and she switched her surprised gaze to her plate.

Her maid spoke, spearing him with a hard stare. "Mrs. Parker is correct. It is best to learn early that not all one wishes can or should come true."

Rufus reeled mentally as if slapped for overstepping. Had Belle confessed about their kissing game to her maid? No, but the woman was intelligent, and if she had seen her mistress when she descended from the upper floor of Clearview, she might have guessed what had taken place. The light of battle in her gaze suggested getting physically close to Belle again would now be impossible.

He stared at his dinner, a leaded weight in his chest.

"How long are you staying in Clearview, my lady?" Mrs. Parker asked.

"Not long," Belle said.

Rufus's head snapped up. "After the New Year breaks, she comes with us to London for the Season."

"That may not be possible," Belle said. "My grandpapa ails, and I am not comfortable being away that long."

"I did not know," he said. *Why had not she mentioned this before?* "I will send word for my physician to attend him."

"He has a good doctor. I saw to that before I left."

"Then there is no reason to rush back."

"Is it time for the Christmas pudding?" Steven asked, obviously having lost interest in the adult conversation.

Rufus was grateful for the change in subject. If she hoped to use her grandfather as an excuse to leave him, she was mistaken.

As Mrs. Parker brought the pudding, which had a piece of holly on top for decoration, Rufus made a mental note to send someone to London to check on Belle's grandfather, the marquess.

The Christmas pudding acted like a signal, and the children's excitement level shot up. Upon receiving their serving, each child immediately demolished their portion and then sat back with a sigh of disappointment.

What a queer custom.

Belle passed him his serving. Their fingers touched, and sparks ran up his arm. She snatched her hand away, as if a similar bolt had struck her. She hid her hand on her lap, and Rufus hid his exultant grin. She *was* as affected by him as ever. And he intended to ensure Belle never forgot that—or found reason to avoid him.

His cheer returned, he gaily sliced into a piece of his pie. *Clunk!* He had hit metal.

"You have found it," Margaret said. "He has got the silver coin. You will be rich and happy. Now you can get my doll."

"Margaret, shush," her mother said.

"The coin is good luck, my lord," Steven said. "That is what I meant when I said you had missed the pudding stirring."

Everyone watched as Rufus fished out his good luck charm and used his handkerchief to clean it.

"Make a wish, my lord," Margaret said.

"And it will come true," her sister finished. "It is tradition. Lady Belle said so."

He held the coin out for all to see. "I believe Lady Belle missed the best part of this tradition."

"What part?" Steven asked.

"Everyone knows that whoever gets a wish must hold the coin, make his or her wish, and then toss it into the air. Whoever catches it also gets their wish."

He closed his eyes and then flipped. The coin sailed high and landed accurately on Mrs. Parker's lap.

"Oohh, Mummy, you get a wish now!" Margaret said.

Mrs. Parker retrieved the silver coin, and in a trice her children's suggestions erupted.

"A doll."

"A pony."

"New dresses."

"Shoes."

"More pudding."

"A pot full of silver coins."

"I only have one wish." Mrs. Parker's grave voice silenced her offspring. "For Mr. Parker to come home safe and soon."

Rufus raised his mug of cider. "To Mr. Parker's return."

The toast broke the solemn silence and brought cheer back to the table. The conversation ventured into livelier channels.

Rufus looked over at Belle, saw the merriment in her eyes, and he had a startling vision of her looking at him like that over the breakfast table, toasting him over a cup of hot chocolate. There was a ring on her finger—*his ring*—and a warm flush colored her cheeks a delightful rose. The result of his kiss. He gulped, his throat suddenly dry. What if this was just a dream, one that would never come true if he was convicted of murder?

* * * *

Belle set her cup of cider on the table, observing the sudden flash of sadness in Lord Terrance's eyes. He hid it quickly as he turned to speak to young Steven, but Belle had seen that change in expression. Up until a moment ago, he had looked happy to be here. What had begun as a test of wills between them, and then an awkward encounter with Mrs. Parker, had transformed into a gathering of happy friends for an evening's entertainment. What had changed?

With a frown, she glanced around the table at their other companions, trying to gauge what might have upset him. Somewhere along the way, Steven had lost his fear of his lordship. He now spoke to Lord Terrance, man-to-man, about a cricket match he and the village boys played last summer, as if the two were bucks in a London club chatting about a fisticuffs event at Gentleman Jackson's.

Even Mrs. Parker appeared relaxed, and her plate, which had remained untouched through most of dinner, now sat half empty.

Belle pushed aside her worry about his lordship's shifting moods and allowed the children to entertain his lordship in the front parlor while she and Mendal helped Mrs. Parker clear the table and wash the dishes. It was a most companionable time. When they rejoined the company, little Margaret was asleep in Lord Terrance's arms, Earnest snored by his lordship's feet, while the other children listened avidly to one of his stories.

A pang squeezed her heart. If they did not leave soon, she might do something foolish, like fall in love. There must not be any more such cozy evenings. Even with Mendal present, this evening felt as dangerous as his kisses.

"It is late, my lord," she said. "Time to allow the children to find their beds. And Mrs. Parker still recovers from an illness. She, too, must rest."

He agreed and stood, still holding Margaret. He carried the child, who never stirred, to her cot where her mother settled her for the night. They then trucked outdoors and wished each other good-night with genuine regret.

Lord Terrance said he would fetch his mount and the carthorse. Mrs. Parker stood with a lantern to light the night as the boys packed the empty baskets back into Belle's cart and hugged Earnest goodbye. The children tore a promise from her to bring the hound to the farm soon to play.

On his return, Lord Terrance strapped on the carthorse and then mounted his gelding.

He rode ahead, guiding the way along the dark, snow-laden pathway to ensure Belle and Mendal took the safest course.

Belle could barely keep her gaze from his lordship's proud back instead of the road. After the second time the horse stopped and looked back in confusion because Belle had directed it off the roadway, Mendal took the reins.

"I believe we should leave for home soon," Belle said, unable to stand the quiet.

"That may not be the wisest course," her maid replied.

"Why ever not?"

"I watched you tonight, my lady. You are afraid of how Lord Terrance makes you feel. So I wonder if going home is the right action to take."

Belle wanted to snap that she was not afraid, but then realized that Mendal was right. She was terrified of how Lord Terrance affected her with a simple touch, even accidentally.

"You should be pleased by my decision to cut short our visit, Mendal, instead of calling me a coward."

"I did no such thing, my lady. It is wise to be afraid of being alone with his lordship. That must not happen again."

"Then you agree we should leave Clearview."

"Not at all. I believe we should stay, at least until after Christmas."

"But you said . . ."

"That you should not be alone with Lord Terrance. I am happy to act as your chaperone."

"Why stay if he is dangerous?"

"Because you love him."

Belle sat still. Her hands, buried in her muff, trembled from cold as much as from Mendal's declaration. Was it true? Had she already made the fatal mistake of falling in love with Lord Terrance? "Are my feelings so obvious?"

"Only to me, my lady." Mendal patted Belle's knee. "It may not be as clear to his lordship. We must stay until it is."

Belle gave a frustrated sigh. "Mendal, there is no future for us. He thinks my ability to see ghosts are a figment of my imagination. Yes, he desires me, but my beliefs, my special senses—I do not, could never, fit into the restrictive little box he has fashioned for his future wife."

Her voice broke on the last sentence, and she glanced at the scenery. *And all the hoping and wishing and coin tossing cannot make it otherwise.*

It was Mendal's turn to sigh this time. "I admit this is a difficult situation, my lady. But it will work itself out if we but stay a little longer. There, we are almost home."

An iron gateway loomed in the distance, while Clearview's dark turrets demarked the starlit horizon. Belle recalled how frightened she had been the first time she approached that imposing structure. Now, Clearview was her home. More so than her grandfather's townhouse in London. How had this come about? More importantly, how was she to deal with it?

Each turn and every house they passed imprinted on her, forming an unbreakable bond. The longer she stayed, the more brokenhearted she would be to leave, for she had done the unthinkable. She had fallen in love with Terrance Village, its people, its countryside, and most appalling of all, with its lord of the manor.

* * * *

A persistent scratching on her bedroom door woke Belle. Still half asleep, she slid out of bed, slipped on her dressing gown, and lit a candle from the dying embers in the fire. Earnest sat by the closed door, and for a moment she wondered if the dog had woken her. Did he need to go out? The scratching came again. Not Earnest. She had a visitor.

"Coming," she called, and used her bare foot to push the sleep-warmed dog aside until she could open the door.

"Belle," Susie said. "I thought you would never wake."

"Susie, what is the matter?"

"Matter?" she said. "Why, we have been waiting for an age. They sent me to find you in case you had forgotten our game." She gave Belle a stern glance. "You had!"

"Oh, dear. I am so sorry."

"You do plan to join us? Mother and Phillip are already in the games room. It would not be the same without you."

Belle invited Susie inside and shut the door to keep out the cool drafts. Her tired mind grappled with the unappealing concept of waking up. Exhausted after her evening out, Belle had fallen asleep without a thought to Susie or the countess.

She glanced at her bed with longing. Her body craved nothing more than to crawl back under those warm covers. She vaguely recalled dreaming about having a meal alone with Lord Terrance as he served her a lemon tart and sealed each serving with a warm kiss.

"Belle, are you still awake?"

She must have drifted into a daydream while leaning against the door. "Sorry. Yes, the billiards game."

Bits of information made its way into her consciousness. On the ride back from Mrs. Parker's home, despite what Mendal advised, Belle had decided to return home as soon as possible. Before she could do that, she must discharge the ghost at Clearview. Mr. Jones might know what had troubled his uncle prior to his death. And that reminded her, she had wanted to speak to him about her vision of the murdered man in the barn.

Preparations for the Parker visit had forced her to put aside such concerns. She could not afford to waste any more time. If she dawdled too long, it would give her heart too much time to irrevocably love a man who could not love her back.

Aside from offering her an opportunity to speak to Mr. Jones, there might not be many more occasions to play billiards. She wanted to enjoy every spare moment with the countess, Susie, and Phillip Jones.

With that in mind, she allowed Susie to help her put on a simple gown. She wrapped a warm shawl overtop and laced her slippers. By the time she finished dressing, her mood had improved considerably. With Earnest by their side, she and Susie ran along the corridor and curved stairs, swallowing their laughter.

"There you are," Lady Terrance said as they entered.

The kitchen had already been raided. The side table lay heavy with platters filled with roast meat and cheese tarts.

"Good evening, your ladyship." Belle curtsied.

"Did you have a pleasant time with the Parkers?"

"A most delightful evening. They are very good folk."

"Rufus was out for dinner as well," Lady Terrance said.

Susie took her turn. She struck her cue ball. With uncanny accuracy, she potted the other two balls. She softly crowed her delight and held out a hand to collect her winnings.

While the countess took her turn, Phillip Jones came to stand beside Belle. "Dashed mean spirited of Rufus not to take me with him," he said. "Not a sociable cousin, these days. Do you know where he took himself off to?"

Thankfully, before Belle could answer, the countess spoke. "He has kept to himself much of late. I worry he has not dealt adequately with his father's passing. Does he speak to you about the matter, Phillip?"

"No, Aunt. Rufus rarely confides in anyone about matters close to his heart. A lonely existence, being the earl. Glad the burden is not mine."

The game continued, and coins exchanged hands. As the night wore on, Susie showed her color as a true gamester. Each time she won, she mimicked clapping and would count her winnings, then pile the growing stack of bronze coins on the mantle.

Belle laughed at her antics. Susie seemed happier. It was due to the increased time she spent in company. Living solely among plants, although most peaceful, had dampened her lively spirit.

Then it was Belle's turn, and as she took her place, she said, "Mrs. Parker mentioned the amusements that existed in Terrance Village once."

"We did have some good times," the countess said with a reminiscent smile.

"Oh, the parties we held at Clearview," Susie said. "Of course, I was too young to join in. I strayed no further down than the first five steps. I remember peeking through the railings to see the ladies in pretty gowns, the handsome men."

"When you come to London," Mr. Jones said, "you shall no longer have to watch from upstairs. You will wear the prettiest dress and dance with the handsomest men."

The countess took up the billiard cue. Since Susie was busy counting her coins, Belle had another moment alone with Mr. Jones.

"Sir," she said in a soft voice, "while you were in the village the other day, did you hear of a murder?"

He gave her a side-glance. Although his manner was no different from his normal ennui, Belle sensed keen interest behind his bland features. He knew something of the crime.

"A most tiring affair," he said. "How did you hear of the matter, Lady Belle?"

She shrugged. "Gossip is everywhere. Did Lord Terrance know the victim, speak with him that day?"

Though he had not moved a muscle, his tension built. Her questions upset him. How intriguing.

"He was with the man earlier that morning."

"Ahh," Belle said, pleased. *This is why I connected Lord Terrance to the murdered man, not because he had harmed him.*

"Would you enlighten me about a matter in return?" He matched her soft voice.

"I will gladly try."

"What attracts you to the upper reaches of Clearview?"

Belle took a moment to breathe before she responded. "How is it you know I go there, sir?"

"That does not answer the question."

She remained silent, wondering how best to respond. "Your cousin has forbidden me to speak of the matter to his family."

"He has confided in you?" he asked, interest caught.

"On the contrary. You were there when he made the stricture. The day I arrived, he said I was not to speak to anyone about ghosts and such like while I remain under his roof."

"Ahh, you speak of that." His gaze returned to the game.

"If not that, what did you think he might have confided in me about?"

He shrugged. "My cousin seems distracted of late. I had noticed that he is unhappy that the villagers are frightened of him. Has he mentioned the matter to you?"

Belle cringed. So, Lord Terrance had taken his nickname to heart.

"Something else troubles him, too," Phillip said before she could reply to his earlier question. "I wonder what it could be."

"Why do you not ask him?" Belle said.

"If he wished to confide in me, I am sure he would. I have discovered that when people do not like to be intruded upon, they resent it if you press the matter."

Deep despair emanated from him, sweeping past her in a blast of sorrow and evoking her vision. It flared, showing her an unfamiliar drawing room, where a woman with golden ringlets cried, a heartbreaking sound. As quickly as the image formed, it was squashed. Mr. Jones had himself back under control and turned his bland smile in her direction. "Also it is too much effort, do you not think? To care about other people's worries?"

"True," Belle said, but she was reeling from that last vision. The blond-haired woman had seemed so unhappy, as if she were trapped in a never-ending spell of utter despair. Belle's body was heavy with her grief, and her curiosity about Phillip Jones and his relationship to this woman spiked. Had he played a part in that woman's anguish? She suspected so, and, therefore, could not let the matter simply drop. "I am often concerned about those I love."

"What do you do in those circumstances?"

This was a heartfelt question, so she took her time to give a proper answer. "Offering to help, sir, is sometimes worth the risk of rejection and the pain that follows."

"If help is refused, or unwanted?"

"Then one must wait until it is."

He nodded. "For one so young, Lady Belle, you are wise."

"It is easier to give advice," she said with a jovial smile, "than to take it."

"And what advice have you not taken?"

"That might have to wait for another night. Speaking of troubles, however, I wondered what troubled the late Lord Terrance before he was killed in that accident in London?"

This time Mr. Jones did not respond. He closed and tucked his emotions inside him as tightly as a baby is bundled on a cold winter day.

"I am sorry if my question upset you, sir," she said. "I did not mean to offend."

He shook a careless hand. "No offense taken. But it does make me curious as to why you asked it."

She could not speak about the ghost or her suspicions about his murder. So, how to explain her interest? "Oft times, after a sudden death, matters are left unfinished."

"Yes, but why do you worry about such things?"

"You said that you were interested in what troubled your cousin. It could be his father's unfinished business."

"Yes, I see your point. You would make an excellent Bow Street Runner, Lady Belle. They, too, have an uncanny ability for uncovering hidden motivations."

"I shall take that as a compliment. But you have not answered my question."

"No, I have not."

Susie left her coins on the mantle and came to stand beside them. "What do you two whisper about? Mother said not to bother you, but I feel left out."

"Nothing of particular note," Mr. Jones said. "We merely passed the time while we waited for you to finish calculating your vast fortune. So, Suz, are you excited about the trip to London? Do you intend to fleece your friends in Town, as you have fleeced us tonight?"

She laughed at his teasing. "Actually, I am a little nervous about the entire sojourn," she said in a quiet voice. "What if I say the wrong thing or step on someone's toes? I am glad you will be with me, Belle. I would not have the courage to attend otherwise."

Susie's comments startled her. All this while Belle had been concerned about how to deal with Lord Terrance's proximity if she went. Not once had she considered how Susie might need her in London.

"It is merely a matter of practice," Mr. Jones said. "Once you have attended one or two events, it all becomes a bore." He yawned behind his hand.

"You say that because you have been to hundreds," Susie said in a resentful tone.

"Now, see here, young lady," he said in mock affront. "I am not that aged."

"Phillip is right." Lady Terrance rested the cue on the table and faced them. "What you need is confidence, Susie, and that comes from experience. And what better place to obtain such an experience than right here at Clearview? We should hold a ball here, a Christmas Ball."

"But Mother, we are still in mourning."

"Your father, bless his soul, passed away over six months ago," her mother said. "I must stay in half colors, but you are permitted to wear something cheerful and bright."

"A ball at Clearview?" Mr. Jones said. "Whom would we invite?"

"There are plenty of gentry nearby," Susie said. "Since father's death, we have received cards aplenty from well-wishers in the area."

"It is too bad we cannot involve the locals," Belle said. "When I visited Mrs. Parker tonight, she did not even intend to decorate her home. She said the villagers are low in spirit."

The moment the words left her lips, she regretted them, for the countess looked sad. Even Susie seemed despondent.

"I am sorry," Belle said. "I did not mean to upset anyone. I am sure the villagers celebrate in their own fashion."

"They mourn the passing of Mr. Darby." The countess walked away to stare out the balcony doors into the dark night.

That was the man whom Mrs. Parker said had died in London. About the same time as the late Lord Terrance. Belle did not believe in coincidences. Oft times, her talent worked in mysterious ways, connecting dots that at first glance did not line up.

"I had heard that Mr. Darby was your particular friend, Aunt," Mr. Jones said. "My condolences. I thought it most curious that both he and uncle died within a day of each other."

Belle approached the countess. "That must have been difficult, losing both your husband and a friend."

"I am all right now," the older woman said. "I have mourned both. It is time we all moved past these sad events." She turned back to the room, and her shoulders stiffened. "I have made a decision."

They all waited expectantly.

"It is time to look to the future," she announced. "The best way to do that is to celebrate the life we still possess. We will indeed hold our Christmas Ball, and, along with the local gentry, we shall invite the villagers."

Susie's mouth formed an 'O.'

Mr. Jones's smile spread across his face in a slow wave. "Aunt, you are a genius."

"Convincing your son to hold a ball may not be easy," Belle said. She knew instinctively that somehow Lord Terrance would find a way to blame her for this expanded ball. "He is adamant that you not be disturbed so soon after your husband's death."

"Oh, Mama, will Rufus put a spoke in it?"

"He seems to have softened of late." Her mother's gaze rested with unsettling intensity on Belle. "Put to him in the right manner, I do not see why he should object."

"Pray, what do you suggest is the right manner?" Belle was at a complete loss on how they could convince his lordship to go along with this mad plan.

Her ladyship squeezed Belle's shoulder. "I am sure you will think of something, dear."

Belle was not as confident. Every encounter with Lord Terrance seemed to end with the tables turned on her, so she was doubtful she could ensure a successful outcome for this latest gambit. Still, nothing ventured, nothing gained. At least this time, there was unlikely to be any kissing involved. Belle was not entirely pleased about that, for a tiny traitorous part of her wished he would turn the tables on her once more and steal another passionate kiss.

Chapter Eleven

Although she had a late billiards night, Belle woke early the next morning. While a housemaid cleaned the cage, with Lady Sefton perched on Belle's gloved arm, she fed the bird.

The owlet's bandages should be ready to come off within the next week, and then the owl would need a larger area to practice flight. With a gentle touch, Belle stroked the owl's good wing. She would miss Lady Sefton when the time came to set her free.

With mysterious round eyes, the owl gazed at her as if in complete agreement with that sentiment. However, all contact between tame and wild things could only be fleeting.

Once the cage looked and smelled fresh, Belle sent Earnest down to the kitchen with the housemaid for his breakfast and settled Lady Sefton onto a clean perch and shut the cage door.

She then washed her hands in the basin her maid held out, but Belle's thoughts were on the task Lady Terrance had given her. She would need reinforcement, so she requested the morning dress made in a military style. It had a rich green braid across the front that was a shade darker than the dress and sported an embroidered epaulet and wristband. Over it she wore a smart white jacket and was ready to do battle.

On her trip downstairs, something else nagged. Mr. Jones had not answered her questions about how he knew she had been in the upper reaches of Clearview or what had troubled the late Lord Terrance. Speaking with Mr. Jones was as fruitful as conversing with the ghost, though more entertaining.

She liked Phillip Jones and instinctively wanted to trust him. Still, much about the man remained a mystery.

Earnest bounded over to her after his meal, and she gave him his homemade ball— tightly rolled piece of cloth tied with bright fluttering ribbons. The hound held his toy between his strong jaws as proudly as if he carried a standard into war. Appropriate, since it was time for them to face Lord Terrance and put her plan to talk him into a Christmas ball into effect.

* * * *

In the breakfast parlor, Rufus glanced up as the door opened. Finally, someone else to keep him company besides his dour aunt. To his deep pleasure, Belle strode in with Earnest at her heels. The hound carried a fanciful ball and looked as pleased as his mistress, who looked enchanting in a dress that reminded him of the cavalry.

Rufus stood. She glanced at him, then at his aunt, and back to him. A cheerful smile flashed across her face, and he wished he had the right to greet the sight with a kiss. *One day soon,* he promised himself, *as soon as I have caught my father's murderer.*

"Good morning, my lord." She curtsied. "Mrs. Jones."

"Come, have a seat." He held out a chair beside his.

Before Belle could accede, his aunt said, "I believe she should sit by me, Terrance. It would be unseemly to have her so close to yourself." She snapped her fingers at a footman to indicate he should pull out a chair beside her.

The servant's gaze skittered between Mrs. Jones and his master while Lady Belle had paused as if to consider the two offers.

"Sit where you please." Rufus released the chair and returned to his seat. What did he care where she sat? Let her bow to convention. He had eaten alone for years. He could not imagine why he thought that state of affairs would change just because he was now in love.

From the corner of his eye, he caught the footman sending Lady Belle a pleading glance. *Fool.* He should know that a woman could never solve a man's problems.

She walked to the side table, and the footman and the dog followed. She pointed to delicacies, and the servant dutifully filled her plate. Once finished, she made a direct line to the table's center and sat in the chair the footman drew out.

Rufus had to admire her Solomon's choice. The lady had a mind of her own. He liked that. If she had chosen to sit beside him, he might not have held her in as high esteem.

"Lovely morning," she said to both him and his aunt.

His aunt greeted Belle's comment with a muffled, *"Hmph."* Obviously, Henrietta Jones did not care for independence. Her loss.

"I had a restless night, last night," Mrs. Jones said. "I heard all manner of odd noises coming from upstairs. On waking, I spoke to a maid but she said none of them go up there anymore because they are afraid."

Rufus frowned. Could Ellison have spread rumors of ghosts after he had expressively forbidden him to talk of such things? He glanced warily at Belle, but she kept her gaze trained on her plate. His shoulders dropped their tense stand, for it showed she kept to her word about not speaking about such matters.

"Have you ever heard such twiddle twaddle?" his aunt said, with a raised neck and eyebrow. "The servants are probably too lazy to go up there to clean and have made up stories of strange goings-on. No wonder Constance is upset. She is not made of my steady constitution. The maid even said she had heard furniture moving about up there despite no one being assigned to work on the third floor. You should have a word with them, Terrance."

"I will, Aunt," he said, with grim determination.

"I had a lovely evening with the Parkers yesterday," Belle said, in a jovial voice. "They are a local family."

"Are they of our society?" Mrs. Jones asked.

"They are Lord Terrance's tenants. Mrs. Parker has four adorable children. I brought them food from Clearview as a Christmas gift from the countess. They were very grateful."

"Ah," Mrs. Jones said. "A charitable act. Most acceptable. Though staying to share the meal seems excessive." She gave Belle a considering glance. "Without parents to guide you, no doubt you lack the delicate sensibilities of how ladies should behave in society. I suggest that while here, you take the opportunity to learn proper conduct for one of your station. I would be happy to be of assistance."

Rufus choked on a mouthful of egg. His two companions sent him concerned glances, and he waved away their concern. Once he stopped coughing, he said, "Excuse me."

"You are excused," Mrs. Jones said.

"Thank you for your offer, Mrs. Jones," Belle said. "That is most generous of you."

"It may amuse me during my stay," the widow said.

"Speaking of amusements," Belle said, "Mrs. Parker spoke about one of the festivities the villagers used to have at Christmastime. It is a shame the practice died off."

"What the villagers choose to do is of no matter to us," Mrs. Jones said.

"This time of the year should be spent in celebration," Belle said.

"You have something particular in mind?" Rufus asked.

"A Christmas Ball might be appropriate."

Both he and his aunt greeted her comment in silence. Then, unable to contain himself, he laughed. "No one would want to come to this old mausoleum at the best of times, Lady Belle, let alone in the middle of winter."

To his astonishment, his aunt joined in with a harsh laugh and said, "Child, you do have the strangest starts. A ball? At Clearview? How preposterous. Terrance is correct. This is far into the North Country. No one of importance lives nearby, and those farther away will not travel so far in bad weather."

"The storm has ended," Belle said. "The snow begins to melt. In a week or two, the roads might be clear enough for people to come from farther away."

"You forget," Rufus said, "my mother is still in mourning."

"It is more than six months since your father passed away, my lord," Belle said in a gentle tone. "And with winter upon us, a ball might put some merriment back in her life. This is also a good way to introduce Susie to the type of entertainment she can expect in London."

"Out of the question," Mrs. Jones said. "I came to the country to rest, and a ball takes a great deal of planning. Besides, you cannot expect anyone of any real social connection to arrive here on such short notice. And I refuse to act as hostess to a room full of country bumpkins."

"Aunt Henrietta is correct." The words ground in Rufus's gullet. "Not for the reasons mentioned, however, but simply because Clearview is hardly the place to hold a ball. This house is more likely to dampen spirits than lift them."

To his relief, the discussion veered into local happenings. He listened absently, his mind playing with the idea of dancing with Belle. Though a ball might be fun, preparations for one would be a distraction. He had yet to resolve the mystery of his father's death. He needed to make another trip to the Briar Inn to make more inquiries about Mr. Brindle's death.

His aunt's comment about a stranger in the village drew his attention. "That would be the magistrate, Aunt, who has come to make a report."

"Report on what?" Mrs. Jones asked.

"A man was murdered two days ago. One of our old tenants."

"That is not an appropriate discussion for the breakfast table," his aunt said, her expression appalled.

Rufus apologized for mentioning the matter.

Belle had gone still. He hoped he had not alarmed her. Why had he mentioned it after keeping silent all this while? Then he remembered that Belle already knew about the occurrence. After she fainted in Susie's room and before their kiss, she had questioned him about Brindle.

Time had shown him that she had too much discretion to upset his family with the news. He should have trusted her. Still, their argument had led to their interlude in the upper gallery. He did not regret that happening. Her current silence on the topic seemed out of character.

"Have I upset you by the news?" he asked her.

"She is acting in a proper fashion for a change," his aunt said. "Young ladies cannot show unseemly interest in men's business. Kindly change the subject."

"Earnest and I are going for a walk after we eat," Belle said.

"Who, prey tell, is Earnest?" Mrs. Jones asked. "And why do you refer to him by his Christian name? Mr. So-and-So would be the appropriate manner in which to address a young man. As well, I do not believe it is wise for a young lady to walk alone in the countryside with a stranger. While you are under our protection, you must be guided by our judgment in these matters."

"She refers to the dog," Rufus said, his humor returned. "I am sure it is allowable for the lady to address the hound by his first name."

"Hmph!" His aunt gave the dog a hard stare.

Rufus doubted his aunt approved of Earnest any more now that she knew he was a dog. "As for the walk, I would be happy to accompany you. To give you the protection you require."

"Unnecessary," Mrs. Jones said. "I merely meant she should take her maid, as would be proper. Besides, I hoped we could have a word after the meal, Terrance. There is some business I wish to discuss."

"It can wait, Aunt," he said. "As Lady Belle has said, we should not waste such a good morning indoors."

He could go to the Briar Inn after they returned. This time he wanted better results from his foray into Terrance Village, and suddenly he thought of a way to ensure a better outcome. Why not use Phillip's annoying talent for ferreting out secrets on Rufus's behalf, instead of against him? Phillip should be awake by the time he and Belle returned. Surprisingly eager at the idea of having assistance in his quest, Rufus stood with a wide smile and held out his hand to assist Belle to rise.

* * * *

Though going for a walk with Lord Terrance offered Belle the perfect opportunity to reintroduce the subject of the troublesome ball, she had learned her lesson about going anywhere alone with Lord Terrance. She no longer had any illusions about her ability to withstand his brand of persuasion. So, she sent word to Mendal that he planned to accompany her on her walk. Never one to like the outdoors, especially in winter, Mendal was nevertheless down in a trice, booted and cloaked.

Lord Terrance looked put out to discover Mendal's inclusion. Henrietta Jones, however, who happened to be out in the hall as they made their departure, nodded her approval.

The sun shone bright against a cloudless blue sky, which gave the morning air a coldness that refreshed rather than chilled her spirits. They followed a narrow path bordered by woods on one side and Clearview's wide open grounds on the other. Snow lingered by the shade of the tall trees, and Belle was grateful for her sturdy calf boots that crunched through the snow and left footprints to attest to her passing.

Their path took them into an enclosed laburnum. The ground inside was fairly dry and easy to negotiate. The snow had not made its way past the tree branches grown together overtop the circular roof. A glance behind showed that Mendal walked with ease, no longer stumbling through the snow.

All too soon they exited the enclosure, and Belle gave a hardy toss of the ball that sent Earnest sailing after his prey into far distant groves. He disappeared within a snowy copse.

"The dog is happier since you arrived," Lord Terrance said.

"The house frightens him," she said and glanced back. A curtain fluttered on the third floor window. They were watched—and not by an earthly figure.

Every time she noticed his father, the son was beside her or soon appeared. Did the ghost worry about his son? Was he in danger now, as his father had been?

She moved closer to his lordship and checked every shrub and bush for a crossbow aimed in their direction. Then she sighed and relaxed her bunched shoulders. She empathized too much with the ghost's worries. Even were Lord Terrance in danger, surely no one would dare harm him on his home grounds.

"The dog is wise," Lord Terrance said suddenly, as if he had brooded about the matter. "If I had a choice, I would not stay in that house, either."

"You dislike your home?" she asked in surprise.

"I detest it. I do not understand what mother and Susie find comforting here."

"I believe they find it peaceful," Belle said. "Lately, I, too, have formed a fondness for the place."

He gave a surprised look. "What appeals?"

Belle considered the double-edged question. Was Mendal correct in that Lord Terrance was unaware of how much she had grown to care for him? She could not openly confess her love, but could she allude to it?

"Clearview can seem imposing at first glance, my lord, with its turrets and gargoyles and its haunting presence. But delve past those superficial layers, and one quickly discovers fascinating corridors filled with rich character, solid masonry that would protect one against assault, and a joyous spirit that enlivens all who enter."

"Are you referring to *my* home?" He gave a doubtful laugh.

Instead of answering, she asked, "Why do you dislike the place?"

He did not reply immediately. Finally, he said, "I was ever under my father's scrutiny here. I failed miserably at every aspect of being a good, dependable son."

"I take it you were not close to your father," she said.

"Hah! He could not stand the sight of me. I disappointed him at every turn."

Belle's heart ached at his sadness. His father had crushed his boyhood confidence. Instinctively, she took his arm and squeezed in sympathy. She would have withdrawn, but he tucked her fingers into the crook of his elbow so they walked arm in arm.

With every step, the back of her forearm brushed his side. Heat rushed to Belle's cheeks, but pulling away seemed churlish. Suddenly, she sensed the manor house loom behind them, as if Lord Terrance's father brooded over an upstart, unsuitable female taking liberties with his son.

We walk in public, she silently told the ghost with a proud tilt of her head. *I am not running off with him to Scotland for a clandestine marriage.*

Considering the manor ghost's fierce protectiveness of his son, Belle could not accept his lordship's estimation of his father's affection for him. "I am certain your father loved you."

"He wished I could be more like Phillip."

Though he said the words as if it were a statement about the weather, the hurt behind his words buffeted her. "Sometimes, parents favor one child."

"You are kind to worry about me." He smiled with such tenderness, her heart swelled. "You may have a point. My mother holds my sister closer than she does me." He shook his head when she would have protested. "As for my father, neither Susie nor I could ever please him."

"It is difficult to interpret a parent's motives. And now, with him gone, we can only deduce his intent by his past actions, but please, do not assume you know what is in your mother's heart until you actually ask her."

He waved in a dismissive gesture. "Why do we discuss such maudlin matters? It is a beautiful day. Choose a more cheerful topic."

He does not believe me. She made a mental note to speak to his mother about her and her son's relationship and switched topics. "You were surprisingly well-behaved with Mrs. Parker and her children."

"They were frightened of me."

"At the start. By evening's end, Margaret was completely malleable."

He smiled. "She is a sweet child."

Belle gulped around a sudden knot in her throat. She had to change the subject again, or she would kiss him, Mendal and the ghost be damned. "Before you arrived, Mrs. Parker spoke of Christmas celebrations that were held here for the villagers."

"That was a long time ago."

"What about the ball?"

"What ball?"

"The Christmas ball."

"I thought we settled that matter. My mother would never countenance such an event at this time."

"It was your mother's idea. She wants Susie to practice mingling prior to her London debut."

He dropped her hand, his shoulders stiff, and his expression going hard. "There will be no ball at Clearview. I am sorry, but this is an inconvenient time for such an event. I beg you to drop the matter."

Belle took a deep breath and curbed her temper, which would have preferred to call him on his obstinate attitude. Instead, she mentally yelled at him, *Why must you be so stubborn?*

"It would cheer the household," she said in a last ditch appeal to his compassion. "And, according to Mrs. Parker, the villagers desperately need a celebration."

"Villagers? What do they have to do with a ball at Clearview? They can hardly expect to be invited." This time he stepped away, anger flaring in his gaze. "Ah, now I see that this is indeed my mother's plan. You may advise her ladyship that there will not be such a rum go at Clearview, now or ever. Although my father may not be present to curb her unconventional behavior, her son intends to act on his behalf."

"That is unfair." She let out a huff of impatience, her intention to remain calm vanishing into the winter air. "What is so wrong with a separate section cordoned off for the villagers' party? Mrs. Parker said this last year has been hard on folks. A celebration will help them forget their troubles and show them that you, as their lord, will stand by them during the lean times. It is important they believe that. Besides, these types of balls have been held for centuries, where the lord of the manor celebrates the year with his people."

"It will not be so at Clearview," he said with finality. A devilish light replaced the ferocity in his eyes. "Lady Belle, are you starting a row with me? Why," he added in a seductive voice, "I do believe you angle for another kiss."

She took a step back in consternation, for that was exactly what she had hoped would happen last night. "I do not!" *Anymore.*

Mendal had stopped when they had, and she looked off into the bush, but the position of her head suggested she listened.

Belle walked on. How could he always twist her words and actions to suit his wishes? *Angle for a kiss, indeed!* Even if she did dream of his lips taking possession of hers, she kept such thoughts buried deep inside her heart, and she wished he would stop rousting them out for inspection.

"Another change of subject is in order," she said.

"As you wish." Laughter layered each word.

Villain! She racked her brain for a neutral subject and hit on one. "Tell me about the murder in the village."

"I thought we were to avoid maudlin topics."

He could be so stubborn. Worse than his father. But she knew when to give up gracefully. "Since you are dismayed with every one I pick, what do you wish to talk about?"

"Let us see. How about our trip to London?"

She wanted to groan. Was this stroll doomed to be unpleasant?

Earnest ran up, covered in twigs and dirt, carrying his muddy ball from which all the ribbons were torn off.

"And where have you been all this while?" she asked the hound in a stern voice.

He shook his head and firmly planted his two front feet on the ground, determined she would throw his ball.

With a laugh she obliged, and he ran wild across the meadow.

"He loves you," Lord Terrance said in a soft voice. "Is that your magical power? Do you have that effect on all who cross your path?"

"Would that it could be so," she said. "Most who get to know me end up avoiding me."

"How can you say so?" He seemed astounded by her assertion. "I find exactly the opposite happens."

Belle's cheeks warmed. She dared not take him literally. He was undoubtedly being effusive with his compliment.

"I do not fish for kind words, my lord." She looked away. "I merely explain what I have experienced."

"By experience, do you refer to your betrothed? He is a fool for letting you out of your binding. If you were mine . . ."

"I am not."

"No," he said, "you are not." He picked up a stick, and despite the fact his dog was nowhere nearby to fetch it, and with a vicious swing, he threw it high and far.

"I am sure you would be glad for that to never come to pass," Belle said, despondent. "As do most gentlemen in Town since word spread of my behavior with Lord Fitzgerald."

"He should have offered."

"He did."

Lord Terrance stopped abruptly. "Then you are engaged still?" He swung her to face him. "Why pretend you have put marriage out of your mind?"

"I am not affianced to anyone, not to Jeffrey, and not to Lord Fitzgerald. I turned down his suit."

He looked at her with patent disbelief. "Why? Despite his rakish reputation, Fitzgerald is an honorable fellow, a viscount besides, and he came into the world well hosed and shod. What was your objection?"

She shrugged. "That entire debacle in London proved that I am not suited for marriage."

He let out an angry snort and gave her a shake. "You cannot seriously mean to spend the rest of your days alone?"

She broke his hold and briskly tramped on. "I have my grandfather," she said over her shoulder. "He is all the company I need."

Ahead, a turn took them through the woods. Belle chose that path and ducked to avoid snow-laden branches.

He kept pace, though Mendal scrambled to adjust to their lengthened strides. The maid squealed when a load of snow dropped on her head.

Belle glanced over her shoulder and gave Mendal an apologetic look. Then frowned at Lord Terrance whose lips twitched. The path soon broadened, and they followed the edge of a half-frozen pond. She slowed to a leisurely walk to give Mendal time to catch up.

Lord Terrance was quiet, seemingly lost in thought. And they were not happy ones, if his scowl was any indication.

The path led to a main road, and they all paused to consider their next choice. Return home or head closer to the village? A look at Mendal told Belle which direction her maid would prefer. Earnest appeared beside her and dropped his ball. Breathing heavily, his red tongue lolled after his morning's exertions. Lord Terrance remained lost in thought, so home might be the best choice.

A horse's clip-clop on the muddy earthen road drew her eyes toward the village. Belle stepped off the road to let the traveler pass.

* * * *

Rufus recognized the newcomer, and his mood spiraled down. Martin Winfield. Must he run into the fellow every time he stepped outdoors?

"How do you do," Winfield said. In a dark double-breasted cutaway coat, buff-colored breeches and riding boots, he was presentable. He tipped his hat to Belle. "A fine morning to be out."

"How do you do," Belle said.

Rufus nodded.

Earnest growled, and Winfield's mount shied and stepped back.

The hound had squeezed himself between Rufus and Belle, his teeth bared and ears back.

Wise dog. Rufus would have liked to mimic that response. He did not care for his neighbor, not since Rufus, at twelve years of age, saw Winfield beating a hound to death.

Rufus's father had found his son burying the pup and assumed he had done the killing. He had taken him to the barn for a painful beating because even though Rufus staunchly denied having done the terrible deed, he refused to say who had.

He had protected Winfield that day, but henceforth refused all Winfield's overtures to befriend him.

"Earnest, be silent." Belle soothed the dog with a pat. "He does not take well to strangers. Pray, do not be alarmed."

"Your dog needs discipline, Lady Belle," Winfield said and dismounted. He led his shying mount father away and tied him to a tree, then strode back, whip held tightly in one hand.

To Rufus's surprise, Belle shifted in front of Earnest. He could have told her not to bother. If Winfield struck the dog, the man would end up far worse for his troubles. Winfield would never dare to cross Rufus so publicly.

"The dog is mine," Rufus said. "As for discipline, his performance is all I could hope for. Rousting trespassers is part of his duties."

"And a well brought up hound, he is," Winfield said with a practiced smile. "I am sure he will give you many years of good service. Are you on your way to the village?"

"We were about to return home," Rufus said. "Do not let us keep you if you are on your way there."

"Not at all, not at all," Winfield said. "There is not much happening hereabouts. Entertainment is hard to come by."

"You will be returning to London soon, then?" he asked.

"I had not planned to leave yet."

"I understand your comment about activities in the village," Belle said. "I hear it did not used to be so lacking. I had hoped we could hold a ball at Clearview to celebrate Christmas for the local society and invite the villagers to join us in food, drink, and games."

Rufus sighed at the stubborn woman for dredging up that beleaguered subject once again.

Before he could denounce it, Winfield, with a thoughtful look, asked, "A ball? What a capital notion. However, it would never do to hold such an event at Clearview. Lady Terrance is still in mourning, and it would not be appropriate."

Listening to the exchange, Rufus ground his teeth in frustration. The man said exactly what Rufus had argued all morning. First his aunt agreed with him. Now Winfield. If that was not ample evidence he was in the wrong, he could not imagine what else was needed.

Rufus glanced down the road. How to cut short this conversation?

"Now that I think on it," Winfield said, "why not hold the ball at Windhaven? We have ample room for tents outside for the locals, and the ballroom is large enough to house the local gentry. My mother would be honored to have you and Lady Terrance, and dare we hope, the reclusive Lady Susie, to celebrate the Christmas season with us."

"Tents in the winter would be too cold for the villagers," Belle said. "Especially in the evening."

Rufus stared at her in astonishment. She did not seriously consider his offer?

"They are hardy folks," Winfield said. "I am sure they will manage. They will be honored beyond comprehension simply to be invited."

Belle stiffened.

Good. Finally, she saw sense and would put this encroaching mushroom in his place and soundly reject his offer.

"That is a splendid idea," Belle said instead.

Rufus started. She agreed? *With Winfield?* He had assumed she had good instincts about people. Winfield was watching Belle with a calculating gleam, and Rufus's shoulder muscles bunched, as if he were about to enter a boxing ring.

Chapter Twelve

Rufus did not at all care for the idea of Belle and Winfield being on such agreeable terms. She had no idea that Rufus's neighbor possessed a cold, calculating heart. Worse, despite his sad lack of character, Winfield was reputed to have a winning way with the ladies.

"Yes, a ball at Windhaven might do," Belle said in a thoughtful voice. "I must insist, however, that we find a spot indoors for the villagers, else I could not enjoy the evening. I would worry about them."

"I suppose . . ." Winfield began.

"That will not be necessary," Rufus interrupted. "The ball will be held at Clearview, and the villagers can be more than adequately provided for in the green ballroom."

Both Belle and Winfield turned to him in surprise.

Winfield found his voice first. "Do you forget the mourning period?"

"I hold the ball, not my mother. And I assure you I have not forgotten in the least how long ago my father died. However, as Belle pointed out, it is time we continue an old family tradition of holding Christmas celebrations at the manor."

Winfield shook his head. "It would be too much work for your mother. A ball at Windhaven is the better plan."

"I think not," Rufus said, "and my mother will have my aunt and Lady Belle to help her. Besides, a ball such as this would be a costly enterprise."

Winfield stiffened. The silence stretched with neither man breaking eye contact. The air sizzled.

Finally, Winfield said, "Do not concern yourself on my behalf, Terrance. Investments fall and rise as often as gossip flits about Town. My finances are ample for the need."

"Still, it is my duty to hold this event at Clearview." Having won his point, Rufus relented and broke the staring match to glance at Belle. She looked as if she held her breath. "We had better return home and advise my mother of our plans. With Christmas only three weeks away, we have much to do to set things in motion. Good day, Winfield."

He bowed and took Belle's arm, barely giving her time to curtsey and grab a breath to say goodbye.

"Earnest, come," he said. A snap of his fingers brought the pup to heel.

He escorted Belle along the lane. They took the shorter route back toward the manor that crossed over a small vaulted bridge. Her maid hurried to catch up, stumbling in the snowy roadway, and he slowed their pace slightly so she could, though he would have preferred to get farther ahead of her so he could indulge in a kiss with Belle.

He glanced down at Belle, and the harsh truth of his affection for her swept over him. *He* wanted to wed her, not the other way around. Yet, unless he cleared his name, there was no chance she could consider his suit. His efforts to find his father's killer took on more importance. His future with Belle depended on discovering what took place last spring in Richmond Park.

Yet, how was he to uncover the truth while in the midst of planning a ball?

* * * *

Belle remained quiet on the walk back to Clearview. Her silence was partly due to astonishment that Lord Terrance had agreed to the ball, and partly due to fear that anything she said might make him change his mind.

Her thoughts were in a frenzy to make sense of what had happened. Lord Terrance had actually agreed to hold a Christmas Ball at Clearview. She was glad, for she had not wanted to accept Winfield's insensitive offer. Imagine, suggesting the villagers would enjoy the festivities in the cold. *Hardy folk, indeed!*

She had never liked the man, not even when they had met in London, and she liked him even less now. She had only agreed to have the ball at his home because she hoped that if she did, it might make Lord Terrance see that not everyone viewed a ball as such an outlandish idea. Could that ploy have really worked?

She gave him a side-glance, trying to read his thoughts. He maintained a stony cast, and she could not discern if he was angry or not. Each step that took her closer to Clearview, however, brought excitement. They were going to have a ball! She could hardly wait to tell Lady Terrance and Susie.

When they arrived home, Felton advised them that Lady Susie, Mr. Jones, and his mother kept the countess company in the drawing room, and that her ladyship had requested her son and Lady Belle join her on their return.

The instant Belle and Lord Terrance entered, Susie rushed over from the settee to take Belle's hands. Her eyes were moist and her cheeks flushed. "Oh, I am so glad you are back."

"Whatever is the matter?"

"Nothing of importance," Mrs. Jones said. "Susie is being excessively emotional."

"She is disappointed, that is all." Lady Terrance looked none too happy herself. Two high spots of color on her cheeks suggested she, too, had a surfeit of emotions boiling under the surface.

"Please, Susie, tell me what troubles you," Belle said in a soothing tone. "As I am up in the boughs, I might be able to pull you out of your doldrums."

"Aunt says we cannot hold our ball and that Rufus supports her in this." Susie displayed a pout to her brother. "It is not as if I like the things. I just had my heart set on having one with people I know before being plunged into the midst of the *Ton*."

"Is that all?" Belle asked. "Then I can bring back your cheer. Lord Terrance has changed his mind and agrees to hold the Christmas Ball at Clearview."

Susie's mouth opened and closed as her gaze swept from Belle to her brother and back.

Belle looked directly at Lady Terrance before she imparted the next thrilling bit. "This celebration is not only for the local gentry, but the villagers, too, will be invited."

Lady Terrance sat very still on the settee, a play of emotions sweeping across her face. Slowly, moisture filled her eyes, and then a lone tear spilled.

"Have you gone mad?" Mrs. Jones broke the pregnant silence. Her gaze speared Belle. "What did you do to my nephew? He may act the simpleton, but his mind could not be swayed so easily."

"Why, thank you, Aunt," Lord Terrance said and bowed. "As for my decision, the fresh air clarified the matter."

Susie squealed and ran into his arms. "I do so love you, Rufus. Thank you, thank you, thank you."

He laughed as she rained kisses on his face. Then, hugging her close, he addressed his aunt. "Aunt Henrietta, it is good to hold high standards, but the villagers need our support. This last year has been hard on folks. A celebration will help them forget their troubles and show that we, as leaders in this society, will stand by them during the lean times."

Rufus glanced at Belle as he said that last, and her heart melted, for he had clearly heard her earlier entreaty.

"It does not matter how he came to the decision." Lady Terrance stood and approached her son. "It only matters that you did." She gently kissed his cheek. "Thank you."

He looked taken aback by his mother's affectionate gesture. "I am glad the news pleases you, Mama. I thought nothing I did would ever please you again."

She slanted her head, as if in thought. "How interesting, my dearest. For I had begun to think you never wished to waste your time pleasing *me* again."

"Well done, Rufus." Phillip Jones slapped him on his back. "This visit is proving to be most enjoyable."

"I can see that my opinion holds no sway here," Henrietta Jones said in such a soft voice that Belle suspected few heard. She had only noticed because the pain from the woman was so palpable, it swept over Belle in a wave.

The lady stood and moved to the window, her back ramrod stiff. She took a handkerchief from her sleeve and surreptitiously dabbed at her eyes.

No one else had caught that telltale gesture. Belle's heart wept for Henrietta Jones's pain, but she did not approach her. The proud woman would not take kindly to any overtures right now. Perhaps later.

"We have plans to make," Lady Terrance said. "Invitations to send out, meals, decorations, and themes to chose."

"We will need new dresses," Mrs. Jones said.

At Lady Terrance and Susie's surprised silence, she exhaled a loud sigh and returned to her seat. "You cannot expect to attend a ball dressed like a villager, even if they are the guests of honor. If we are to hold a Christmas Ball, it must be done right. This cannot be a slap-dash affair, Terrance. It will cost you a pretty penny before we are through."

"Anything you ladies require will be at your disposal." He gave an exaggerated bow.

When the discussion turned to the evening gowns' latest cut, he gestured to his cousin, and they spoke in soft tones. Then they wished the ladies good day and left the room, saying they had business in the village.

Watching them leave, Belle suddenly recalled what Mrs. Parker said about Mr. Nightingale's dismissal and how the villagers saw it as unfair. She then recalled Mr. Jones's comment that Lord Terrance worried that the villagers disliked him. Like pieces of a puzzle, the two concepts connected, and she excused herself to hurry out.

"Lord Terrance," she called before he stepped outdoors.

* * * *

Rufus turned to find Belle running toward him, out of breath and delectable. He stepped back into the foyer.

"I will see to the horses." Phillip gave a roguish smile and closed the front doors behind him.

Rufus handed his hat and coat to the butler and said, "I will speak to the young lady."

Felton nodded and removed himself to the stairs, standing close enough to come if called but out of earshot.

He was glad for the butler's discretion. Without that watchful presence nearby, he might be tempted to steal another kiss from Belle. In fact, he wanted to do a great deal more than kiss her. The blush spreading across her cheeks suggested that he was once again easy to read. This time, he was glad. "You wished to speak with me?"

She nodded. "Since we had our meal at Mrs. Parker's, I have meant to mention Mr. Nightingale."

"What about him?"

"Before your arrival, Mrs. Parker suggested that he was the most loyal servant you could wish for."

He frowned, but she held up her hand to halt his words. "All I ask is that you hear me out. What you do afterwards is entirely your decision."

He nodded and capped his doubts, listening to her as she said, "I was glad of what you said about wanting to support the villagers. But you must be made aware that Mrs. Parker and other villagers do not trust you. Right or wrong, they believe that, like your father, you do not have their best interests at heart. They see your plan to dismiss Mr. Nightingale as an example that if any of them displease you, you will simply replace them."

Rufus listened with growing unease because what she said explained the villagers' response to him with startling simplicity. They painted him with the same brush they had his father, irrespective of how little they knew of his character.

She glanced at her hands, as if to collect her thoughts. "I only say these things because Mr. Jones mentioned that you are concerned about the villagers' opinion of you."

He reeled back in shock, and all of his suspicions about Phillip's relationship with Belle rolled over him like a cold wave as he asked, "When?"

She looked up, her expression confused. "What?"

"When did you speak with Phillip?"

"What does that matter?"

"To my recall, you have not been alone with my cousin to have an intimate conversation about what concerns me."

He moved closer, and an old suspicion cracked the surface of his happiness. His cousin's sly smile when the lady's name arose in conversation in the taproom. Phillip's familiarity with Belle even though they had all only recently met.

"When did you speak with my cousin?" It was important she answer. His trust in her depended on it.

Her gaze skittered away before she spoke. "I believe you were not there at the time."

She was prevaricating. She had a secret. And it involved Phillip. A cold certainty about their relationship invaded him and made him sick to his stomach. Though he did not want to know her answer, he asked in a hard voice, "Are you in love with him?"

Her gaze, roaring with fury, rose to clash with his. "How do you dream up such absurd notions?"

"You have not answered my question."

"No, I am not in love with Phillip Jones. I consider him a good friend, that is all." Her words came out fast and furious. "I view him much as I do your sister or your mother. I have no other interest in him. He does not provoke me. He does not make my blood roil. When I am not with him, I do not give him a second's thought. I do not dream about him in my sleep. He does not stir my passions. *He is not the least bit like you.*"

As if suddenly realizing what she had said, she stopped short.

Warmth spread through Rufus, and he wanted to swing her around the entryway and shout for joy. She had as much as admitted that she loved him.

"There is no need to smile like that, my lord." She backed away. "I did not mean to say what it may have sounded as though I said. That is, I . . ."

"What did you not mean to say, Belle?"

With her head held high and her back straight, she assumed a mantle of dignity that made him want to smile wider as she replied, "All I wanted to convey was that you should reconsider your decision about discharging Mr. Nightingale. It is you that brought your cousin into the conversation and confused me. Now, I must go. Pray do not let me detain you further. Good day, my lord." She gave a curtsey and ran back to the drawing room.

Felton approached with his hat, coat, and gloves. The grin on the old retainer's face matched the one Rufus failed to suppress. Without a word, he accepted his gear and left.

Already mounted, Phillip waited by the courtyard stairs. Rufus took Goodwin's reins from a stable boy and sprang onto the horse's back.

"By your expression," Phillip said as they rode away from the estate, "I take it your words with the lovely Lady Belle went well?"

"She said you were her friend," Rufus replied.

His cousin's eyebrows lifted in pleased surprise. "Truly? That is excellent news, for I consider her mine. A friend, that is. Nothing more."

"I know," he said with smug satisfaction.

Phillip laughed, and they road along the lane toward the village. "So, where are we off to?"

Rufus glanced around as he considered the question. He had stayed in London too long. How could he have forgotten the peacefulness of this region? The verdant groves, variegated meadows, and the leafless woods seemed enchanting in their winter melancholy. The cloudless blue sky suggested the storm had indeed passed, though it remained cold enough to mist his breath.

He reined in to watch two sparrows confront each other on a fence. Each raised its tail and lowered its head so that their entire bodies assumed a more or less horizontal position. One fluffed its feathers, making itself look twice its size.

The stance reminded Rufus of the Parker boys' play fight. It was how he often acted in Phillip's presence.

"Shall we sup at the Briar Inn?" Phillip asked. "It is almost noon."

"A good plan." Rufus liked the quaint inn and its portly innkeeper. "It will give us a chance to speak about an issue that troubles me."

"You wish to confide?" When Rufus glanced at Phillip in surprise, his cousin shrugged and said, "You have not asked for my counsel since we were children."

"I have had other matters on my mind," he said, not sure how to explain his withdrawal from their childhood kinship.

"For five years?"

The number shocked him. *Had it been that long?*

Trying to live up to his father's approval, and always failing, must have worn down his desire to expose his hurt. Especially to Phillip, who never displeased his uncle.

In Rufus's father's eyes, Phillip had a knack for proper dress, an arrogance of expression that easily hid his true thoughts, and a gift for befriending the right people. All attributes that his son lacked.

The sparrows flew by them, chirping to each other, apparently no longer in disagreement. Time he, too, put aside his old hurts and treated his family as family.

"I need your help," he said. "There is a rumor going about that I killed Father."

"I know," Phillip said.

Rufus swung his head to look at him. All this while he thought he was alone on this quest, and Phillip *knew?*

"Though the King tried to hush it, the news has spread about all the clubs," his cousin said. "I squashed as much as I could before I posted here."

Thank heavens his mother preferred the countryside. She would not have heard the news yet. The repercussions of this ball multiplied. Not only would it be a distraction, but it might also bring Town gossip into his home and within his family's earshot.

He shifted his shoulders as a weight, heavier than before, settled there. "I have a little time to clear my name."

"So I heard."

Rufus gave a huff. "It might help to tell me what you know so I do not waste your time repeating common knowledge."

Phillip chuckled. "That story of a hunting accident seemed strange since Uncle was an excellent marksman, not an inexperienced cub to be caught in the line of fire. What interests me is, why do you search for the killer here, instead of in London?"

"The leads in Town withered on their vine," Rufus said, "so I followed the one that pointed me to Terrance Village. My father came here in a hurry shortly before he was killed, but no one seems to know why. I hoped to elicit information from the locals, but I have not succeeded there, either. The villagers are unwilling to confide in me. The only man who did died the day we spoke."

"The drunk found in the stable," Phillip said. "Your suspicion that someone in Terrance Village is involved could be right then."

Rufus nodded.

"What makes you sure that person is not me?" Phillip asked.

Today seemed a day of shocking conversations.

"If something were to happen to you, thanks to Uncle's will, I would gain a more handsome yearly stipend," Phillip said before he could respond, "and the London townhouse would be mine, since it is not entailed and is willed to me should you die before me. Then my mother need not worry about losing the home she has known all of her life."

That last struck home, no doubt as intended, and fully justified. *But, dammit, I had a perfectly good reason to do so. And besides, why must I be forced to live with a woman who dislikes me?* "I gave her another house. One as opulent as my London townhouse."

"It is not her home. Although she may not say so, it hurt her deeply that you did not wish her to reside with you as your father did." Phillip gave him a serious look. "My point is that with so much to gain, I am the perfect suspect. So why do you not consider me the villain?"

"Because I trust you," Rufus said.

"Can you afford to?"

"If I cannot trust you, I cannot trust anyone. You are a brother in my heart."

They rode in silence from then on. When they came to a crossroad, Rufus drew Goodwin to a halt. "There is one item I must deal with before we sup."

Phillip tilted his head and raised an eyebrow in question.

"My agent, Nightingale, resides in that direction." He gave his cousin a mischievous look. "He is under the misapprehension that I am about to dismiss him. Indeed, since I read his most recent report, not only do I intend that he continue in my service, but that he run an important errand for me."

"Regarding your search for Uncle's killer?" Phillip asked.

Rufus shook his head. "No. I am satisfied you and I can deal with that. I owe one of my tenants two Christmas presents. And one for Lady Belle. London is a long ride from here, and Christmas is only a few weeks away."

Ignoring his cousin's obvious curiosity, he laughed and urged his mount toward Mr. Nightingale's house. "I shall meet you at the Briar in one hour."

* * * *

After speaking with Lord Terrance, Belle could not concentrate on the ball. The chatter between Lady Terrance, Mrs. Jones, and Susie fizzled away.

She had as much as admitted to his lordship that she loved him. His expression all but shouted that he had understood her meaning and rejoiced in her embarrassment. *What a vexing man.*

Belle stood and paced the drawing room from one corner to the other. The walls, furnishings and ornaments confined her at every step. She had only wanted to ask him to make peace with Nightingale so it would ease his relations with his tenants and villagers. That they feared him hurt her as much as it did him.

"Belle, what plagues you, child?" Lady Terrance asked.

When she turned to face her, all three women wore varying degrees of curiosity. "Nothing," she said and sat beside them. She pointed to the fashion illustrations that Susie held. "That is a pretty shade of rose. A gray border could symbolize a degree of mourning, and yet still show off your coloring to advantage."

The discussion veered to the amount of gray or black to be used on the dresses, and Belle's thoughts again wandered.

She had come to Clearview to rid this house of its ghost. She had found a way to keep Lady Terrance distracted at night, but had she done anything to make the ghost leave? *No.* The only time she and the spirit had come face-to-face, she had cowered in fear.

Had she spent all her time mooning over Rufus Marlesbury to avoid dealing with his father? Possibly. And apparently, her broken engagement had taught her nothing.

Susie's animated face and Lady Terrance's happy chatter drew her gaze. It was easier to concentrate on the troubles of the living than the dead. But by doing so she shirked her duty to this family. It was time she did as she had promised.

With resolution, she stood, and, as expected, the three women's attention swerved toward her.

"I am fatigued," Belle said. "Will you please excuse me while I rest?"

"Of course, dear," Lady Terrance said. "What a sad hostess I am to keep you here when you are tired from your walk. Shall I order our noon meal to be served early?"

"No, thank you. I am not hungry. Carry on with your discussion. You can apprise me of your ideas this afternoon. I shall be rested by then and eager to go over all the plans."

She gave a curtsy and left the room, with Earnest as her shadow. On the third floor, Earnest whined and darted in front of her. He leaned against her legs, forcing her to stop or go sprawling onto the dusty carpet.

"If you are afraid, go downstairs, Earnest. I must do this." She picked up her skirts and moved around him. Unhappy he might be, but the wolfhound kept to her side, a comforting bulk.

She made her way along the twisting corridors, swishing open curtain after curtain from the widely spaced windows to let in sunlight. Dust plumed, and she coughed, but the light broke up the gloom. More importantly, it marked her passage so she could find her way back through the catacomb of corridors quickly if the need arose. She listened for the whisper of a ghostly wind, her skin poised and alert to feel the onset of any unusual chill.

Memory and instinct guided her to the gallery. She stopped by the portrait of King George and walked to the opposite wall where the late Earl of Terrance's portrait hung. With tentative fingers, she brushed its bronze frame.

No spirit swooped through her. No change in temperature.

The last time she was here, with the curtains closed, it had been dim. Now, framed against the rays of sunlight, the late earl's sharp countenance loomed, and his eyes pierced her with recrimination. She could tell there had been no leniency in his make up. One either lived up to his expectations or failed miserably. And his son believed he fell into the latter category.

Earnest trembled. She scratched his ears to calm him, but she, too, was afraid her desire to confront the earl's ghost might come true. However, she must discover what troubled this spirit. Since extracting information from his family had proved to be a complete failure, she had no choice but to go directly to the source in order to discover what kept the late Lord Terrance earthbound.

"My lord," she called out.

Silence.

Would mention of his wife draw him out? "Could whatever troubles you be a danger to Lady Terrance, my lord? Is that why you have been visiting her? If so, I wish to help, but you must first tell me how."

A cold wind blew down the passageway. Mention of his wife did indeed get his attention. The temperature dropped by several degrees, and Belle tightened her shawl about her shoulders. Earnest pressed himself against her right leg, shivering.

"You should have gone when I suggested," she told the dog in sympathy. "Now whatever I experience will be your ordeal also." She ruffled his fur. "Still, let me tell you that I am more glad of your company now than ever before."

His wide-open eyes pleaded for them to leave.

"Not yet, Earnest," she said softly. "Not yet."

A fiercely cold breeze spun Belle around until she staggered. Using the wall for support, she said, "I am here to be of service, my lord. Please, will you trust me?"

The air before her wavered. She did not need Earnest's warning growl to know they were no longer alone.

"If you will not speak of your wife or yourself, tell me about Mr. Darby. I hear he went to London shortly before you were killed. He died the day before you."

A howling echoed down the corridors. Suddenly, the wind whipped the curtains, swishing them closed across one window after the next, barring sunlight and eliminating her safe guide back to the stairway.

Bad sign. Mentioning Mr. Darby might not have been the wisest course. Too late, she saw the danger she had put herself and Earnest in by approaching the ghost this way. Belle grabbed hold of Earnest's ruff and leaned against the wall.

Earnest barked, and she asked the ghost, "What do you want?"

"Traitor!" The word resounded along the dark gallery.

"Who is a traitor? Whom did he or she betray?"

"My country!"

Doors along the hallway flung open and slammed shut, and inside adjacent rooms, furniture crashed against walls. The spirit's wrath was beyond anything she had experienced, but it was nothing compared to the turmoil raging in her mind.

This was not about a restless spirit. This was about a betrayal of the Crown!

Chapter Thirteen

Belle's legs gave way, and she slumped to the floor. She had to tell Lord Terrance about this discovery. Could he already know that his father was murdered? Was that why he seemed so worried? Why his study was in such a mess, with books scattered everywhere? And the library! Mrs. Jones had said that it was in complete disarray and that the butler had told her Lord Terrance had done it. Could he have been looking for clues at Clearview? It made sense that the two rooms he would search first were ones the late earl was likely to have frequented most. If he was looking for clues to his father's murderer, no wonder he had been against holding a ball. She probably *was* the distraction he had accused her of being.

"Does he know?" She scrambled up and ran into the closest room. A puppet show was in progress, as every item in the room swayed in the air. A chair sailed toward her, and she ducked. It struck the wall and splintered.

"Your son," she shouted, her breath coming out in white puffs inside the ice-cold room. "Does . . . He . . . Know?"

Every moving object halted in midair. And then they all crashed to the floor. The chilling room warmed marginally. *Great. What a time to leave.*

She ran out into the corridor and shouted, "Come on, Earnest. We have to find Lord Terrance."

Skirts lifted, she sprinted along the twisting corridors. She made it to the stair landing before the ghost grabbed her by her shoulders, sending shivers shooting up into her neck. She was raised upward midair like the furniture. Her breath choked to a halt.

Earnest ran around beneath her barking and jumping.

"Do not tell," a hollow voice whispered by her left ear.

She hung there, petrified that if he released her, she would plummet down the stairs. As quickly as that thought crossed her mind, she shut it out, lest he interpret that as an easier way to ensure silence.

Belle took a labored breath, knowing that reasoning with his ghostly lordship was unlikely to save her a fall. She tried another tact. "Very well, my lord. My lips are sealed."

"Liar!"

Her temper flared at that accusation, accurate as it might be. "What do you want of me?"

"Find him."

Now that she had time to consider the matter, telling his son of her experience with his father would more likely get her thrown out of Clearview than help her find the traitor.

"All right. I promise not to tell your son, and I will do my best to find this traitor. But then you must do something for me."

The fierce grip loosed enough to get her blood surging.

"No kisses." For the first time, there was a note of amusement in the voice.

Belle's face flushed hot. She was so mortified, she had the impulsive urge to fight loose so she *could* tumble down those stairs and break her neck. Instead, she fought the strident urge to slap the father, as she had wanted to slap the son the first time she had met him. But how did one slap a ghost one could not see?

"You must attempt to go into the Light, my lord."

The words seemed to leave him speechless.

Belle softened her tone. "Your family cannot recover from their grief while you remain earthbound."

He released her so quickly there was no time to scream. She landed half on top of Earnest, and desperately tried to gain her balance, but failed. She pushed the dog toward the landing even as she tumbled down the stairs. The worn carpet chaffed her elbows and cheeks. As if in slow motion, she rolled over each stair, her view swerving from staircase bar to ornately carved ceiling to paisley patterned red carpet.

This is the end. They will find my mangled limbs at the bottom of the stairs. Earnest will howl with grief. My grandpapa will despair.

Something hard blocked her from rolling past the fourth step. Belle lay there for several moments as she silently thanked whatever object had halted her fall. Once her head stopped spinning, she glanced behind to see what had saved her. Her breath stuck in her throat as she realized she was leaning against empty air.

The ghost had saved her.

She was released abruptly, and her back hit the stairs with a soft *thunk,* and pain shot up her side and down her leg. Her vision blurred as she lay on the stairs.

Earnest ran down to lick her cheek.

"I am all right. Are you?" She felt the dog's limbs and body, but he seemed to have fared better than she. She released him and gently sat up, her movements slow, awkward, and painful. She waited a moment for her head to clear and then tried to stand. The moment she put weight on her legs, pain shot up from her right ankle. She stifled a scream and lifted that foot off the ground and leaned against the banister. It was a minute before she could open her eyes without wanting to throw up. Hobbling downstairs was out of the question.

Slowly, she slumped back onto the stairs. How was she to reach her room? She gave the dog a rueful glance. "You will have to bring help." She brought his face toward her and pictured the countess. "Find the countess. I need help."

Earnest wagged his tail and gave her another lick before he turned to go on his errand. She held him back as she checked over her shoulder. Did she want to remain here alone? Then again, what could the dog do for her if he stayed? The last few minutes proved he could not protect her from a ghost.

Reluctantly, she released him. "Go."

Once the patter of his paws died away, all remained silent. No sound, no movement, and most of all, no unearthly visitor.

He had departed as quickly and silently as he had appeared. But what an assignment he had given her.

She lowered herself a step at a time, but after a few, the pain in her ankle became intolerable, and she became dizzy, so she gave up. Nothing for it but to wait.

She sighed heavily, and then cringed as her side ached. She sat and rested her elbow on the knee of her good leg and her chin on her fist. So the ghost sought a traitor. And she was not allowed to confide that to anyone, least of all Lord Terrance. Why not? One more mystery to add to her bag of troubles.

How was she to search out this villain without a name, a description, or some indication of where she should aim her search?

According to the villagers she spoke to at the Briar Inn, the only rogue in the area was Lord Terrance. In fact, one man had even said that it was believed Lord Terror, Lord Terrance, was a traitor.

Could he be a traitor?

No!

She asked and answered the question without hesitation. Having come to know the man and, Belle admitted with a sigh, come to love him, she could not imagine he had it in him to betray his country.

He was too honorable. He valued his name too highly to risk soiling it. And she would bet he loved his country as much as he loved his family. Besides, surely the ghost would not refer to his son as "traitor"? He would have said, "My son killed me, the bastard."

The Terrance men did not mince words. Except for Phillip Jones. She knew little about him other than that he played a fine billiards game and possessed a keen sense of humor. He also seemed inordinately interested in her activities and Lord Terrance's whereabouts. However, that could merely be curiosity and familial interest. According to Lord Terrance, his cousin was short of blunt. Was he capable of betraying his country to fill his pockets? Her instincts said a firm, *No*.

She leaned back and rested her elbows on the step behind her. All right, not Phillip Jones. How about his Mrs. Jones? She seemed to have no love for her nephew, and she, too, was short of funds. Susie said her aunt deeply grieved her brother's death.

Still, she had been reliant on the old earl for her creature comforts. Being the poor relation could wear on a person's soul. Also, if she removed her brother and nephew, her son could inherit.

Was that why she had posted herself here to Clearview when she obviously did not care for country life? Had the chance to be rich enough to live in style and never want for another pence proven too much temptation? But could that high stickler for propriety betray her country? Or murder her brother?

Once again, her instinct said, *No*.

Belle's leg throbbed from toes to hip. She moved her bottom to the side and eased the weight off one hip, all the while keeping her injured ankle and side still.

In the meantime, her mind insisted on going over the suspects one by one. There were the servants to consider. And what about Mr. Nightingale? She had spoken on his behalf to Lord Terrance, but what did she really know about him? Then there was Ellison, Lord Terrance's valet. Mendal said the man was a perpetual drunk. His loyalty could have been bought for a pint or two.

Outside the manor, there were villagers and local gentry. The baker and his wife and the innkeeper all appeared to be simple, honest folk. None of the villagers she had met seemed capable of such infamy as betraying their country.

As for the neighbors, on the top of her list of suspects she easily placed Martin Winfield. She found nothing likeable about him. She had not cared for him when in London, and closer acquaintance in Clearview had not endeared him either. But did a healthy dislike of a person mean they were evil?

Running footsteps on the stairs suggested her wait was over. Belle straightened, glad to give up her quest for answers. Her head now ached as much as her leg, and her reflections had brought her no nearer to finding the traitor.

Earnest reached her first and gave her a warm, welcome lick. A minute later, Lady Terrance rounded the corner.

"My dearest Belle," Lady Terrance said upon sighting her. She hurried to Belle's side. "Oh heavens, you poor child." She leaned against the railing, took several deep breaths and laid a hand on her chest. "My, I have not climbed so much and so fast since I was a child."

"Are you well?" Belle asked.

"I believe that question is my prerogative. By the by, quite impressive, this dog." She leaned over to smooth Earnest's forehead as he lay on the step beside Belle. "He barked until Susie opened the door. Then ran to me, ignoring all others. With my hem in his jaws, he dragged me out and up the stairs. Gave Henrietta and my daughter quite a fright, not to mention, myself."

Belle scratched the large shaggy gray puppy that lay panting beside her. "He is the best of dogs."

"Woof," Earnest said, and his tail thumped the step.

"Now see here," her ladyship said, "we have discussed the dog but not your ill health. Where are you hurt, child?"

"Only a slightly twisted ankle," she said and smiled ruefully. "I am so sorry for troubling you."

"Pish posh," her ladyship said. "These things cannot be helped." She checked the stairs leading upward behind Belle with a half-curious, half-nervous glance. "Though one does wonder if you found what you were searching for up here."

With difficulty, Belle kept her thoughts and findings to herself. She would keep her promise to Lord Terrance about not speaking of such things to members of his household. And her promise to the ghost to keep mum about her hunt for the traitor.

"If you would be so kind as to give me some assistance on my good side," she said, "I am sure I can make it to my room."

Before either could move, a commotion on the stairs heralded another arrival.

"Dear Lady Belle," Martin Winfield said as he sprinted to reach her.

Earnest stood and growled. Winfield held his riding crop threateningly. Afraid the man might strike, Belle pulled Earnest close.

At the same time, a stirring began behind her. The hairs on her neck stood on end, and not because of Winfield. They needed to remove themselves from these steps promptly. But how to do that with Winfield blocking the way?

"Ladies," he said. "If you would both step aside, I will deal with that wild animal."

"You will do no such thing." Lady Terrance stepped protectively in front of Earnest. "He is a hero for rescuing my Belle. You, sir, will kindly show the hound the respect he deserves and put down that weapon."

Mr. Winfield immediately lowered his arm. "My pardon, your ladyship, I thought you were in danger. They said the dog dragged you here."

"Yes, to find Belle, who has hurt her ankle. That explains why she and I are here, but what brings you to our doorstep? If you are looking for my son, he has gone to the village. I am surprised Felton did not inform you of that."

"Oh, he did," Mr. Winfield said with a wide, charming smile that appeared like a rainbow after a storm. "I actually came to see if I might offer my services for the ball preparations. Pardon my abrupt entrance, but when I heard you might be in trouble, I took the liberty of coming to your rescue. Needlessly, I see."

"It matters not why any of us are here," Belle said, afraid this conversation had gone on far too long. "I simply wish to return to my chamber." She forced herself to *not* look behind her. "Lady Terrance kindly offered to lend me her arm."

"Oh, allow me." Mr. Winfield stepped forward.

Earnest poked his head between Belle and Lady Terrance to growl and bare his teeth.

"Earnest, no," Belle said. "Stay. Sit."

He ignored her orders, which was so unlike him. He had been very good of late, especially when she used her stern tone. She half wondered if Earnest disobeying her command had something to do with the ghost's presence. But then why growl at Winfield instead of the looming presence behind them? And why would the ghost show up again now, just when Mr. Winfield arrived? Now she saw the icicle that fell when she first arrived with new eyes, for the one who had been standing beside her that day had been none other than Mr. Winfield.

Earnest made to leap at him, but both she and Lady Terrance restrained the dog.

"That animal should be shot," Winfield said. "He is a danger."

"He only seems to be a danger to you," Belle said, out of breath from sitting on the large dog to keep him from flinging himself at Winfield. The dog's jaws were agape, sharp white teeth flashing above drooling gums.

"What the blazes is happening here?" Lord Terrance suddenly asked.

With all the noise Earnest was making, Belle had not heard him come up the stairs. She hoped he would not ask what had brought them all up here.

"Aunt, Lady Belle, are you both well?" Mr. Jones added his bulk to the crowded stairway.

"We do seem to have a bit of a problem with Earnest," Lady Terrance said. "I do not understand why. He seemed wonderful before Mr. Winfield arrived."

Lord Terrance gave his neighbor an angry glance then turned his attention to the dog. "Earnest, sit."

Earnest sat. For the first time, the hound's gaze moved away from Winfield. He gave a sad whine when his sight met his master's, and with a lick of his chops, he lay down.

Lady Terrance slumped beside him on the stairs, looking exhausted.

Belle did likewise. In the excitement, she had forgotten about her leg, and now it throbbed worse than ever and made her queasy. *That is all I need. To cast my accounts on the closest gentleman's boots.*

A glance up informed her she would be violating Lord Terrance's polished black Hessians. The world began to swim, and the sound of chatter faded. There was a moment of pain, then she was floating in the air. Was she in the ghost's grip again?

"Be still." Lord Terrance's voice was so close to her right ear that his breath brushed her cheek.

"Careful, Rufus, do not drop her," Lady Terrance said.

"That is hardly my intention, Mama," he said, but he held Belle tighter.

Belle wound her arm around his neck and settled her head against his shoulder. Her heart pounded, and her blood rushed to her head at being held so fiercely and protectively by this man. She never wanted him to let her go. She tenderly ran her free hand down the length of his neck.

"If you do not stop that right now, I *will* drop you," he whispered. "There is only so much restraint you can expect from a man."

"What was that?" Mr. Winfield said. "I did not quite catch your words."

"I asked Lady Belle to lie still. It is difficult enough to negotiate these winding steps without her squirming."

"I would be happy to relieve you," his neighbor said.

"That is unnecessary, Winfield," Mr. Jones said. "This is family business. If Rufus requires assistance, he will gain it from me."

"No need to jostle my Belle any more than necessary," Lady Terrance said.

"*My Belle,* indeed," Lord Terrance muttered.

"Your mother is most kind to tolerate my mishap." Belle clenched her fingers to keep from caressing him. Her head was thick, as if her mind swam in a bowl of jelly.

"How is it that you gain everyone's love the moment you meet them?" he asked her. "I have tried for years to . . ."

"To what, my lord?"

"Never mind." He had reached the first floor.

Belle let her lips, resting so close to his neck, brush against his skin. He sucked in a sharp breath as she savored the warmth of his skin.

He groaned. "Stop that," he said in a low, harsh growl, and strode along the hallway in long strides, practically running.

"Oh, my lady," Mendal cried and rushed to meet them. She must have heard Lord Terrance's heavy strides and come out to see what was happening.

"Your lady needs to reach her room," Lord Terrance said. "Ready her bed."

The maid gave another cry and ran to do as he bade.

"Phillip, see the doctor is summoned. And show Winfield out."

In short order, Lord Terrance saw to it that Belle was ensconced under her sheets, her injured foot raised and awaiting the physician's inspection. He then left without another word.

When the doctor arrived, he duly inspected Belle's ankle and her side and confirmed her sprain and bruises were the result of her fall. He prescribed plenty of rest and departed.

She was glad to see him leave, worried he might want to bleed her, as so many in his profession did to patients at the slightest sign of illness. She had forbidden anyone from doing that to her grandfather.

She frowned at the thought. Her grandpapa had yet to reply to any of her missives. But then he was a poor letter writer. How did he fare all alone without her to care for him? She wanted to see him and make sure he was well, but until she resolved her dilemma with the ghost, she could not leave Clearview. And the ghost seemed in no hurry to depart until he—or now Belle—found his traitor.

She shivered and lay on her good side, remembering again the ghost's cold grip.

As if sensing Belle needed comfort, Lady Sefton shifted in her cage and hooted softly in her throat. Earnest then jumped up on the bed and lay down, his body heavy and warm against her back.

Belle sighed and closed her eyes. Tomorrow, she would worry about the ghost, the ball, and the manor house. All she wanted was to relive being carried in Lord Terrance's arms. If they had been alone, would he have responded to her kiss against his neck?

A smile stretched her lips as her thoughts drifted off into a satisfying dream in accompaniment to the dog's deep, steady breathing and the owl's soft stirrings.

* * * *

Despite a week having passed since her injury, Belle was still not completely healed. She could do naught but sit and let everyone else arrange the upcoming ball, which was now set for Tuesday, the fifteenth day of December. This, Mrs. Jones had said, would give ample time for their guests to return to their home for Christmas, if they so desired.

Belle, frustrated by her injury, could do no more than lounge on the luxurious Grecian couch in the drawing room, while all the activity in preparation for the ball whirled about her.

She could not even discuss her worries about Mr. Winfield with anyone, because her main source of knowledge came from a ghostly encounter, which she could not talk about, and Earnest's instinctive dislike of Winfield, which could hardly be presented as evidence before a court of law.

She had learned a little something about the man from Mendal after she sent her to speak to the servants about him. Apparently, Winfield had been a childhood friend of Lord Terrance, but they were no longer friendly. No one knew what happened to end their friendship. Winfield had an elderly mother who lived with him, and he was hard-fisted when it came to paying his servants. None of which pointed to the man being a traitor to England.

As for the ball, that progressed better than Belle's investigation. Invitations had been written, and the Royal Mail carried summons to friends and family as far away as London, while servants hand-delivered invitations to the local gentry. The vicar, happiest to hear that the celebrations also included the villagers, agreed to carry the word to his parishioners.

On the morning of Friday, the twenty-seventh day of November, Belle, Mrs. Jones, and Lord Terrance were assembled in the drawing room when Susie ran in to complain that she did not feel comfortable visiting the village by herself for her dress fittings.

Her mother, busy working with the housekeeper, could not be convinced to chaperone her, and Belle, in her invalid state, was useless as well.

Belle hid her grin at Susie's mournful tone. Lord Terrance caught her glance and smiled too.

"I would be willing to accompany you," Mrs. Jones said. "I have some experience in the matter of ball gowns."

The offer sent her niece into tears, and then Susie gave her brother an anguished look before she rushed out.

"Well!" Mrs. Jones said in a huff. "I cannot help worrying that the child will not take during the Season. Not if she continues to react in such a missish manner."

"The invitations included members of the *Ton,* and that might have put her in a pucker," Belle suggested. "Susie likely hoped to ease her entry into their midst by practicing her debut with the local gentry with whom she is more familiar."

She did not say that having Susie's dragon of an aunt order colors and lace that the young girl might not care for probably played a significant role in the outpouring of tears.

"Have the seamstress come here," Lord Terrance said.

Belle agreed that Susie would feel more at ease to have the fittings done at Clearview and was pleased that he was willing to do this for his sister.

Her leg ached, so she moved it toward a pillow. Lord Terrance rushed over to help. He gently settled her leg, his hand warm against the back of her ankle.

"Thank you," she said.

He had been most attentive since her injury. Was it her imagination, or did he search for a reason to touch her? He often brushed against her when he tended her ankle or plumped the cushion at her back. He insisted on carrying her to and from her room each morning and evening.

Not that she objected. Especially the carrying. Something about being held in his arms made her feel safe and cherished.

Most of her life, Belle had shared little physical contact with people, so she found the constant handling most welcome. And since the carrier was Lord Terrance, it was inordinately exciting. She did not have the courage to again kiss him while he conveyed her, though.

From his smiling glances, she wondered if he wished she would.

Her sprained ankle did have one clear advantage. Lord Terrance had been most impressed with Earnest's response to Belle's injury, and he took the dog on daily walks and runs and even on sojourns into the village.

For Earnest's part, though he professed to miss her by exuberantly licking her face upon his return, he seemed happy to be away from Clearview manor as much as possible. After their last traumatic ghostly encounter, Belle could not blame him for his defection.

Mr. Jones arrived in the drawing room dressed in his dashing flair. Both men bid the ladies farewell, and Earnest followed them out the door.

Having to lie about day in, day out did have its advantages, however. It gave her the rare opportunity to not only visually observe her companions without appearing nosy, but to also practice her special senses.

Mrs. Jones certainly acted the lady of the manor, or the "dragon," as Susie called her. Whenever Mrs. Jones and Lady Terrance were together, the countess would bow to Mrs. Jones's words and then do as she pleased once Mrs. Jones left. Mrs. Jones, on the other hand, was frustrated and disappointed when Lady Terrance ignored her suggestions, especially since the lady would not argue the point. Her craving to be accepted and loved by her family practically palpated in the air.

As for Susie, she believed her aunt never heard her wishes. Her fears were routinely reinforced since Mrs. Jones and her niece did often disagree. For Mrs. Jones's part, she desperately wanted Susie to "take" in society.

Once, while niece and aunt argued, Belle caught a glimpse of a homely young lady of Susie's age. In that instant, she understood Mrs. Jones's greatest fear. The elderly woman identified with Susie most, for she had once been young and awkward, with no one to guide her. The result had been a decision to marry in haste.

She did not want her niece to resign herself to a similar fate. Mrs. Jones wanted to offer Susie the guidance and vast experience of mingling with the elite that she now possessed. That Susie did not care for her advice left Mrs. Jones gloomy. After their encounters, the older woman's fears for Susie hung in the air like a stormy cloud.

On the few occasions that Belle saw Lord Terrance and his aunt interact, she had been most puzzled. In Mrs. Jones's presence, Lord Terrance presented a bland countenance.

Mrs. Jones mirrored that behavior. The moment he glanced away or left the room, however, a cold depression settled on the lady. It was then that her grief at her brother's passing surfaced. Belle wondered if her nephew reminded Mrs. Jones of her brother.

Belle wanted to run over and give the woman a warm hug on those occasions. She did not follow through for two reasons. One, her ankle prohibited such exertions. Two, even were she to offer consolation, Mrs. Jones would reject such a gesture.

So, Belle had no choice but to spend her days idly. All this time to think had also made her reconsider her suspicions of Winfield. The ghost had not specifically named him as a villain, so what if she were wrong about him? Just because she did not care for a fellow did not mean he was capable of murder and treason.

So, she began to examine the motives of everyone she encountered. To family, servants, and visitors alike, she posed questions about their background in a chatty manner and caught their stray thoughts to examine for deeper meaning.

Was this man other than he appeared?
Did she harbor murder in her heart?
Would he willingly betray England?

As for Lord Terrance, for the past week, both he and his cousin seemed excessively intent about their daily journeys. They left shortly after breakfast and did not return until close to suppertime. Yet neither seemed happier for their outings. They were up to something, but to her mounting frustration, both men kept their thoughts well under cover.

As the days passed, Belle sensed a growing unease in the urbane Mr. Jones. Lord Terrance, she still could not read, though he, too, grew quieter and looked more discouraged each time he returned home.

She wished he would speak to her about what troubled him. Every time she questioned him about what he had done that day, he changed the subject. All she could do was hope that whatever trouble the two men stirred, they would remain safer than Lord Terrance's father had.

Chapter Fourteen

It was the day before the ball, and it had arrived faster than Belle could have imagined. Agitation flitted from room to room, stirring anger and frustration. A torn sleeve brought tears and a dropped vase recrimination when a fortnight earlier neither would have garnered more than a raised eyebrow or a sigh.

Belle was no more exempt from this growing agitation than the others. She had grown no closer to finding out who was the traitor the ghost hunted and, therefore, had not been able to discharge the ghost of Clearview. She sensed a general unease in the air about Lord Terrance and Mr. Jones, but she could not discern its cause.

On the positive side, her leg had healed nicely, which meant dancing with a gallant partner no longer posed a problem. Her dress, a lovely confection of lace and pale dreamy primrose silks flowed like a dream. She could hardly wait to see Lord Terrance's expression when she made her entrance.

During the weeks since her injury, she had no further ghostly encounters. Nor had she made any headway into discovering the so-called "traitor." At least, now that her ankle had healed, she could venture upstairs again to solicit more information from the taciturn spirit.

Not that she was in any hurry to do so. The terror of her last encounter was vivid. Partly because of that, she had decided to wait until after the ball to disturb the ghost of Clearview, wanting the planned entertainment to proceed without incident.

The upcoming ball had also acted as an excellent distraction for the countess. Belle did not know all the details, but Susie said that Lady Terrance planned many games and a play to entertain her guests. She had heard the entire village mirrored their excitement. This Christmas ball would be like none ever experienced in Terrance Village, because this time, many villagers had been invited to be a part of the festivities instead of merely watching the elite of society enjoy themselves. Something that Susie said her father would never have permitted had he been alive. Belle crossed her fingers and hoped he would not choose tonight to show his objections.

While Belle fed Lady Sefton her midday meal, Mendal handed her a summons from Lord Terrance. He requested that Belle come directly to the foyer. She returned the owl to its cage and hurried downstairs.

Skirts held up, she raced down the last few steps. Hopefully Earnest was not in trouble again. His lordship had taken the dog for a walk earlier this morning, and she had seen neither since. Man and dog finally saw eye-to-eye, but could some trouble have ruined their rapport?

When she reached the bottom of the steps, no one was in the foyer, not even a butler or footman in sight.

"Lord Terrance?" she called out.

"Lady Belle." He came out of his study. His shining blue eyes said they hid a delicious secret.

Earnest, who followed his master, wagged his tail while portraying an equally happy grin.

"What has happened?" she asked, her agitation shifting from dread to excitement.

Lord Terrance stepped aside, and from behind him an elderly man stepped forward. It was the Marquess of Alford.

Grandpapa!

He appeared frail, with high spots of color on his cheeks. Belle's tears misted her vision, and she blinked rapidly to keep him in sight. She ran to give him a warm welcome hug.

His arms wrapped around her so tightly that he had to be healthy and hearty, despite his feeble appearance.

"You should not have traveled in this weather," she scolded lightly.

"The most enjoyable journey I have ever experienced," he said with a wink to Lord Terrance. "His lordship sent a coach, a doctor, and his agent to ensure my every need was met. His London chef, who was on his way here to oversee the ball's feasts, was also with us in the second coach, and he cooked my every meal on the way here."

Belle wanted to thank Lord Terrance. If she had not already been in love with him, this thoughtful action would have sealed the deed. But in the ensuing commotion of happy greetings, she lost sight of the elusive gentleman.

All too soon, her grandfather said he wished to retire. "We will have ample time to catch up on news this evening."

She escorted him upstairs, where he could rest from his long trip. Lady Terrance had given him the room across the hall from Belle's.

On her return downstairs, Felton informed her that his master had been called away on business.

Disappointed, Belle wandered to the front parlor and lay on a chaise to gaze out the window while Earnest lounged on the carpet beside her. For once, the dog had stayed instead of following Lord Terrance like an enamored puppy.

The view out the window showed scarce evidence of the freak storm that had blown her into Terrance Village over a month ago. She spotted tufts of snow-covered ornamental shrubbery and brown vines on a trellis climbing the manor house walls. Cut-back shrubs were interspersed between garden seats resting on intricate ironwork legs and flowerbeds that edged a white-speckled lawn.

One plant caught her eye, and she sat forward, unable to distinguish if what she saw was real or a vision. While all its partners had been trimmed back for the winter, one rose bush had a branch that still held a blooming rose. Most of the velvet, dark pink petals had fallen, but there were a couple still clinging to the stem.

How extraordinary! The sight made her hopes rise that perhaps all would turn out well for Lord Terrance and his family. She had honed her skill at sensing people's thoughts during her impromptu confinement, so during the upcoming ball, when most everyone from the village would be here, she could practice what she had learned. See if she could identify the traitor the ghost sought if he—or she—was among the guests. By the end of the ball, the entire mystery of the ghost of Clearview might be resolved.

She sat back, well pleased with that plan. Come spring, this garden would come alive with brilliant tones and fragrances, and that rose bush would be in full bloom. How she wished she could be here to see it. For now, she was pleased the roads had cleared enough for their guests to arrive. Several families were already ensconced on the second floor.

Thankfully, the ghost had chosen not to bother anyone so far. Hopefully, he would keep away from the guests. She did not want the ball to be a disaster for Lady Terrance or Susie.

The butler entered the room and said, "My lady."

"Yes, Felton?"

He handed her a note. "A message for you from a tenant farmhouse. The runner said it was urgent."

Surprised, she sat up, unfolded the paper, and read.

Lady Belle,

Pardon my presumption in summoning you so abruptly. However, it is vital that you come to the farm forthwith.

Your most humble servant,
Mrs. Parker

The first thought that popped into Belle's head was that one of the children was in trouble, and Mrs. Parker needed her help. "Felton, have a horse readied for me."

"Yes, my lady. Is anything the matter?"

Belle had already run out the door before he finished speaking, and she did not slow down to answer him. Instead, she gripped the note, lifted her skirts, and raced to her room.

Again, she could not help wondering what could have happened for Mrs. Parker to summon her in such an abrupt manner. If the note had been from Lord Terrance, then she might have assumed he had another pleasant surprise for her. But coming from Mrs. Parker, the missive sounded ominous.

Mendal, busy folding linens, turned in surprise as she stormed in. "My lady, what is wrong?"

"Get my riding dress. I have to leave now for the Parker farm."

"What has happened?"

"I do not know." She gave Mendal the letter before slipping out of her gown. "I hope the woman's children are all right."

"Mrs. Parker's illness might have returned," Mendal said. "Should we summon a doctor for her?"

"No," Belle said. "Let me discover the problem first." With one murder already having taken place and a traitor in the village, a constable might be more appropriate than a doctor.

"I should accompany you," Mendal said.

"No time to take the cart, and you hate riding a horse. You can meet me there later."

Belle ignored her maid's grumbling and hurried Mendal through the change of clothes.

"I will request that a footman follow you," Mendal called as Belle rushed out the bedroom door. Again, she did not slow down to answer.

In short order, Belle mounted her horse and rode at a gallop toward the Parker farm. She barely noticed the servant who rode hard behind her, trying to keep up.

She arrived feeling hot, her heart racing and her breath wheezing as harshly as her mount's. Another horse was tied to a post outside the farmhouse.

The gelding looked familiar, and when she dismounted and raced to its side, she recognized Goodwin. Lord Terrance was here.

A wave of relief swept through her. She paused and took a deep breath, resting her hand against the animal's warm, sturdy side.

"I see you made it here in excellent time." Lord Terrance stepped out the front doors and gave her a roguish smile. He had worn that same expression before he produced her grandfather.

Her heart beat a light tattoo of joy. He had another surprise? Had he found that doll Margaret wanted?

He wore a crisp white cravat, woolen waistcoat, and tightly fitted breeches beneath a deep green Carrick coat with many shoulder capes that fluttered in the cool wind. Arms folded, he studied her in a relaxed manner.

Compared to him, she was warm, bothered, and rumpled. How had he convinced Mrs. Parker to send that note? Belle had a mind to be angry. How could he worry her so?

"No words for me?" he asked.

"I thought something had happened to Mrs. Parker or her children."

"Something has." He came around to where she stood.

She laid her hands on his folded arms in a pleading gesture. "Is Mrs. Parker all right? Tell me she is unhurt. And her children?"

"They are fine," he whispered. He bent his head as if to kiss her worries away and then looked over her shoulder.

Belle followed that glance to the servant who had followed her. With a smirk, the man obligingly dismounted and diplomatically turned back to his master and walked both his mount and Belle's to cool the horses after their strenuous ride.

When she faced Lord Terrance again, his lips pressed against hers in the gentlest of homage. Then he raised her off the ground and brought her to his height while he plundered her face with an assault of kisses.

Belle wrapped her arms around his shoulders and groaned in pleasure. For weeks, she had dreamed of him kissing her like this. His mouth returned to torment hers as he cupped the back of her legs and swung her into his arms.

It reminded her of him carrying her to and from her room. Each time her legs had weakened in anticipation of a kiss. Instead, he had always been circumspect, never once straying from showing proper respect for her person and status.

Encounter after encounter, her frustration had grown. If he had wanted to prove how much she craved his touch, how much she no longer wanted to remain a single lady, how easily she would submit to his embrace, he had succeeded ten times over. Belle now released all her pent-up passions and ardently returned his kiss.

Children's laughter intruded into her concentrated seduction of his lordship. Lord Terrance pulled back enough for her to catch sight of their young audience.

Belle's cheeks heated in embarrassment at her impassioned response and the position she was in, held up so intimately in their master's arms. She struggled to get down, and he gently allowed her feet to touch the ground.

"Did she guess what you were thinking, my lord?" Steven, the eldest boy, asked. "That is how she won a kiss from me last time. Of all that she had brought, she guessed what I wanted most."

"She did indeed guess what I was thinking," Lord Terrance replied. "Better than I thought she would."

Belle stepped away to control her roiling emotions. How could she have responded so wantonly? What had come over her? One moment she had been frightened for Mrs. Parker, and the next overwhelmed by all her frustration at wanting this man. How would she ever live this down? His accusations when she first came to Terrance Village taunted her. She had just acted like a veritable Cyprian, as he had once accused her of being.

What must you think of me? she wondered as she gazed up at him.

"I think you the most delightful of lovers," he whispered, as he pressed his lips against her sensitive ear.

She jumped away, shocked by his words and the realization that she had spoken her question aloud. She touched her hot cheeks and avoided his eyes. She wanted to be anywhere but here. And what did he mean by *the most delightful of lovers*?

The thought of such a relationship with him brought to mind utterly scandalous visions. Blood coursed through her in shock and thrill. She reined in those emotions. She would not become his mistress. Had her ardent response given him that idea? What a fool she was.

"My lady," Mrs. Parker said, stepping outdoors.

Belle caught the woman's compassionate gaze. Had she witnessed hers and Lord Terrance's behavior? *Oh, it did not bear considering.*

"Will you ever forgive me for that note?" the woman asked. "I wanted to explain myself, but his lordship said it would be better to surprise you. Instead, I see I have upset you abominably."

"I thought something horrid had happened to you or your family," Belle said.

The four children laughed and danced around, arms extended, proving her fears false.

"I see they are fine, as are you," she said, smiling at the children's antics. "For that I am pleased."

"Something *has* happened," Mrs. Parker said with a wide smile. "Something wonderful."

She gestured through the open front door to someone inside, and a man stepped out. In his worn cloak and patched breeches, Belle would have thought him uncommonly weary, but his ecstatic smile disabused her of that thought.

Then, from behind the stranger, stepped Mr. Nightingale. The young man wore a proud expression.

Belle glanced at Lord Terrance in concern, for he had not been very pleased with Mr. Nightingale lately. Lord Terrance, however, appeared complacent.

"This," Mrs. Parker said, recapturing her attention, "is my husband, Mr. Parker." Her hands firmly clasped in front of her, she seemed ready to burst with happiness. "Your Lord Terrance has made my Christmas wish come true. My husband is home safe with his family. No words can possibly express my gratitude."

As tears welled into Mrs. Parker's eyes, Belle ran over to hug the woman. "I am so glad for you."

"And I have my doll." Little Margaret held up a rag doll by one of its red braids. Then she wrapped her arms around her father's legs. "I like him better."

The other children quickly agreed with that estimation and joined their sister in hugging their father.

"I am also pleased to be back with Mrs. Parker and my family," Mr. Parker said. "Getting a job in London was not as easy as I had hoped." He looked at Lord Terrance, and for a moment looked nearly as teary-eyed as his wife when he said, "My lord, I truly appreciate you giving me another year to pay off what I owe. I promise to make this farm the best in the country next year, even if I have to be out here every hour of every day."

"Glad I could be of service," Lord Terrance said. "And I hope you know that if you need help again, you are to come to me straightaway."

"The Parkers know that now, my lord," Mr. Nightingale said. "The rest of your tenants will know before sunset. I will be on my way."

"Will you be attending the ball tomorrow, Mr. Nightingale?" Lord Terrance asked.

"Ball, my lord?" The man tipped his head in inquiry.

"My mother hosts a Christmas ball tomorrow, and everyone from the village is invited. There will be food and games, and, I believe, she has arranged for a play to be enacted. As such, there will not be much time for us to speak privately."

"Speak about what, my lord?"

"I have plans for farm improvements. New disciplines I have read about. I want to build milking parlors in Terrance, which will be a better system for promoting hygiene in our dairy farms."

Mr. Nightingale's eyes widened, and he stepped closer, paying rapt attention.

"I hope you will attend our meeting as well, Mr. Parker," Lord Terrance added. "No, I insist on it," he said. "I have some farming theories I want to test out, and I would like to try those techniques on your farm first. I hope you will do me the favor of assisting my agent with this rather large-scale project. Are you both in agreement?"

"Yes, my lord," both men said in unison, their smiles widening even more.

Belle could hardly contain her own smile at their enthusiastic response. She caught Mrs. Parker's gaze, and they shared a moment of silent understanding before returning their attention to the men.

"I, too, have some ideas," Mr. Nightingale said. "I have read good things about four-course rotation for planting crops. Your father did not care to change our current system, but I have it on the best authority, a Mr. Thomas Coke from Norfolk, that they have used this system widely, and it has done excellently."

"Bring your notes to Clearview the day after the ball," Lord Terrance said. "I might send both of you to inspect Mr. Coke's properties and see for yourselves if it is a profitable operation."

"Thank you, my lord," Mr. Nightingale said. He made to leave, then came back to shake Lord Terrance's hand and then, surprisingly, gave him a hug.

Belle bit her lip to keep from laughing at the surprise on Lord Terrance's face and Mr. and Mrs. Parker's shocked and half-frightened expressions.

Mr. Nightingale stepped back, his face pale, as if he had been dismayed by his temerity. When he realized Lord Terrance had not taken offense, his shoulders relaxed, and, with a beaming smile, he left, muttering about row planting and turnips and something about phosphate of lime.

"Shall we return to the manor?" Lord Terrance asked her. "It is almost suppertime."

Belle agreed and bid the Parkers goodbye. Lord Terrance helped her mount and then leaped onto Goodwin.

On the ride back, she remained silent, absorbing all that had happened. Lord Terrance, too, remained quiet, as if what had happened between them were an everyday occurrence.

Belle did not know what to say. Anything she uttered would confirm that she loved him. How would he react to such news? Would he be pleased or embarrassed? He obviously found her desirable. *The most delightful of lovers,* he had said.

After denouncing her during the snowstorm, he seemed to have changed his mind about her motives in coming to Cheshire, and he had just hinted that he wanted her to become his mistress. But could he ever see her as a suitable wife? *Not as long as she believed in spirits,* she thought with an inward sigh.

Though she craved his caresses, she was not sophisticated enough to simply be his lover, nor could she bear the disappointment and shame such a union would generate both within her family and his.

Yet, if she were to admit to him that she loved him, it would make the road easier for him to seduce her. No, she did not believe that. The Lord Terrance she had come to know would be too honorable to take advantage of her weakness. He would want to protect her. Worse, he might pity her.

That would result in no more stolen kisses. And after the ball, he would see to it that she returned home with her grandfather. That might be the best course of action to safeguard her heart. However, the ghost of Clearview still remained. She could not risk being sent home until she cleansed the manor. It would be best all around if she kept her feelings to herself. Then, once she had rid the house of its haunting, she would leave on her own, with no one aware, except Mendal of course, that she departed Clearview with a broken heart.

* * * *

The next evening, while preparing for the ball, Rufus's valet seemed intent on ensuring that his master outshine every other gentleman present. He produced a fine cambric shirt that hugged Rufus's frame and enclosed his neck in a high standing collar.

Rufus was uncertain whether he could turn his head without poking out an eye.

A brilliant white waistcoat and black knee breeches from Westin's had been pressed to a point and flawlessly fitted his figure. Finally, Ellison helped him don a dark blue velvet coat.

The effusive compliments from the valet, who for once seemed sober and enjoying his work, made Rufus conclude that Ellison was even more anxious about this ball than he was.

"It is just a dance," Rufus said.

"My reputation is on the line, my lord," Ellison replied.

Bemused, Rufus left his valet to tidy the room where every available surface seemed covered with discarded shirts, breeches, and cravats, and made his way to the drawing room to await the rest of his family.

After twenty minutes of pacing, he was no closer to his decision about what to do about Belle. Despite his and Phillip's efforts for the past several weeks, he had failed to clear his name. And his time was running out. In less than two weeks, the suspicion that he was a murderer would be made public. The way things looked now, he was more than likely to be facing a hangman's noose than being in a position to declare his feelings to Belle.

He felt a surge of frustration so powerful it made him want to yell for Felton to check to see if everyone else had forgotten about the night's festivities. Thankfully, Phillip strode in before he did something so foolish.

"Sit," his cousin said, looking well-presented and composed. "All that walking looks tiresome."

"Did you see Belle on the stairs?" he asked.

"No."

"Mother?" he asked in exasperation.

"No, and not Susie either."

The door to the drawing room opened, interrupting his retort. Rufus held his breath, waiting for Felton to announce Belle. Instead, the butler announced the Marquess of Alford, Belle's grandfather.

"Good evening, my lord." Rufus bowed. His gaze strayed behind him.

"Good evening, Lord Terrance," Lord Alford said. "I believe my granddaughter is not yet ready. Ladies, you realize? Cannot rush them."

"Of course. My mother and sister have not arrived either. The guests will be here any moment, and there will be no one but us to greet them."

"I am sure we will do a credible job, Rufus." Phillip stood to bow to the marquess.

"My lord," Rufus said, "it is good that we have a moment to speak before the ladies arrive. There is a matter of grave importance I wish to discuss with you."

"I shall leave you to it then," Phillip said and went toward the door. "I shall check with Felton that everything is in order for the evening." He gave Rufus a thumbs-up sign of encouragement behind the marquess before he shut the door.

The elderly gentleman appeared lean and a little pale, attesting to his recent illness.

"Would you care to sit, sir?" Rufus asked, concerned.

Lord Alford accepted the offer with a look of gratitude.

Rufus took a chair nearby. "My lord," he said and paused, his throat suddenly constricted. He cleared it and tried again. "My lord, about your granddaughter. I wish to say I have the most honorable intentions toward her. Since she arrived here, she . . ."

"I had heard that you had your differences," Lord Alford interrupted. "I hope you realize that I sent her only because your mother is a dear friend, and she was concerned about the manor."

"I wish my mother had come to me first."

"Sometimes it is easier to speak with those who are not so close about certain"—he waved his hand in the air—"umm . . . things."

"Tell me you do not place any credence on her wild imaginings, my lord," Rufus said, arching a brow. "I forbade your granddaughter to discuss spirits with my family. She has been graceful enough to accede to my wishes."

"She has?" Lord Alford asked, sounding surprised.

"Why, yes. I have high hopes that she might never mention ghosts again." Lately, he had successfully given Belle other, more earthly desires to occupy her thoughts.

The old gentleman eyed him askance. "Are we still speaking of *my* Belle?"

Damnation! Why was he the only one who did not have permission to address her as *my Belle*? "Indeed," he said aloud. "My lord, I hold your granddaughter in the highest esteem. I care deeply for her."

"But how can you care deeply for her when you place no credence on what she believes?"

"What?" he asked in confusion. What was the old man chattering about?

Before they could finish their conversation, the drawing room doors opened, and his aunt, mother, and sister entered. The two gentlemen stood, and Rufus was astonished by the ladies' beauty.

"Aunt," he said, "as handsomely turned out as ever." His attention swung to his mother. "Mother, you look . . . well, to put it simply, lovely. And Susie, there will not be a lady present who could rival you."

"Oh, thank you, Rufus." Susie rushed to give him a hug. She seemed to do that a great deal of late. He liked it.

"Careful, child," Mrs. Jones said, "or you will ruin all your maid's efforts to bring you to this point of perfection."

Susie smiled and gave Belle's grandfather a pretty curtsey. "Good evening, my lord," she said to Lord Alford. "I am so pleased you could come for the ball."

"As am I," he said. "You are as delightful as your mama said, my dear." He nodded to Lady Terrance. "Constance, I hope you keep well? And thank you for taking such good care of my granddaughter."

Lady Terrance took his hands. "Thank *you*, Alford. Having your granddaughter here has been a godsend. She is adorable. You should be proud of her."

"I am, my dear, I most certainly am."

"Grandpapa!" Belle said as she appeared in the open doorway.

Rufus's breath caught at sight of Belle in her ball gown.

Her yellow gown fit her upper figure like a second skin, the material falling to the floor and pooling behind her. Her silky bodice lovingly hugged her bosom, while a slip of lace tantalizingly hinted at a deep cleavage. Every man who came to the ball would want to uncover its secrets.

He wanted to wrap her in her flowing scarf and take her upstairs so no one else would be as entranced as he. Instead, not only would he have to watch other men pay her homage tonight, he was not free to claim her as his own, not while he was still under suspicion for murder.

Chapter Fifteen

Rufus stood back as Belle ran to greet her grandfather. Then the ladies crowded together, all very pleased with each other's appearance.

Phillip returned to the room and raised everyone's mood further with his fulsome compliments.

Rufus came forward and bowed to Belle. "Good evening. You look lovely."

"Thank you, my lord," she said and curtsied, blushing.

"I hope you will save me a dance?"

Before she could respond, Phillip said to Susie, "As I hope you will save one for me, dear cousin. Rufus and I will be the envy of the ball, leading the prettiest ladies out onto the dance floor."

Susie giggled and hugged Belle. "I cannot imagine why I thought I would hate such entertainment."

"My lord," Felton interrupted. "The first guests arrive."

"Then we had best form the reception line." Rufus led his family to the foyer, while Belle and her grandfather walked into the grand ballroom.

Once everyone had been received, Rufus inspected the various ballrooms and listened to the happy chatter. The house overflowed with guests. He could not take in the change. Where once Clearview had been dour and gloomy, now its rooms sparkled in bright candlelight and sang with cheer.

The green ballroom was filled with villagers who welcomed him as if he were their best friend. No one ran and hid as he approached. News about the Parkers had apparently traveled among the villagers, elevating their opinion of him.

The weight of his father's disappointment in him withered under the villagers' uninhibited approval, as one man after another shook his hand and voiced support for his plans to rejuvenate the farms and properties around Terrance Village. Many had ideas for improving their establishments, which they wanted to speak with him about. Rufus called Mr. Nightingale to his side, and as he moved about the room, he instructed his agent to take notes.

He was still mingling with the villagers when Lady Terrance entered the green ballroom, and everyone grew silent. She carried a mask and wore a cape to portray her as a doctor. Right behind her came a green, scaly dragon puppet born by three village women. Laughter erupted.

Rufus watched in astonishment as his mother and the dragon

women proceeded to entertain everyone with a unique rendition of the old play, *Mysterie of St. George*. He could not contain his smile at her and her friends' antics.

He leaned against the wall, his gaze fastened on his mother's happy countenance. She thrived on these people's affection for her. How long had his father denied her this contact? Certainly as long as he could remember. And why? Because of some silly rule about the behavior of a lady of the manor?

He was about to quit the room, when a heavy-set man waved to catch his attention.

"Milord," the man said.

"Yes?" This gentleman looked familiar, and he sought to remember where he had seen him. Ah, yes. The day Belle arrived at Clearview, this man had accompanied her. He was also the baker who had made him dessert the day Brindle died.

"Pardon me boldness, milord," the man said. "Allow me to introduce meself. Ah am Mr. MacBride, the local baker. Ah consider Lady Terrance, yer mother, a good friend, if ah may be so presumptuous."

"Any friend to my mother is a friend to me." Rufus held out his hand. "I believe I have tasted your pastry. You bake a wonderful lemon tart."

"Thank you, milord." Mr. MacBride appeared pleased Rufus had remembered the small treat.

They shook hands, and then the baker straightened his jacket. "What ah wished to speak to ye about is Mr. Darby."

Rufus's interest kindled. "The late blacksmith?"

"Yes, milord. He, too, wuz a friend of yer mother's. A good friend." Mr. MacBride stepped into an alcove of plants and gestured for Rufus to follow. "Mr. Darby wuz killed. Same time as yer father. In London Town."

"Yes, so I heard." Rufus, his excitement rising, followed the man behind the potted plants.

"I also heard that ye be seeking information about yer father's last days before he left Terrance. After word came of what ye did fer the Parkers, me wife insisted ah speak with ye, milord. About the matter of Mr. Darby, that is."

"What about him?" When the man looked reluctant to continue, Rufus said, "Please speak freely, Mr. MacBride."

"Mr. Darby came to see old Lord Terrance the day before his lordship returned to London."

"Do you know what they spoke about?"

"Mr. Darby, though a good friend, kept mostly to hisself. He did not confide in people. The day he wuz to see the late earl, though, he did tell me wife that he had come across some troubling bit of news."

Rufus's pulse shot up. This was the clue he had been searching for. Now, when he had done nothing to seek it out, it fell right onto his lap. "What news?"

The audience boisterously clapped as the play ended.

"What news did Mr. Darby share?" Rufus asked again.

He cursed inwardly when a man tripped over the potted plant and against Mr. MacBride and said, "Oh, pardon me."

"Good evening, Mr. Langley," the baker said. "Milord, may ah introduce ye to our new blacksmith, Mr. Langley."

"We have met." Rufus nodded to the lean man. The fellow had terrible timing. He wanted to shout at him to go away.

"Pardon me for interrupting," Mr. Langley said. "But, Mr. MacBride, your wife sent me to find you."

"Strange. She wanted me to speak with his lordship. Oh well, women change their minds faster than the wind changes directions. If ye will pardon me, ah will be right back, milord."

In frustration, Rufus watched him skitter back to his wife's side. *What rotten luck.*

"This is a lovely ball you have thrown for us, my lord," Mr. Langley said.

"Thank you, Mr. Langley. Are you enjoying yourself?"

"How could one not?" the man asked. "You have excellent food, and your mother has kept us wonderfully entertained."

"Excuse me, Mr. Langley," Rufus said, knowing he was being rude, but anxious to find the baker and finish their conversation. "I had better see how the rest of my guests fare. Good evening."

He made his way through the crush in the direction he had seen Mr. MacBride depart, but after circling the ballroom twice he could not locate the baker. Perhaps his wife was unwell, and he had taken her to a side chamber to rest. It would be impossible to guess which one.

Tomorrow, he would seek out the baker and learn more, he decided. Tonight, he had a dance to claim with a lovely young lady.

The crush in the grand ballroom was as bad as in the green ballroom. People milled about in small groups or reposed on double rows of chairs by the walls. Several couples danced in the center to the music played by an orchestra in the balcony. He spotted Belle as she traipsed around the floor in the arms of none other than his tall, blond, rakish friend, Lord Fitzgerald.

Rufus's head was ready to explode. The man had disgraced Belle and himself on Rufus's London doorstep, and now he had the temerity to dance with her in public? Did he ogle her as he had that night? Rufus did not care that Fitzgerald had offered for Belle's hand or that it was she who had refused him. He wanted to call his friend out. How could her grandfather have given the bounder permission to dance with her? And who invited him here in the first place?

"Rufus, stop frowning." Susie tapped his arm. "Belle might believe that you dislike her if you glower at her."

He smoothed out his facial expression and said, "Who invited Fitzgerald?"

"Mother did," Susie said. "She invited all your friends."

Rufus felt his temper flare hotter, and he clenched his fists when he saw the bounder had his palm flat against Belle's back. And must her smile be so charming? "How could Mama know my friends?"

"Aunt Henrietta told us."

Stunned by the comment, Rufus turned his attention to his sister. "And how would Aunt Henrietta know who is intimate with me?"

"She knows all your friends," Phillip said.

Rufus had not noticed his cousin's catlike approach. How did he move so softly, and what did he mean, his mother knew him that well?

"She knows every gentleman who routinely shuns her invitations to parties," Phillip said cryptically.

"I beg your pardon?" Rufus said.

"Your friends support you by eschewing my mother's company. They care for you, and since you have held a long standing grudge against your aunt, they show their support by not attending her functions."

"I did not know that." He had not realized his aunt had suffered so because of their enmity. The idea was disturbing on many levels, not least of all because he did not hate her. If anything, he desperately wanted her approval because she was the last direct connection to his father. In fact, her disapproval was a mirror of his father's constant disappointment in him, and while it was too late to change his father's mind, there was still hope he could bring his aunt around to perhaps at least tolerate him.

"I will speak with them," he said in a firm voice. "It will not happen again."

"I am sure she would not care if they attended or not," Phillip said, "as long as you did."

Rufus laughed. "Then you know your mother less well than she appears to know me. She would care for my presence as much as she would Napoleon's. You are all she needs by her side."

"Then it is you who does not know my mother," Phillip said calmly. "The only reason I attend all her affairs is to give her moral support. It hurts her deeply that her only nephew abhors her company and publicly avoids her parties."

"I do not . . . I never . . ." He stopped, unable to finish as the truth sank in. His absence had indicated to his aunt, and apparently also his friends, that he did not care for her. They were all wrong.

And so was he. Until now, he had thought it was his aunt who did not care for him and voiced her disapproval to all and sundry. Instead, it seemed he was the main culprit in their quarrel.

Susie drew his attention with a touch on his arm. "You have not danced with me yet."

The compassionate look in her eyes suggested she understood how much their cousin had upset him.

"Would you do me the honor of this dance, Susie?" he asked, and offered her his elbow.

"I would love to." They joined the flow of dancers.

She moved gracefully, and he found it hard to reconcile the young girl who preferred to keep her plants company with this beautiful young woman who skillfully followed the dance's rhythm.

"You make me proud, Susie," he said.

"How so, Rufus?"

"By being the sister I always knew you to be. Father would be happy to see you tonight."

Her bright smile dimmed. "I make myself happy tonight," she said. "Belle says we cannot count on others for our happiness. Father, too, must look within himself, not outside, for his peace."

He frowned, not quite taking her meaning. What their father might have sought during his lifetime was immaterial. She did have a point though. It was time he stopped wanting to please his father and settled for behaving in a manner in which Rufus Marlesbury approved.

His glance was immediately drawn to his aunt where she was busy whispering behind her fan to one of her cronies. The music stopped. He left Susie with Phillip and made his way toward Henrietta Jones. Was it his imagination, or did the level of noise in her vicinity suddenly drop?

She turned to greet him. "Terrance."

"Aunt," he said and bowed.

Her eyebrow rose in inquiry. "Is Susie in trouble? She seemed happy a moment ago." She gazed anxiously around the ballroom in search of her niece.

"She is with Phillip," he said. "I came to beg a favor."

"Of me?" She blinked several times as if to control some discomforting emotion.

"Yes." He kept his gaze firmly on her and hoped his friends watched him. "I wondered if you would do me the honor of dancing with me."

The closest old biddy gasped. Rufus ignored her and everyone else and held out his hand, palm down.

After the briefest hesitation, she placed her hand on the back of his, and they walked to the room's center. A country tune began, and they joined in.

The second time they came closer, his aunt's gaze, which had followed his movements throughout, faltered and flickered away. Then she looked at him again and asked, "Do you have something you wish to say to me?"

They took a turn round before the four dancers met and then stepped apart. When next they drew close, he said, "Merely to comment on how well you dance, Aunt." He gave her the first genuine smile he had since he was a child. "I hope you will invite me to one of your London events this coming Season. I am sorry I missed so many in the past."

The dance had almost finished before Henrietta spoke again. When they drew close, she whispered, "Thank you, Rufus. You will get the first invite."

At the tune's end, he returned her to the midst of her astonished friends and bowed deeply before departing.

Next, he went in search of Belle. Several of his friends surrounded her and her grandfather, and he mock-berated his friends to step aside. Then he bowed to the marquess.

"Good evening, my lord. Lady Belle." Finally, Rufus faced her companion. "Fitz."

"Terrance," Viscount Fitzgerald said genially. "So you gained enough sense to invite Lady Belle into your house."

The allusion to Fitz's and Belle's previous misconduct was not lost on those who crowded close, most especially the marquess. Rufus could not quite meet the old gentleman's eyes. Nervous laughter broke out among his friends, and Belle blushed prettily.

"I will have you know that Lady Belle is welcome in my home anytime she wishes," Rufus said. "She no longer needs your less than stalwart support to gain entrance."

Fitzgerald's laugh sounded delighted by the direct hit, and he bowed gallantly to show no ill feelings.

"My lord," Rufus said to the marquess, "may I be permitted to lead Lady Belle in the next dance?"

"Well, steady on there, old fellow," Mr. Bosworth said. Rufus's chum from Eton, Bosworth stood a head shorter than Fitzgerald, but he made up for the shortcoming by his wider girth. "The cotillion is promised to me."

"And I am sure you are quite happy to relinquish it to me." Rufus glowered at him.

Bosworth held out his hands in supplication. "If the lady has no objection, you will find none here. I see your disposition has not changed much since we last met, though your taste in ladies has seen a marked improvement."

His friend's slight nod toward Rufus's aunt spoke volumes. He inclined his head in silent communication that his feud with his aunt was indeed over.

"I believe the field is clear," the marquess said with a congratulatory smile.

Rufus thanked him and held out his arm for Belle.

* * * *

She placed her hand on his and allowed him to lead her onto the dance floor. She had dreamed about dancing with him all night long. Whatever the future might hold for them, Belle meant to thoroughly enjoy this one dance, for it might be all she had to treasure of the two of them together for the rest of her life.

As the tune for the "Sir Roger de Coverley" began, Lord Terrance's hand settled on Belle's back, and he drew her close.

Her breath caught in her throat, and she immediately forgot the ball and every other man she had danced with tonight. They followed the couple ahead and, in turn, formed the arch. She followed his lead as if her feet were designed for that purpose.

The faces of the other dancers and the crowd's shouts of laughter receded until only he existed in the swirling, whirling, world of music and light. They spoke not a word, simply dipped and turned, moving as one.

When the music ended, Rufus gestured toward Martin Winfield, who had just arrived with his mother. "You might soon find one more dance partner than you wish."

"We could get some fresh air," Belle suggested.

With an approving smile, he led her onto the balcony. Several couples were present, seeking a moment of quiet conversation from the ballroom's noise and bustle. Despite the chill in the air, Belle did not protest as he guided her out into the moonlit garden. The area was well lit, and they stayed on the cool cobblestone pathway.

If only this night could go on forever, she thought as she gave Rufus a side-glance. He seemed relaxed but lost in thought, and she felt a slight sting that his attention had been so easily drawn away from her.

"If the crush is any indication, the ball seems a success," she said, still warm from the heat generated from dancing. "Thank you for allowing your mother to host it."

He looked at her and smiled. "It is I who should thank you for pursuing the matter."

They stopped beside a large copper beech tree. "I saw your dance with your aunt," she said. "That gesture meant more to her than you can imagine."

"It was brought to my attention that I have played a part in our enmity." He raised his hand, and the backs of his fingers skimmed her cheek as he brushed a tendril of her hair. "Tonight, I hold only good intentions toward those I love."

She felt a lump form in her throat at his words. She so wanted to be one of those people. How difficult it would be to leave this man. To walk away knowing she might never see him again. And if she did meet him, he might belong to some other woman.

"Why so sad on such a wonderful night?" he asked, frowning down at her in concern. "Are you not enjoying yourself? Has someone upset you?"

She shook her head and gestured about them. "I was just thinking that I would miss all this when it comes time to leave."

He caught her hand and brought it to his lips. "You do not ever have to leave."

Her heart jumped like a startled hare. What did he mean?

"Belle, I am asking you to . . ." His words were cut off by a scream from the ballroom.

"What the devil?" he said, releasing her as his head jerked back toward the manor.

"We had best find out what has happened," she suggested, lifting her skirts.

He nodded, and they ran inside. A crowd of people milled about the doorway to the ballroom.

"What is the matter?" he asked.

A gentleman on the outskirts shook his head. "I do not know, my lord. I have not been able to get close enough to see."

"Excuse us," Lord Terrance said firmly and pushed into the crowd until they came to a maid who cowered on the floor, crying hysterically.

Belle crouched and gently touched the woman's arm. "What is wrong? What has happened to upset you so?"

The maid grabbed Belle's shoulders, her eyes wide with terror. Before she spoke, Belle saw an image of what had frightened her.

"A ghost!" the maid said. "I seen a ghost, and it wants to kill me."

Belle doubted the spirit planned to hurt the maid. From her glimpse into the woman's thoughts, the ghost had swooped past and through her, as it had once done with Belle. But it was on the hunt for someone else. Still, that would have been a terrifying experience for the poor woman, and so Belle sympathized with her.

"This is some havey-cavey ball, Terrance," Martin Winfield said, walking up, "with maids running about in hysterics."

Belle studied the man who looked out of breath and pale, as if he had recently been running himself or been frightened. Had he seen the ghost, too, but did not wish to admit to so startlingly an encounter?

"My mother is most distressed," Winfield continued. "I shall have to take her home. No doubt the rest of your guests will do likewise."

"Do as you see fit," Lord Terrance said. He ordered everyone away from the maid, saying she needed quiet, that she was obviously upset. Probably by a shadow. Nothing to worry about.

With Felton's help, he assisted the maid into the library. Belle followed. All the way there, the frightened girl continued to babble on about her experience.

Lord Terrance settled the maid on a chair and said in a firm voice, "There is no such thing as ghosts."

"There is, my lord, I have seen it. I swear." She broke off to slump into the chair and cry.

"I will fetch the housekeeper." Felton hurried from the room, shutting the door behind him to keep out onlookers.

Belle knelt beside the woman. The maid appeared trapped in a state of horror, poor thing.

"What is your name?" she asked in a tranquil voice aimed at calming the hysterical girl. "Can you tell me that? It is an easy question to answer, my dear. Your mother has surely called you by it many times."

The girl took a deep shaky breath. "I am Melinda."

"Such a pretty name," Belle said. "Now, Melinda, I know you are frightened, but we need your help. Can you tell us what happened?"

"Yes, my lady." The maid sat up and straightened her shoulders, her expression growing determined. "I do not want that thing to hurt any of you."

"Thank you, Melinda," Belle said, patting the young woman's hand. "You are a good soul. Now, to make sure none of us are harmed, tell us where you saw this ghost."

"You are not serious?" Lord Terrance's tone bordered on derisive. "Why encourage her in her delusion?"

Belle ignored his interruption. "Where, Melinda. Where did you see it?"

"Upstairs, my lady, on the third floor. I was changing the guest room linen on the second floor when the housekeeper asked me to dust the portraits hall. Seems some guests had gone there and complained they were dusty." She gave Lord Terrance an apologetic glance. "It is because the servants dread that floor, my lord. Not because we are lazy."

"Of course you are not lazy. Go on with your story." Belle encouraged, but she had her suspicions about where the maid and ghost confrontation took place.

"Well, all went well until I reached the picture of your father, my lord. Then this shadow swooped into me." Her shoulders slumped again as the memory brought a fresh array of tears.

"Now see what you have done," Lord Terrance said. "She has gone off into hysterics."

Belle stood and hurried to the door.

"Where are you going?" he asked. "You are not leaving me with this crying woman."

"Felton will be here shortly, my lord," Belle said. "Keep her calm. I must find the ghost before he ruins the ball."

She slipped out the door to the hallway before he could protest and hurried toward the stairs.

As she climbed them, she thought about the matter and knew that having all these people in the house could have stirred the ghost's ire. He was not the most sociable of spirits. Or had the one person whom the ghost thought a traitor come to the ball?

She stopped at her room and took the precaution of collecting Earnest. Not that he could be of much help, but he had been present the other time she looked for the ghost, and they had a partnership in the endeavor. Besides, she did not care to confront the ghost alone, and no one but her grandfather would likely come, and his health was not sufficient to confront ghosts.

With Earnest in tow, she and the hound then hurried toward the stairs.

Just as they reached them, Lord Terrance ascended from the ground floor. "There you are." He looked stern and forbidding. "So, what you said about not talking about ghosts was a lie?"

"No lie, my lord. I said I would not speak of such things with your family, and I have not."

"But you have not given up the notion my home is haunted?"

"Clearview *is* haunted. By your father."

His head jerked back as if she had slapped him, and she said gently, "I am sorry to break the news in such a bald fashion, but it is the truth. I have seen and spoken with him on two occasions, and I have sensed him several other times. He has visited your mother every night since the day his body was brought home for burial. I have distracted her at night so that he would not bother her, but that does not change the fact that the spirit is here."

* * * *

Rufus stared at Belle as each of her statements washed over him in a fresh wave of despair. He thought he loved her, but he did not even know this woman. And then the revelation of her words hit him, and his breathing constricted. This was the secret he had sensed within his family.

"You, Mama, Susie and Phillip," he said, knowing the answer already. The familiarity between the four that was inexplicable. "This is your secret. You have all been working to rid my house of a ghost?"

"I am sorry," she said.

"After you promised you would not involve them in your ghost stories, you broke your word."

"No, I did not."

She reached for him, but he stepped away. She folded her arms, as if to avoid the temptation to reach for him again. "I never once spoke of a ghost to them. Well, once, to Susie the day after I arrived, and she told me your mother was not sleeping. I told her I needed her help in distracting your mother. All we did from then on was play billiards into the small hours. A game at which your sister excels. She has fleeced us of many a coin."

"You included Phillip in these games? A man who is a stranger to you?" That idea of their secret games burnt an acidic hole in his chest. "Yet you could not include me? Was I a joke then, between all of you? How we fooled Rufus. Leave him out of our play."

A tender, treacherous look crept into her gaze. "It was not like that, my lord. Phillip caught me raiding the kitchen that first night. Then Susie trudged in, and we were forced to let him into our secret. It was only meant to be Lady Terrance, Susie, and me."

"Of course," he said. "Now I see why my mother refers to you as '*my Belle.*' You belong to everyone but me. You trust my sister, my mother, and even my cousin, but not me. You thought me incapable of helping you. Of taking care of anyone."

"I do trust you, Rufus."

Now she called him by his name, when it sounded as much an insult as when his aunt called him "Terrance."

"You have lied to me every day that you have been here," he said. "That is not trust. Were your kisses lies as well? Did you seduce me to keep me from catching onto your game?" When she did not answer, he grabbed her shoulders and pulled her to him. "Did you?"

"No! Rufus, I love you."

"Hah!" He gave a harsh laugh. He moved farther away from her, unable to countenance her close presence. The memory of her grandfather's words surfaced.

"How can you love me," he asked her, the words tainting his mouth with poison, "when you do not know what I care about? What matters to me are truth, honesty, and acceptance, none of which, by your own admission, you have ever shown me."

"I wanted to help your mother." Her tearful gaze pleaded with him for understanding. "You made me promise not to speak of ghosts. How could I confide in you about my findings?"

"And what have you found?" he said in a scoffing tone.

She took a deep breath, as if preparing for a terrible disclosure. Despite her lies and betrayals, he leaned forward, wanting to hear her justifications. *Damn it, I still love you.*

"The ghost haunting Clearview is your father. I believe he is searching for his killer in this house, someone whom he calls a traitor."

His mind whirled, and he could not understand what she implied. *I live here and I'm the only one who is under suspicion of murdering my father.* She could have heard about that rumor in London. *Since there is no such thing as a ghost, did this mean she suspects that I not only killed my father but that I might also be a traitor?*

"Get out." He said the words through clenched teeth.

"I beg your pardon?" she said, looking confused.

"Leave Clearview. Do not cross my sight again. Nor contact my mother, my sister, or my cousin. They will no longer be your lackeys. And never, *ever* speak to me again. Have I made myself clear, Lady Belle?"

Face blanched, she stepped back.

Earnest whined and sat on the landing beside her, tail wagging, eyes beseeching.

He pointed to the hound. "And take that traitor with you."

Chapter Sixteen

Rufus had not slept a wink all night. He paced in his bedchamber, lit by a lone candle set high on the mantle. It was still pitch black outside, a condition that matched his mood and future outlook. The ball had ended hours ago.

Once news of his argument with Belle spread—it had been loud enough and the place packed with people—first his guests left, and then his friends abandoned him for the Briar Inn. They were not the only ones upset with him. The moment he had asked Belle to leave, he had wanted to retract his words.

Come sunrise, Belle, too, would depart his home, and he was endlessly rethinking letting her go. He was discovering that he did not care that she had lied to him. Or that she believed in ghosts. Or held a low opinion of him. He was on the verge of begging her to stay.

Ellison entered then, wearing a frown that looked as if it had taken permanent hold on the man's craggy face.

"What is it?" Rufus was in no mood to tolerate one of his servant's harangues.

The valet held a lit candelabra, which he set on a nearby table and produced a note from his breast pocket.

Rufus took the letter and dismissed the surly valet. The missive was marked urgent on the outside with his name beneath. That precise lettering pricked an uneasy chord of alarm. He recognized that writing. A similar penmanship had lured his father to Richmond Park on the night he died.

He knew because on Rufus's return to the London townhouse, he had learned that his father had left on an urgent, mysterious errand. He had found that scrunched up note on the study desk. The writer purported to have Rufus in custody and had threatened to murder him unless his father brought specified shipyard documents that were in his custody.

Rufus could not believe his father was being blackmailed over a commercial enterprise, and someone had used Rufus as bait. He had raced to the meeting place to assure his father he was safe. He arrived too late, and a moment later, a bow street runner found him crouched over his father's lifeless body.

The next morning, Rufus received the summons from the Regent. As the son of an earl, Rufus had not expected to be hauled into gaol despite his suspicious presence at the crime scene or the incriminating blood on his gloves. But neither had he expected a royal summons about the case the very next morning.

Troubled, and deep in grief, he had brought the letter as proof that a villain was at play in his father's murder. That evidence had gained him six months leniency in which to clear his name, else he might have been clapped into irons and thrown into prison that very day.

Rufus moved toward the lit candle and ripped open this newest missive, expecting another trap.

My lord,

Come to the southern edge of the mere. Take the old mill road. Come alone. I have news that is only for your ears. No one must know we are to meet.

Your obedient servant,
Mr. MacBride

Rufus would have bet his last shilling that Mr. MacBride had not penned this note because there was not a Gaelic phrase in sight.

Rufus took the candle to his writing desk and sat to pen his own gambit in this murderous game of cat and mouse. This puzzle had been difficult to piece together, none of it making sense individually, but a grander picture was forming in his mind. For if the Regent was interested in these events, then treason must somehow be at the root of it.

Rufus gambled that whatever this killer was after, he had not yet obtained it despite committing two murders, nay three—his father, Darby, and most recently, Brindle. And the coincidental timing of Darby's death, which, according to Phillip, had occurred in London the day before Rufus's father was killed, added the late blacksmith as a vital piece in this puzzle box.

So he wrote that he had his father's shipyard documents, and if "Mr. MacBride" wished to ever lay hands on them, he had better come to Clearview at ten this morning, else those documents would be surrendered to the Crown.

He surmised that whoever used the hapless baker as a pawn, could most easily be contacted at the MacBride residence, and he rang for Ellison to hand-deliver his letter.

* * * *

An hour before ten, Rufus, his nerves on edge, gazed out his tall study windows onto the courtyard where Belle and her grandfather prepared to depart Clearview. The dog barked in protest. For once,

Rufus agreed.

He wanted to lean out the window and shout, *Belle, please stay.* But pride, and a looming battle with his father's killer, prevented the plea from escaping.

A footman carried a large birdcage to the carriage. Inside those bars, an owl fluttered its wings. No longer sporting bandages, the bird looked ready to take flight.

Belle must have taken good care of it for the bird to heal so quickly. He had seen it often enough, whenever he carried her while her ankle mended, but he had been too focused on controlling his desire to crawl into her bed, so he had never asked after the recovering bird.

Earnest jumped inside the conveyance last, the door shut, and the vehicle lumbered along the long drive.

Rufus squashed the urge to chase after them and turned away from the window.

An emptiness born of their departure swept into Clearview, an ill wind that stole into his study and settled in his heart like a weighty lump of iron. He shrugged to dislodge his sorrow. Now was not the time to become mired in despair. There would be time enough for that later.

Today, he had a murderer to catch.

He rang for Felton.

The butler entered, his face a mask of disapproval. Once rumor had spread among his servants that their master had ordered Belle to leave his home—likely from Ellison, who had an earhole for any hint of gossip—every servant had apparently been issued one of those masks. "Yes, my lord?"

"I expect a visitor this morning. See that he or she is shown to the third floor drawing room."

That should not only keep him far enough away from eavesdroppers, but it should keep his family and servants from being harmed by stray shots.

For a moment, surprise shifted his butler's mask, but then he readjusted it into place. "I shall order a maid to ready the room."

Rufus nodded his dismissal, and the butler bowed and retreated.

Before the old retainer shut the door, Rufus said, "Felton."

"Yes, my lord?"

"I shall count on you to see that my guest and I are not disturbed."

Now worry wreathed Felton's face. Years of service, however, prevented him questioning his master. He obediently acknowledged the order and left.

Rufus waited until the upstairs room was ready, and then he climbed to the third floor. Upon reaching his destination, he looked about.

Candles blazed on the mantle and side tables. The room sported a few high-backed chairs positioned against the walls and a settee and armchairs by the hearth where a healthy fire blazed. Sparks spit, and coal shifted.

He pulled out the letter he had received this morning and read it one last time. Then he balled the paper in his fist and tossed the crumpled sheet into the fire. It crackled and burst into flames. Taking out his father's watch, Rufus checked the time. The games were about to begin. He hoped that this appointment with a traitor would end in the capture of his father's murderer and not in Rufus's demise.

* * * *

"Grandpapa," Belle said, as the carriage reached the village outskirts, "may we stop at the Briar Inn?"

He was seated across from her and looked at her in surprise, his faded version of her violet eyes catching and holding her gaze. "I thought you could not wait another moment to depart Terrance Village, my dear. Did we not leave a note for the countess instead of waiting for her to rise so we could leave quicker?"

She stared out the window with what felt like a lump of coal constricting her throat. The trees and homes blurred.

"Belle, my dearest child," her grandfather said, "will you not tell me what has upset you? Was it Lord Terrance?"

"What makes you ask that?"

"Yesterday, he mentioned he had only honorable intentions toward you. I took that to mean he planned to propose."

Belle stared at him, startled. Then Rufus *did* love her. She turned to look out the window again and bit her scrunched up handkerchief to keep from crying out.

No, he had *loved* her. In the past tense.

She had ruined everything by going on about the ghost. Even now she could see his hurt expression when he realized she had lied. She hid her face, for her tears would not cease.

"My lady." Mendal sounded teary, too. "A man in love with you is nothing to cry about. How I wish you had a mama to talk to at times like these."

"Mendal, why must you bring that up now?" Belle asked and cried even harder.

"Now, now." Her grandfather patted her knee. "If you would but tell us what ails you, we might be able to be of aid."

"All I want, Grandpapa, is a chance to release Lady Sefton," she said between gulping sobs. "The owl is well enough to be set free. I do not want anything caged around me ever again. It is too cruel and unkind."

"But the cage is for the bird's safety, my lady," her maid said. "It healed quicker because it was safe inside the bars."

"Love is a cage," she said in a muffled voice. "It seeks to trap you and keep you confined, never allowing you to soar."

"You have it backwards, Belle, my dear," her grandfather said. "Love does not seek to tie you down but to allow you to be everything you were meant to be. And now I see where our problem lies. Lord Terrance does not believe in your talent. He told me as much."

When she did not reply, he nodded as if in understanding. "I hinted to him yesterday that he did not know you as he should. You are correct, child. It is best that we leave. I should never have asked you to come to Clearview. This is my fault."

"No, Grandpapa," Belle said. "Please do not say that. I came because I wished to be of help. Not that I have done much good at Clearview. I did not discharge the ghost, and if anything, I have turned one family member against the other and caused more disruption rather than bringing harmony into his home. Lord Terrance is right to send me away."

"Ahh," he said.

They traveled in silence from then on until the carriage reached the inn's courtyard.

Belle asked her grandfather to procure a private parlor as it might take her a while to settle the bird in the stables where it would find ample rodents to hunt until the winter weather had passed. She wanted to ensure the owl could fly properly and find a place to perch away from harm.

Mendal wanted to come with her, but Belle sent her after the marquess, saying she wished to do this alone. "I will be fine, Mendal. See to Grandpapa's needs."

Seeing that her maid was still worried, Belle called a young stable boy of about nine over and gave him the cage. "There, now I have an escort. What is your name, lad?"

"Dobby, miss."

"Well, Dobby, if anything untoward happens to me, will you promise to run to the inn and find this lady?"

"Yes, miss."

"All right, Mendal?" Belle asked. "And I shall have Earnest with me."

Mendal gave the dog a dubious look and then fished out a silver coin to show to the stable lad. "You will get this when the lady returns unharmed. Understand?"

The boy's eyes became fixated on the prize. "Yes, miss! I promise to take proper care of her. On my honor."

Earnest followed them toward the stable. He wagged his tail, but Belle could tell by the sadness in his eyes that he would have preferred to stay with Lord Terrance at Clearview. Although afraid of the house, Earnest was now attached to its master.

You and I, both, she silently commiserated. "But he has thrown us both out of his home, Earnest, and this time, I will not buck his wishes."

Like her, Earnest must learn to settle for her company alone. The years ahead stretched lonely and forsaken. She doubted that either she or Earnest would ever be as happy as they had been at Clearview these past few weeks. She recalled her words to Susie about the need to create one's own happiness. It was time she practiced living those words.

Belle informed the stable master that she intended to release the owl within his stables, and he immediately balked.

"But the owl could be an asset, sir," she said. "It would keep down the number of voles, shrews, and wood mice and might even deter strangers from the stables at night."

His frown cleared at that last suggestion. "There was a murder on the premises, recently," he said. "I suppose a night guard who is unlikely to fall asleep could be a valuable asset."

"Excellent thinking," Belle said.

Dobby carried the cage and led the way up the steps leading to the loft. Belle and Earnest followed behind him. She was glad to get away from the mucky scent of hot horses and manure and inhale the dusty but sweet scent of fresh hay.

Once the cage was settled on the straw-laden floor, she opened its door. Then she shooed the stable boy and Earnest back, and all three sat and waited for Lady Sefton to venture outside her familiar confines.

Belle watched the owl, speaking gently and picturing cozy corners where the owl might find a safe resting place.

Lady Sefton twisted her head in all directions, scrutinizing the rafters, the straw beds, the horses and men far below. Finally, she hopped onto the straw-laid floor.

"Ah!" Dobby whispered. "She is beautiful."

Belle patted his shoulder in approval, confident that Lady Sefton would now have a new caretaker.

The owl fluttered her wings and took to the ceiling. She faltered in flight, and Belle sucked in her breath. But then Lady Sefton soared toward the tall timbered ceiling and found a perch by an opening near the top.

Earnest barked once in congratulation, and the barn owl fluffed her feathers to show her satisfaction with her new abode.

Belle closed the cage door. Lady Sefton's flight to freedom symbolized the end of a chapter—a sad parting for both of them, but Belle was happy the bird would live in her natural environment.

"I suppose we should return below," she said to Dobby.

He nodded, scrambled up, and headed for the stairs.

She stood and then staggered, her breath knocked out of her as her current surroundings shifted out of focus, and a new one appeared. Instead of the loft with piles of sweet smelling hay bales, she was in a darkened room that stank of stale sweat, blood, and fear. And in a far corner of this room, a woman, whose wrists were rubbed raw because a rope bound her hands tight, quietly sobbed.

The vision faded as quickly as it came. Belle hesitated. She could run down and ask the stable master to look for a woman somewhere in the stables who was being held prisoner. However, that conversation would likely go much worse than the one about Lady Sefton invading his stable. But neither could she simply leave if there was an innocent woman somewhere here, possibly about to be molested or killed. And who was to say it was the stable master who held the woman captive?

She glanced below, where men brushed horses, cleaned equipment, or mucked out soiled straw. Each stall either housed a horse or remained empty. None held a prisoner.

Dobby came back and looked below. "What is the matter, miss?"

"I am not sure yet, but we are going find out." She hurried downstairs. A crude man might have the temerity to manhandle a poor servant girl, but he would hesitate before he attempted the same with a lady from the nobility—and in front of witnesses.

Earnest and the stable boy followed Belle down from the loft and along the stables. She nodded absently to the stable master, who was speaking to another man, and moved on before he could stop her. She did not slow until she reached a side entrance into an area where packed earth covered the ground instead of straw.

"No one is allowed there 'cept with the blacksmith's permission, miss," Dobby said. "You should not go in there."

"Wait here for me," she said. "If I am not back in a few minutes, find Mendal and tell her that she is to find some strong men and come looking for me. Do you understand?"

The boy nodded, his wide-open eyes gleaming with excitement.

Satisfied he would obey her instructions, she and Earnest ventured into the blacksmith's arena.

The place was quiet. To the far left, doors were flung wide open so sunlight cheerfully swept in. This area was large enough so that a wagon could be rolled in to have work done on it.

She turned right, toward a darker section, and came upon a workbench at one end beside which sat a water tub and an anvil. A table to the side held all manner of strange tools. Racks hung on the wall with horseshoes and steel rods. On the anvil's other side, a good six feet away, was a large forge and a coal bin.

She eyed the several doors leading off from this section. One in particular drew her. She opened that door, and hinges creaked. She walked in absolutely certain the bound woman was nearby.

There were no windows inside, so it took a moment to adapt to the darkness. She squinted. Was that a cot? And two piles of lumpy bedding piled on the floor beside it.

"Maybe this will help."

Belle yelped and swung around. A laborer, wearing a large black leather apron overtop his clothes, stood in the doorway with a lantern in one hand and a doubled-barreled fouling piece in the other. His light fell across the room and outlined the two lumps by the bed as Mr. and Mrs. MacBride. Belle's heart thudded in fear for them and for herself. This was more than a servant girl being molested. The MacBrides were tied and had rags stuffed into their mouths. Their terrified gazes pleaded with her for help.

The laborer shut the door behind him.

Earnest growled and bared his teeth.

He aimed his pistol lower. "I suggest you hold onto that dog if you do not want him dead."

Belle laid a restraining hand on Earnest. The look in the man's sinister eyes suggested that neither she nor Earnest had much longer to live.

"Someone will look for me soon," she said.

The intruder laughed. "I hope you are not relying on young Dobby to assist you, milady. I have already dispatched him on an errand that should take him far away. He seemed most disappointed, but he is not foolish enough to disobey me."

"Who are you?" she asked.

"Mr. Langley, the blacksmith." He gave a bow that was no more than a presumptuous tilt of his head.

"I am sorry to have intruded, sir," Belle said, trying to play to his arrogance. "But why do you keep these good people tied up?" If she distracted him enough, Earnest could leap up and dislodge his weapon.

"Why?" Mr. Langley repeated. "For gold, of course. Why else would a decent man do evil deeds in this blighted life? Now, my master, he has motives other than wealth."

"Who is your master?"

"Never you mind. You will not live long enough to use the information, so there is no need to burden you with it."

She tilted her chin upward. "If you harm me, Lord Terrance will not rest until you are captured." Surely the earl's name carried some weight with this villager.

Apparently her threat only amused Mr. Langley, for he laughed. "Shortly, he will be no more alive than you." He vaguely waved his gun. "My master is off to dispatch him, as he did his lordship's father. By the time anyone is wise to the murder, we will all be richer and too far from England to worry about repercussions."

She shivered with terror. They planned to kill Rufus. Fear for her own safety vanished. She would have rushed the man, but she sensed they were no longer alone. Someone else had entered the room, and whoever he was, he was no longer alive. Could it be Brindle, the man she had seen murdered in this stable? Spirits who were killed unexpectedly often lingered at the site of their demise.

And then the air above Langley's left shoulder shimmered.

The blacksmith followed her gaze just as the shimmer materialized into a square-shaped iron piece aimed at Langley's head. Langley shouted in alarm and jumped aside as a ghostly hammer struck. The weapon missed his head and smashed across his right hand.

Mr. Langley screamed and dropped his weapon.

Belle released Earnest. "Get him!"

The hound leaped at the ruffian and brought him to the ground.

"Earnest, stay!"

The hound stood over Langley, his powerful jaws within tasting distance of the man's throat and dripping saliva.

Quickly, Belle grabbed the fowling piece. Placing it on the cot and out of Langley's reach, she released the MacBrides. Once they were untied, she sent the sobbing baker's wife to fetch the stable master.

She then gave Mr. MacBride Langley's weapon. The man's hands trembled more than hers, but he took the fouling piece with a fierce, determined expression. In threatening his wife, Langley had apparently crossed the MacBride retreat line.

Satisfied Langley was not going anywhere, she was about to go find the stable master, when a ghostly whisper stopped her.

Little time left. A hefty spirit appeared beside Mr. MacBride, holding that ghostly hammer.

This is not Brindle was Belle's first thought. Her memory had shown that murdered man as slender and gaunt. She gave a small shake of her head. Terrance Village seemed hectic with restless spirits. Fortunately for her and the MacBrides, whoever this ghost was, he was not Langley's friend.

The baker turned, and on seeing the ghost shadowing him, he screamed and dropped the fowling piece. The weapon hit the ground and fired, barely missing Langley's foot.

Langley swore and, shoving Earnest to the side, lunged for the weapon, but that ghostly hammer descended again.

Langley backed away frantically, and the steel slammed on the ground, barely missing his fingers.

Belle retrieved the fowling piece and placed it back into Mr. MacBride's grip. "Sir, are you able to hit him with this if he moves?"

The baker waved it at the ghost. "That . . . that is Mr. Darby!"

Belle nodded, finally understanding this spirit's wish to help her, as well as why he had appeared here, of all places. Though this man had died in London, he was the blacksmith Langley replaced. This stable had been his domain.

I could not save his lordship, the ghostly Mr. Darby said. *Now you must save my Constance.*

My Constance? She frowned. Did he mean Lady Terrance? Why would she be in danger? Langley had said the killer meant to harm Rufus. Then a fresh vision blasted her, and she cringed from its heat.

Oh dear heavens! Clearview was about to go up in flames—and Rufus and his family and servants with it!

Leaving Langley in Mr. Darby's ghostly, and Mr. MacBride's shaky, care, she raced into the main barn and passed the stable master, who was running toward her with Mrs. MacBride.

There was no time for talk. She had to stop Clearview from being burned to the ground and all its occupants from being burned alive. She spotted a stable hand with a saddled horse. Shoving him aside, she mounted, and, with a kick, they trotted out the open barn doors.

Her grandfather and Mendal came out of the inn with Dobby racing ahead of them and yelling, "The lady is in danger!"

"Rufus needs me," she shouted and then urged her horse into a canter that quickly turned into a gallop back to Clearview. Earnest chased after her, barking.

Belle forgot Rufus's order to never speak to him again. She did not care if he hated her. She loved him, his family, and his home, and she would not stand by while they all perished.

A forlorn howl drew her glance backward. Unable to match the horse's speed, Earnest lagged behind.

"I am sorry, Earnest." She sent her message with voice and thought. "Go back. Keep Grandpapa and Mendal away from Clearview. It is too dangerous there for any of you."

Too soon, she lost sight of the dog and forgot about him. The countryside whizzed by, and her horse's hoofs pounded the dirt road, while in her ear, Rufus, trapped inside a burning Clearview, shouted, "Belle!"

Chapter Seventeen

Rufus straightened a tilted frame in the third floor drawing room. This time, the game of cat and mouse would be played on his terms. He had loaded his father's dueling pistol earlier, and it rested heavy against his ribs. He absently took out his father's gold watch and rolled it with one hand while he waited. He checked the watch again. Fifteen minutes to the appointed time.

Would the coward show? Would he face the man whose father he had murdered?

He checked the watch and then restlessly turned it over. On the second roll, he caught a glimpse of an inscription on the back and paused to read.

Before me, my king. Behind me, my liege's future.

A strange saying. He could not recall seeing it before, but then his father had not been one for sharing intimacies. Even ones as simple as showing off his new gold watch to his son. He read the words again.

Before me, my King . . .

He suddenly remembered kissing Belle for the first time beside his father's portrait. And directly across from that portrait was one of King George.

Rufus dropped the watch on the end table and hurried out to the corridor and toward the gallery.

* * * *

On his return to the drawing room, Phillip was there. His cousin held his father's watch in his hand, reading its inscription. Uneasiness crept into the room.

"I have been looking for this for ages," Phillip said. "Where did you find it?"

"Father had it on his person the day he died. What are you doing here?"

"Last summer, when you asked me to look through my uncle's effects for what I might want, I searched for this watch. It was not among his possessions."

Phillip seemed intent on the watch. Rufus moved away from the doorway. He circled the room, remembering the day he found his father's corpse. He had been shocked, saddened, and desperately unhappy. He had searched the body for a clue as to why or how this abomination could have happened. The only thing he had found was the watch. Absently, he had pocketed it.

When it came time to dispose of his father's effects in the London townhouse, his mother and sister had both declined to assist and bade him to deal with that unpleasant detail. He had called together Phillip and his aunt. His aunt had asked for many of his father's collectibles. Phillip had searched carefully through everything and asked if there was anything else Rufus had missed.

"Why do you want the watch?" Rufus asked now.

"Uncle said he had intended to will it to me."

Rufus gave his cousin a startled glance. "Did he know his time was near?"

Phillip glanced up at him and smiled. "No, nothing like that. He simply said that if anything were to befall him, he wanted me to have the watch. Will you excuse me a moment?"

Rufus nodded as Phillip left the room. He waited. His cousin would be back. Within a few moments, he was.

"You found it then?" Phillip said.

Rufus stood perfectly still, not wanting to accept the thoughts nagging at the back of his mind. "Found what?"

"Do not play games with me, Rufus." Phillip waved the watch at him. "This is serious."

"I agree, my father's murder is serious. Is there something you wish to confide in me, Phillip?" he asked.

His cousin advanced toward him with a purposeful stride.

"This seems to be the week of betrayals," Rufus murmured, and backed away. "But Belle has beaten you to breaking my heart. Nothing you say could hurt me more." He laughed, a bitter sound to his ears. "So, proceed, Cousin. Tell me you know how and why my father was murdered. Tell me he trusted you more than me."

Phillip shrugged. "I did not mean to lie to you. There are some things I was simply not at liberty to share. But I need those plans, Rufus." Phillip moved in, right hand outstretched. "If you give me what you found behind your father's portrait, I will tell you all. I promise."

Fool that he was, a small part of Rufus had hoped Phillip would deny all knowledge on this subject. But what Rufus had told Phillip earlier stood. If he could not trust his cousin, he could not trust anyone. He pulled out the sheath of folded papers that he had tucked into his jacket and offered them. "I only glanced at them. They look like the ship plans my father was being blackmailed about."

Phillip snatched the pages and scanned them. "They are. For our new fleet. The vessels are close to completion. These plans and dispatches would tell the enemy our strengths and weaknesses and could turn the war in Bonaparte's favor."

"So I was suspected of being both a traitor *and* a killer?"

His cousin made eye contact. "The Regent gave you time to prove your innocence."

"But not alone?"

Phillip's lips quirked. "I have been of assistance to His Royal Highness in the past, so he sent me to locate the missing documents and ascertain if, indeed, you were a traitor."

"You have the papers," Rufus said, his chest tight. "That leaves you to determine my guilt or innocence."

"I determined that long ago, Cousin. When I was ten and you saved me from a thrashing by confessing that you took your father's snuffbox when I had done it on a lark. You would never betray anyone, never mind England. That type of villainy is not in your makeup. I convinced my mother to come to Clearview so I could accompany her and prove your innocence."

"How touching," a man said from the doorway, the words layered in sarcasm.

Rufus swung around to find Martin Winfield shutting the door behind him. He aimed his pistol at them. "I will take those papers, Jones. So kind of you to fetch them for me, Terrance."

So, Winfield was the killer. Rufus felt a cool thirst for revenge steal over him, and instead of surprise, his estimation of his neighbor's cowardly character was merely confirmed.

Winfield motioned Phillip to stay in place. "I will take those papers. Toss them to me, sir. Gently!"

Phillip hesitated a moment and then threw the packet at him. As the man's eyes followed the flying pages, Rufus drew his gun, cocked, and fired.

Winfield's head jerked at the sound of the pistol cocking, and instead of reaching for the papers, he dove for the floor.

Phillip drew his pistol and aimed it at Winfield. "Lie still."

"I suspect my cousin, too, has murder in his heart," Rufus said and calmly took out the small ramrod and set to ramming another charge and ball down the barrel of his pistol. "I would not move an inch."

Footsteps sounded outside, and then a loud argument ensued. Since Rufus had said he did not wish to be disturbed, Felton, once he had shown Winfield into this room, must have decided to personally bar entrance to anyone else. Unfortunately, Rufus recognized the lady's dulcet tones.

Dammit! Why would Belle never listen to him when he told her to stay away?

Suddenly, Winfield rose from the floor and raced for the door. Rufus took after him. Phillip fired, and the ball hit the doorframe. Winfield flung open the door.

Outside Belle and Felton turned, eyes wide in surprise.

Rufus shouted a warning, but before he could get to Belle, Winfield pulled her to him and aimed his pistol at her head. "I think not, gentlemen."

Phillip, in the midst of reloading, paused.

Rufus was ready to fire but could do nothing with Belle in the way.

"How dare you manhandle me, sir?" Belle squirmed in Winfield's embrace. "Release me this instant!"

"Hold still, Belle." Rufus swallowed hard as an image of her on the ground with a hole in her head, like his father, swam through his mind. "Hurt her, Winfield, and I will . . ."

"Will what, Terrance?" Winfield motioned for Felton to step into the room. "Kill me? Unlikely, old son. In case it escaped your notice, I have the upper hand, as I have had all along. Drop your weapons, gentlemen. Or as surely as I shot your father, Terrance, I will finish her."

As Phillip obeyed and dropped his gun, Rufus's breath left his chest in a gush of dismay. Then he, too, laid his pistol down.

Felton took that moment to bravely charge for the open door. Winfield struck him over the back of his head, and the butler crumpled.

"Damn you!" Rufus said. The old butler's chest moved with labored breaths. At least the fiend had not killed him. "There was no call for that. He is an old man."

"He was attempting to ruin my fun," Winfield said in a reasonable tone and used his foot to shove the butler into the room, then he entered and shut the door. One arm wrapped around Belle, he moved a chair against the door and jammed it against the handle.

To prevent any further would-be rescuers who might have heard that shot and come to investigate, Rufus realized. Careful bastard.

Winfield motioned Phillip and him back before he kicked aside their dropped pistols. Then, one by one, starting with Rufus, he bade Belle to tie them up with slender ropes he produced from an inner pocket. He double-checked each knot to ensure she did not leave any loose. Felton alone remained unbound, but he was unconscious.

Once Belle was also secured to a chair, Winfield turned his attention to the scattered documents on the carpet. He carefully scanned the pages, his smile growing triumphant.

With each passing moment, any hope someone would come upstairs to check on the noise faded. Felton must have informed the servants that no one was to interrupt the master once his guest arrived. Though did he really want his mother or sister to walk in on this madman?

Winfield straightened from the floor and tucked the documents inside his jacket. "After months of seeking entry into this mausoleum and being foiled, this morning's work has made those earlier failures feel less frustrating."

Rufus glance at Phillip. His cousin looked as nonchalant as ever, but Rufus now realized that look of ennui was a façade that hid deep secrets. They might not be in as big a fix as he had thought. Phillip's relaxed demeanor gave him the only ray of hope in this situation.

"Foiled how?" he asked to give Phillip time to act on whatever plan his cousin brewed in his devious brain. "You have only entered my home twice in recent weeks. Once when Belle was injured, and then again for the ball."

"Yes," Winfield said. "That accursed ball. If you had held it at my home, as I suggested, I would have had a clear field to enter Clearview while it lay empty. Instead, you had to have it here. When I finally could search the upper floors, that mutton-headed maid's hysteria ruined my attempt."

So that is why the maid had broken down. Rufus glanced at Belle to see if she had come to the same conclusion, that the maid had probably seen Winfield up here and mistaken his clandestine movements for a ghost.

Belle returned his look and then shook her head.

No? She stuck to her ghost theory despite obvious evidence to the contrary?

"But all that is past," Winfield rambled on. "I forgive you since you did find these papers for me. Your father would be proud of your deductive abilities."

"You will not get away," Rufus said. Had Phillip's right shoulders shifted to an awkward angle? If so, then Rufus needed to keep Winfield's attention on him.

"Do not say you hold hopes of coming after me." Winfield's laugh blared. "We cannot have that, can we? I need several hours to see me safely to my ship. The trouble is, if I were to dispatch each of you, that would amount to a lot reloading, but the noise might bring the attention of your household, where that one shot did not." He tapped a finger against his chin. "Hmm. What to do?"

"Leave, please!" Belle sounded desperate, her voice cracking.

Rufus wanted to wrap her into his arms and hold her safe, to tell her he would protect her at all costs. Unfortunately, he could not do any of that because he was tied to this blasted chair.

Winfield ignored her and gazed around, as if seeking inspiration, and then settled on a lighted candle. He plucked it from a nearby table.

"No!" Belle shouted. "Please, do not do this."

Rufus glanced from her to Winfield in confusion. "What do you plan to do with that?"

"He is going to burn down Clearview, with us in it," Belle said in a defeated voice.

"Very perceptive, Lady Belle. One might even say, psychical." Winfield laughed and indicated the curtains. "What do you think, Terrance? A little distraction to keep everyone busy?"

He stared at the man in horror. "Are you mad? There are dozens of people in this house. You cannot mean to kill them all."

"Once the fire spreads, I am sure they will run for the door like rats seeking refuge," Winfield said in a careless tone. "You four, however, will not fare better than your father or that fool, Darby."

* * * *

Winfield's words brought home to Belle the man's villainy. Her gaze kept returning to that flickering candle. She had to distract him from starting the fire.

"You say you killed Darby?" She flexed her fingers to see if she could wiggle them free, but instead the rope constricted her wrists so tightly that pins and needles shot up her arm.

"Darby?" Rufus repeated. "My mother's friend?"

"Also friend to your father, apparently," Winfield said. "The fool overheard a careless conversation between myself and my man, Langley, and went to warn the old earl. I stopped him, as I will all of you."

"Why?" Belle asked. "What have any of us done to you?"

"Done to me?" Winfield stepped away from the curtain and toward her.

She breathed a sigh of relief. Before she came up here to find Rufus, she had warned Lady Terrance to get her family and the servants out. She might not be able to save herself, Rufus, and Phillip, but the longer she kept Winfield talking, the better the chances Rufus's family and servants had to reach safety.

As she watched Winfield, she sent out her special senses to knock on this man's consciousness. A wave of bottled rage answered her probe. His wrath was born of deep shame at his low birth because his noble mother married a commoner and became disinherited. That shame was fed by a deep-seated fear of Rufus Marlesbury.

Why?

No sooner did she think the question than the response swept her into the deepest corner of Winfield's mind. There, a younger Rufus, surely no more than ten years of age, stumbled across Winfield viciously striking an innocent dog.

Belle cringed from that brutal vision, but it gave her valuable insight into this man's character. From that instant when his cruel destruction was witnessed, a worry that Rufus would tell on him had taken hold of Winfield's scruff and refused to let go.

That constant fear had twisted and ballooned out of proportion until it transformed a cowardly boy into a ruthless thug intent on stripping Rufus Marlesbury of everything he valued, and if that involved betraying England, so be it.

In a flash she witnessed the late Lord Terrance enter an empty copse on a dark night and another man approach him. This was a vision with which she was familiar. She had witnessed it in London and had run to warn his lordship. Instead, she had ended up disgracing herself on the Terrances' front steps.

This time, she recognized Winfield as the assailant. The two men spoke. Rufus's father shook his head at whatever Winfield requested, his lips twisting in contempt.

"My son is ten times your worth," the late Lord Terrance said in a deadly voice. "Threaten Rufus again, and I will see you clapped in irons and your mother sent to the poor house."

She recognized the late lordship's overwhelming ferocity, had seen its effect on his own family. She almost felt sorry for Winfield until the image shifted, and she saw anger narrow his eyes.

Without a moment's hesitation, Winfield raised his gun and fired. The late Lord Terrance fell, looking stunned that this whelp would dare fire on him.

Winfield quickly searched the man's body, and then, not finding his prize, fists raised toward the heavens, he raged. Then shouts, followed by running footsteps, brought him to his senses, and Winfield backed away into the bushes. Rufus ran to his father's body and hunched over it. Winfield reloaded. Before he finished, a hue and cry went up, and more footsteps and shouts came in their direction.

Winfield swore, but he knew he could not risk getting caught. As a last ditch effort, while Rufus's back was to him, Winfield quietly laid the pistol near where Rufus knelt over his father's corpse and skulked away.

"Why do I wish you harm?" Winfield asked her again as if stunned by the question. And well he might be if he carried this much fury against Rufus. But then a shutter fell over his emotions, almost as if he suspected she had delved into his psyche. "I see your game. You wish to delay me until help arrives. Unfortunately, my dear, I cannot spare time for your mind-tricks."

With a sharp laugh, he turned and swept the candlelight at the curtains until a fire roared upward. "I hope you get as much enjoyment in watching this old horror of a house burn as I will."

Belle could do naught but watch in despair as the flames licked toward the ceiling.

Winfield ran to the door and pasted his ear to it. Apparently satisfied at what he heard, he kicked Felton aside and tossed the chair away to open the door.

Earnest stood outside, looking weary and muddy. The dog launched himself at Winfield.

Winfield ducked and easily shoved the tired dog away. He ran out and shut the door. Above the frustrated dog's barks, Winfield's laughter echoed. Then the sound ended abruptly. Shouts followed, and a cry for help, and then there was a fierce, inhuman howl.

* * * *

"In God's name, what was that?" Phillip asked.

Rufus shook his head, as perplexed as his cousin.

"It is the late Lord Terrance," Belle said, sounding weary. "I doubt Mr. Winfield will make it to his ship."

"Belle, this is hardly the time for that," Rufus said, irritated. "I do not want us to spend our last moments fighting."

"I am sorry," she said, looking at him. "You should know that even if we burn, your family and servants are safe. Before I came upstairs, I warned Lady Terrance to get everyone out."

"Good thinking, but what made you warn them?"

"I found the MacBrides tied up in the Briar stable. Winfield's man, Langley, admitted that his master planned to kill you this morning. I could not let that happen."

Rufus shook his head. How did she always manage to get in the middle of his problems? "Belle, I thank you for that, but you should not have put yourself in danger."

"Could we focus on a way to free us?" Phillip asked in that same calm voice he used every day.

Rufus nodded. Smoke spread across the plastered ceiling, blackening the carvings. "Phillip, let us move our chairs back-to-back and see if we can reach each other's cords."

Putting action to word, the two shifted so their backs were to each other. The tall chairs had curved backs, however, and prevented them from reaching each other's wrists.

"I have a better idea," Belle said. "Earnest, come here."

The hound ran to place his heavy front paws on her lap and lick her face.

"Good dog. Oh, Earnest, I am so glad you are well. I told you to stay with Grandpapa. You could have killed yourself following me, you foolish hound."

"Lady Belle," Phillip said, "I do not mean to press you, but could you hurry with whatever idea you have?"

Belle smiled at Phillip over her shoulder and then focused back on the dog. "Earnest, bite the rope."

"That is your plan?" Rufus asked, stunned.

"I am talking to the dog," she said.

"Your plan is a dog rescue?" Phillip asked.

"Shhh, I am trying to concentrate. Earnest. Pull on the rope."

Earnest jumped off her lap and circled her. He licked at her fingers.

"The rope, Earnest. Bite the rope and pull back."

"I do not believe what I am seeing," Rufus said as the hound tore at Belle's binding.

Phillip bounced his chair around so he, too, could watch the dog. After a few tugs, Belle pulled her hands free. She untied her feet, and then petted the dog before she approached Rufus.

"I could not even teach the dog to roll over," he said, dumbfounded. "How did you manage that?"

"Believe me or not," she said, "but Earnest can understand my thoughts."

As Belle came over to work on the rope binding his hands, Rufus found his skepticism fleeing before the factual evidence. Once loose, he caught her fingers and brought them to his lips. "I am sorry for constantly doubting you."

"If you two are finished romancing," Phillip said, actually sounding aggrieved, "could you free me, too?"

"And here I thought you were the great spy, and you do not know how to get yourself out of a little knot?" Rufus teased as he worked on the ropes binding his cousin's wrists.

"Expedience is the ruler in all situations," Phillip said. "I was testing the possibility of dislodging my shoulder and arm bones to free myself, but this seems the better solution."

Rufus gulped because he believed Phillip would have done that if Belle's plan failed.

"The fire's spread too far to put it out without water," Phillip said. "We need to get out, and fast."

Belle stood by as Phillip helped Rufus lift Felton. While they carried the man between them, they all fled down the corridor. They had just reached the landing to the stairs when a bone-chilling scream came from the attic above them.

"Winfield," Belle said with pity in her voice. "Your father has him."

Rufus opened his mouth to object, but then closed it. If he could believe that Belle could indeed speak to Earnest, then why could he not believe her story that his father haunted the manor? And something definitely had Winfield in a panic. At that moment, Rufus decided to believe her. If there were such things as ghosts, then his father was upstairs doing only God knew what to Winfield.

Rufus examined the narrow wooden stairs that led upwards. If his father was haunting the manor, it was his responsibility to save the ghost's victim, even if that man was Winfield.

He shifted Felton's weight entirely onto Phillip. "Ensure Belle and Felton are safe."

Before his cousin could object, he swiveled and sprinted upstairs. He had reached the top floor before he noticed Belle and Earnest coming after him.

"What are you doing?" he asked in horrified exasperation. "This whole house could be ablaze. You must leave, and you must leave now."

"I will leave when you do." Her chin jutted out stubbornly. "Phillip takes Felton to safety."

"Then we leave now."

"No," she said. "You are right, Rufus. We cannot leave Winfield to your father's mercy. Is that not why you came up here? Despite the horrible things the man has done to you and your family, we must save him. But first we will have to catch your father's attention, and with that, I can be of help."

He shook his head as it dawned on him that she had been dealing with his difficult father all alone, and she had continued to do so even when he had given her every reason to turn her back on him and his family. He tenderly took her brave face in his hands. "Belle, my love, I will not risk your life for Winfield's."

"Then do it for your father. If he destroys Winfield, he may damn his soul for all eternity. If you want him to rest in peace, we need him to release his hatred and thirst for vengeance." She gently covered his hands. "Rufus, I may have failed to convince him before now, but with your help, we might be able to reason with him this time."

With a nod, he took her hand and turned toward the attic door, from behind which Winfield's screams could be heard.

"If we must face him," Rufus said, "let us do so quickly, or we will all be doomed to die in this house."

"Agreed," she said and squeezed his hand in encouragement.

Chapter Eighteen

Rufus opened the door to the attic, which served as a storage room. The large, cavernous space was filled with boxes and trunks piled roof high, which made visibility difficult. They moved around stacks of crates, always following the sounds of Winfield's cries.

Finally, Rufus saw him, and he instinctively gripped Belle's hand. The man floated six feet off the ground, a rope tied around his throat that led off to a distance and ended in midair. His fingers were pulling on the noose, to keep it from strangling him while his feet kicked out trying to find solid purchase. His eyes were wide and maniacal. The papers he had killed to obtain were beneath him scattered like white clouds on the dusty gray floor.

Belle pulled out of his hold, gave him a gentle push forward, and pointed toward Winfield. "Both Winfield and your father are up there."

He gave her an uncertain glance and then stepped closer to the only person he could see. Winfield.

Earnest growled and circled Belle, as if unsure what to do.

Rufus sympathized. Even though he told himself not to, he had to ask a foolish question. "Belle, are you sure Father's here?"

"Someone holds Winfield up. Talk to your father, Rufus. You must turn him from his purpose."

He nodded and swallowed to clear the sudden lump in his throat. "Father." He addressed the empty air where the rope ended around Winfield's neck. "Release this man."

Mine.

The whisper, in that familiar voice, spiked the hairs on his neck and arms. He knew that tone of voice, and he also knew that his father in a foul temper was never a good sign. He shook off his reflexive fear and spoke in a firm tone. "I beg to differ, sir. Winfield is mine."

Murderer. Traitor.

"Yes. All those things, as well as a thief and a coward. Still, he is mine. Not yours."

Shot ME!

Rufus summoned his courage to face up to the man who had terrified him his whole life. "And you are dead, Father."

No response.

He paced beneath Winfield in a circle while the rational side of him insisted that he must have imagined his father's words. But that logical side could not offer any reasonable explanation for a man hanging in midair without any visible support, or for Earnest following Belle's command to the letter, as if he understood English as well as his master.

So, if the rational explanations were out, he must believe in the irrational. Which was the world where Belle lived. Rufus drew in a deep breath and stepped into that world with full acceptance. If Belle were mad, so, now, was he.

A joyous sensation burst out of his chest, and he could not attribute that extraordinary feeling to anything other than a sense of finally finding peace. He hurried back to Belle and kissed her cheek.

She gave him a surprised look, then a frown of confusion marred her beautiful face. Apparently she could not read his mind as easily as she could a dog's or a ghost's.

Good! A solid sustainable marriage required some secrets that could later be revealed as surprise gifts.

Rufus knelt to pick up the scattered paper. Once finished, he stood and spoke to his father as much as to himself. "Father, you are dead. Now, whether you approve or not, I am head of the Terrance household. It is my duty to see that Winfield is brought to justice." With the papers clutched in his fist, he indicated Winfield. "Release him. I am capable of taking care of our family. It is time you trusted me to do so."

Son. Always trust. Always protect.

At that amazing admission, a lifetime of hurt that had rebelliously clung to Rufus's shoulders dissipated and drifted away like ashes blown by the breeze.

He folded and tucked the papers into an inside pocket. Then he glanced toward Belle, who smiled her encouragement. Earnest, however, shivered, his eyes pleading for them to leave this doomed place.

Soon, Rufus promised his dog and turned back to Winfield's floating body. His neighbor stared down at him in petrified silence.

"I no longer need protection, father. I am a grown man. And if you do trust me as you say, then prove it. Release Winfield. I will see that justice falls on his head. Allow me to be the man you brought me up to be."

The silence following his request lasted a long while. Then, suddenly, Winfield plunged toward the floor, screaming.

Rufus dove for him, arms outstretched, and caught him. He staggered under the weight.

Then he looked upward and smiled. "Thank you, Father."

* * * *

Belle stood with her gaze transfixed near the ceiling. The old earl appeared, garbed in old-fashioned clothes from over three decades ago.

He looked younger than his portrait, but what caught and held Belle's attention was his pride with his son that shone brightly on his face. In that moment, a blinding light engulfed him, and Belle smiled as the late Lord Terrance left this earthly realm.

This is why I cannot turn my back on my talent, she thought.

She had not realized her shoulders were tense until they relaxed as she came to terms with why she was unable to abandon her "imaginings," as Rufus had once asked her to do.

* * * *

Rufus heaved a terrified Winfield to his feet. The man had gone limp, becoming a dead weight, though his eyes remained wide open. Rufus dragged him toward the door, saying, "Come, Belle, we must get out of here."

When she did not respond, he looked up to where she stared at the ceiling. "Is my father still here?"

"No." She turned to help him with Winfield. "Thanks to you, he has finally found peace, Rufus. He will not haunt this house anymore."

"Good," Rufus said. "Unfortunately, I doubt this house will be around much longer for anyone to haunt."

Together, they dragged Winfield downstairs. Smoke had spread everywhere. The accompanying heat was unbearable.

"Hurry," he said, but left unvoiced his worry that they might already be too late to escape.

As he had feared, on the third floor landing they were forced to halt. The stairs were no longer passable.

"We must find another escape route," he said. "Maybe through a window on this floor."

"No!" Winfield cried wildly and tried to pull away.

Rufus tightened his hold. "Winfield, there is no time left to argue about this."

Winfield fought free, wildly flinging his arms. Rufus let the crazy fool go in order to protect Belle as one of Winfield's fists came close to clobbering her. He pushed her behind him and turned to face the madman.

"You will not win," Winfield shouted. "You can burn in this house, Terrance, but I'm getting out. You cannot stop me. No one can stop me."

"The terror of meeting your father has loosened his mind," Belle said.

"I am not a lunatic!" Spittle dripped out of Winfield's mouth, as if in contradiction to that statement. He pointed at her, his eyes bulging like cue balls. "I see how you trail after his almighty lordship, hoping to catch a little of his fame. It will not work. No one notices you. Nothing you do compares favorably. You might as well not exist."

"Winfield, there is no time to argue," Rufus said. "This fire spreads like a lit fuse. Come man, we can escape out a window from a room behind us." He grabbed Winfield's arm, but the man screamed and lunged toward him.

Belle shouted a warning as Rufus crashed against the banister with Winfield on top of him. Timber cracked beneath their combined weight.

Belle shoved Winfield out of the way, and the fool woman grabbed Rufus's arm. He was afraid of taking her over the railing with him, but she pulled him back onto solid ground.

Earnest ran back and forth, barking in frenzy. Winfield chose that moment of distraction to leap down the stairs and jump over the flames.

"Stop, you fool!" Rufus shouted. "Come back here."

"Time for you to burn, Terrance," Winfield shouted gleefully over his shoulder. And then the stairs buckled beneath him.

Rufus would have gone to help, but Belle laid a restraining hand. There was a faraway look in her eyes as she said, "It is too late."

Before she finished speaking, a crack sounded. In a swoop, Winfield sank through the floor to his hips. He put his arms out to pull himself up, but the entire stairway gave way. He plummeted, screaming and arms flailing. The smoke was too think to see, but Rufus heard him crash onto the marble foyer in a horrific crunch of bones, and his screams cut off.

As smoke and debris billowed up in a tremendous plume, Rufus pulled Belle against his chest and covered his face with his arm. Once the air cleared, Winfield's position became clear. He lay below them unmoving among the crisscrossed fallen beams and charred rubble, his neck and legs twisted at an unnatural angle.

Higher up, the stairway ended abruptly, as if a ghostly hand held it up despite Belle insisting his father was gone.

Earnest whined and backed away, and Belle coughed against his chest.

Rufus drew them backwards onto safer ground and then led the way to a bedroom he used to play in as a child. He was sure there was a way to get out from there. It had worked when he was a boy. "This way, Belle. Earnest, here!"

They arrived to find smoke in the room. He ushered her and Earnest inside and shut the door. "There is a tree outside that window. If we climb onto one of the branches, we should be able to get down safely."

He tore the curtains away to give them unhindered access and then opened the shutters. Daylight poured into the dark, smoky room. He opened the window and lifted her until she sat on its ledge.

"You cannot climb in that gown," he told her.

"I am not taking it off!"

"Then we improvise." He ripped at the bottom of her gown.

"Rufus!" she cried, sounding scandalized.

"You will need to use your legs to climb that tree. The skirts will hinder your movements."

When he was done, only a modest portion of her gown still covered her thighs.

"Go!" he ordered.

Carefully, she reached for the closest oak tree branch beside the window and climbed onto it. "Are you coming?"

"The branch has grown bigger than I remember but it is still too small to hold both our weights. You go first, I will follow."

Heart in mouth, he watched as she crawled along the wide branch. He heaved a relieved sigh as she grabbed the main trunk. Only then did he give himself permission to admire her bare legs.

They were strong, firm and delectable, and he could not wait until she wrapped them around him as she now did with that lucky trunk. He watched with uninhibited enjoyment as she slowly slid down until she touched ground and turned to wave up to him, completely unaware of how tempting she looked.

"Woof!" Earnest said, leaning out the windowsill.

"Yes, she made it." Rufus petted the dog. The large Irish wolfhound puppy would not make it without help. "Now it is our turn."

He used torn curtains to fashion a makeshift sling. First he wrapped it securely around Earnest and then slung the whole around his shoulders so the dog hung off his chest.

Earnest whined.

"Only way, boy."

Together they climbed out. The limb buckled, and Rufus's stomach dropped. But the branch held, and, clutching the dog with one hand, he made his way to the trunk and then down the tree.

The closer to the ground they drew, the more Earnest wiggled. Once they landed, Rufus ignored the dog's complaints, as Belle gave him a lingering kiss that suggested her thoughts were not so far removed from his. The squirming dog got in the way of serious lovemaking, and they had to stop.

Once released, Earnest raced in wide circles barking. Rufus pulled Belle to him again, ready to finish what she had started, but the barking brought running footsteps and a shout. As Phillip raced round the house, they had to step apart.

"With all that racket, I assured your mother that you must have made it safely out," Phillip said, sounding out of breath and anxious despite the teasing glint in his eyes.

"Are you sure Mother and Susie are safe?"

"More worried about you than themselves."

"And Aunt Henrietta?"

Phillip gave Rufus a hug. "Thank you for asking. My mother is fine and more cantankerous than ever because of her fright. Felton, too, has recovered. All the servants and guests are accounted for. I am just happy to see you and Lady Belle got out safety."

"Why were you so worried, Cousin?" Rufus asked. "Were you afraid you would have to take over the family fortune?"

"Do not even joke about your death." Phillip pumped him on the back and wore a delighted smile.

"I have something for you." Rufus handed Phillip the papers he had rescued from Winfield. "Do you think this will help in clearing my name?"

Phillip looked over the papers and nodded. "Assuredly. And you may consider me speaking on behalf of the Regent on this matter."

"I want to hear more about your work," Rufus said. "Later. Oh, and Winfield is dead."

"Good," Phillip said, but his gaze was arrested on Belle. "Interesting fashion plate, Lady Belle. I suspect it will become the rage of London once you arrive."

"Oh!" Belle ran to hide behind Rufus

"What can I say, Phillip, other than that she seems intent on disrobing in front of me at every opportunity."

"It is a sad development," Phillip agreed in a sober tone that had an underlay of laughter. "You might have to marry the girl to ensure she does not embarrass you."

"The thought has crossed my mind." Rufus removed his jacket and offered it to Belle behind his back.

"It was necessary to destroy my gown so I could climb down the tree," Belle said in a pained voice. "Rufus, I mean Lord Terrance, insisted on it."

As Phillip, too, shed his jacket to give to Belle, Rufus glanced at the manor, now engulfed in flames. The sight drowned out his humor. Even the gargoyles on the rooftop, which according to lore, were meant to guard the place against evil spirits, appeared scorched. Some guardians they had turned out to be. The sky remained a clear blue without a cloud in sight to hint at rain that might help extinguish the blaze.

Before long, the manor would be nothing but charred remains. He would miss the place. Ever since Belle had arrived at Clearview, he had grown fond of it. Instead of his father's punishments and recriminations, the house now reminded him of dancing and kisses.

"Clearview is clearly lost," he said. "I shall miss it."

"Come with me," Phillip said. "I have a surprise."

Rufus and Belle followed until they rounded the corner to the front courtyard. The sight there lodged his heart in his throat.

Villagers swarmed over his front steps as they worked to put out the fire. Buckets were passed back and forth, people with blankets put out spot fires, and ladders had been brought in to reach the higher floors.

"Most of the house might be saved," Phillip said. "The worst damage seems to be in the east wing." He clapped Rufus's back. "For a man nicknamed 'Lord Terror,' your neighbors seem very keen to run to your aid."

Speechless, Rufus could only smile. All these people had rushed to save his home. He would not forget this service.

* * * *

Much later, after the fire was all but extinguished, Rufus went in search of Belle. When he found her, he drew her toward the beech tree in the back garden where, during the ball, he had almost confessed his predicament to her.

Instead of the delight in yellow and lace she had worn then, she now had on borrowed servant's garb that smelled and looked singed. Yet she still took his breath away whenever her violet gaze caught his, which had been often throughout the time they worked to fight the fire.

Earnest, who had become his shadow since he carried the dog from the burning house, followed him and sat by his feet. All three turned to study the remains of Clearview.

The surroundings seemed little changed. The burnt east wing walls were fallen in and were charred. The lawn and bushes still looked wintry in their layer of gray ash. The air smelled smoky, and each breath irritated the back of his throat. Instead of a moonlit sky, the sun was on the brink of setting.

"Belle." He turned her to face him. "I have a question I would like to ask."

Belle returned his solemn look with a teasing smile, her arms casually yet possessively wrapping around his neck. "And what would that be, Rufus?"

She had never looked more beautiful than with her sooty face and singed hair. Quite a change from his angel in the snow. Yet, the woman whom he had lambasted then as being unworthy of him, now seemed eminently suitable.

"Annabelle Lilith Marchant." He removed her arms from around his neck and dropped to one knee. "Will you do me the honor of haunting me for the rest of my days as my wife?"

She burst out laughing, then bent to accept his proposal with a lingering kiss. "Yes, yes, a thousand times, yes."

He stood, whooped, and then looked around. The place was crawling with villagers. If he was to kiss her the way he wanted, they needed a better hiding spot. Eyeing the maze, he took a firm grip on her hand and raced toward the opening.

"Rufus!" She sounded breathless. "Do you mean to have your way with me?"

"I do, my lady. Though I did not realize reading my thoughts were part of your special abilities."

She chuckled. "It had not been, until this moment. But is this the right time and place for what you have in mind?"

He stopped abruptly at the maze's edge. "You object?"

She shook her head. "No, but what will your Aunt Henrietta say to my going unescorted into a maze with you at sunset?"

"That it is high time I made an honest woman of you."

She ran a thumb across his lips. "Is that your plan?"

In response, he pulled her close enough so she would be in no doubt about his plans.

Her violet eyes widened with excitement or anticipation, and he hoped it was both. "I intend to stir another blaze between us before this day ends."

"Rufus Marlesbury, are you saying you intend to steal my innocence?" For all her stern tone, she wore that mischievous look she sported when he first asked her to kiss him after her carriage ran him off the road. "What type of lady do you think I am?"

Despite her humor, he answered seriously. "Not a lady, an angel," he whispered and kissed her as no angel had ever been kissed.

Ernest jumped up to join in the fun, and Rufus pulled back with a groan of frustration. "Belle, tell this confounded dog to stop vexing us. You can talk to him. Ask him to go plague Phillip or Mother or my aunt. Anyone but us."

The puppy skirted his shove and, encouraged by Belle's laughter, jumped on them and nearly toppled them to the ground in order to obtain his portion of the affection being so generously shared between the two people he loved most.

Rufus laughed and gave in to the dog. After all, Belle was his for the rest of their lives, and Earnest loved her almost as much as he did.

CPSIA information can be obtained at www.ICGtesting.com
Printed in the USA
LVOW121944190413

330044LV00001B/201/P